PRAISE FOR THE BOOKS OF KAREN McQUESTION

"Karen McQuestion just keeps getting better! *Hello Love* is an enchanting, impossible-to-put-down novel about big hearts and second chances."

—Claire Cook, *USA Today* bestselling author of *Must Love Dogs*

"An emotional and engaging novel about family . . ."

—Delia Ephron on *A Scattered Life*

"McQuestion writes with a sharp eye and a sure voice, and as a reader, I was willing to go wherever she wanted to take me. After I finished the book, I thought about how I might describe it to a friend, and I settled on . . . 'You should read this. It's good.'"

—Carolyn Parkhurst on *A Scattered Life*

"The plot is fast paced and easy to dive into, making this a quick and exciting read."

—*School Library Journal* on *From a Distant Star*

"I devoured it in one sitting!"

—*New York Times* bestselling author Lesley Kagen on *Edgewood*

"I feel like I've been waiting for this book. It's kind of like all my favorite comic books rolled into one awesome package . . . I'm eagerly awaiting the second book, I'm hooked!"

—*The Kindle Book Review* on *Edgewood*

"At first glance *Favorite* is a story of a girl and her family learning to cope with loss. But at some point it morphs into a psychological thriller. It's an unexpected but welcome turn that will leave readers on the edge of their seats."

—Jessica Harrison, *Cracking the Cover*

"This story featuring a strong protagonist who has mastered the art of being the new girl will appeal to girls who are fans of this genre."

—*School Library Journal* on *Life on Hold*

"This is an adventure that is sure to appeal to both boys and girls, and I can't wait to read it to my students."

—Stacy Romanjuk, fourth-grade teacher at Hart Ransom School in Modesto, California, on *Secrets of the Magic Ring*

"An imaginative fable about two witches that should excite young readers."

—*Kirkus Reviews* on *Grimm House*

Good Man, Dalton

OTHER TITLES BY KAREN McQUESTION

FOR ADULTS

A Scattered Life
Easily Amused
The Long Way Home
Hello Love
Half a Heart

FOR YOUNG ADULTS

Favorite
Life on Hold
From a Distant Star

THE EDGEWOOD SERIES

Edgewood (Book One)
Wanderlust (Book Two)
Absolution (Book Three)
Revelation (Book Four)

FOR CHILDREN

Celia and the Fairies
Secrets of the Magic Ring
Grimm House
Prince and Popper

FOR WRITERS

Write That Novel!: You Know You Want To . . .

Good Man, Dalton

KAREN McQUESTION

This is a work of fiction. Names, characters, organizations, places, events, and incidents are either products of the author's imagination or are used fictitiously. Any resemblance to actual persons, living or dead, or actual events is purely coincidental.

Published by Lake Union Publishing, Seattle

www.apub.com

ISBN-13: 9781542041447
ISBN-10: 1542041449

Cover design by Shasti O'Leary Soudant

Printed in the United States of America

For Danielle Marshall

CHAPTER ONE

"Chardonnay," the flight attendant said, setting the glass down in front of Greta and smiling pleasantly.

"Thank you," Greta whispered, pushing away the urge to ask if it was complimentary. She'd been watching, and thus far no one else had pulled out a credit card, leading her to believe alcoholic beverages were just one of the perks of flying first class.

She crossed her legs and examined the people around her. Many were in business attire, their eyes on their respective devices, as if some major transaction might go through at any moment and they needed to be ready. The couple across the aisle appeared to be married, the woman sporting a huge diamond on the hand she waved to get the flight attendant's attention while her husband quietly sipped his bourbon.

Greta wasn't deluding herself. She was aware that normally she'd be back in coach, most likely next to a young mother with a fussy baby. She felt like an imposter, an actor portraying the kind of person comfortable flying in the expensive seats. However, only a half an hour in the air, and she'd already decided that first class was definitely the best way to travel from Wisconsin to New York, especially since someone else was paying for it.

She sipped the wine slowly and shook her head when offered another. She did allow herself a second snack, which she tucked into her purse for later. When the hot towels were delivered, she watched the businessman next to her to see what he'd do, then copied his movements.

"Pretty luxurious," Greta said to the man as she wiped her hands and wrists. "This is my first trip to Manhattan."

He was a portly gentleman wearing a button-down shirt and a tie loosened at the neck. He responded after handing the towel back to the waiting attendant. "It's a great city. It can get expensive, though. If you're planning on shopping, I hope you brought a platinum card."

Greta handed her towel back. "I don't think I'll have much time for shopping. I landed an internship at the Vanderhaven Corporation, and I'm staying with my cousin's family."

The man looked at her with new eyes, surprised. "The Vanderhaven Corporation?" He nodded approvingly. "Good for you, young lady. You're off to a great start."

She settled back into her wide, comfortable seat and closed her eyes. She could have told him so much more, but she didn't want to sound like she was bragging. Besides, would he even believe that she was related to the Vanderhavens and would be staying with them for the summer? She herself found it hard to believe she would soon be living with Cece Vanderhaven.

Cece Vanderhaven. A distant cousin and maybe, very soon, a friend.

The businessman would have heard of Cece, of course. It was likely everyone on the plane knew of her. She was on magazine covers, and her photo was plastered all over the internet. Her social media accounts were called Cece's World, with no last name required.

Over the years, Greta had kept a watchful eye on Cece's images online. She knew her fascination bordered on obsession, but there was just something about Cece that kept drawing her back. Part of it was Cece's beauty. It didn't matter whether she was climbing out of limos at charity events or leaving a club at three in the morning; she always looked gorgeous. Always. It defied logic that someone could go through life without a hair out of place, her skin glowing and perfect. And if that wasn't enough, her professional accomplishments were mind blowing. Cece and Greta were the same age, twenty-three, and Cece was already a big-name fashion designer with her own skin care line and signature fragrance. She'd gone to a university for one semester when she'd quit to start her own company: Firstborn Daughter, Inc.

Greta admired Cece's quirky fashion sense. One time Cece had been photographed at a club with black lacquered chopsticks poking out of her messy bun, and the look had inexplicably started a craze. That summer Greta saw chopsticks in women's hair seemingly everywhere—the cashier at Walgreens, girls at the mall, a host on the *Today* show, and models in every fashion magazine. When Cece stopped doing it, everyone else did too, because after that, it just looked passé.

When Cece announced, after a year of living on her own, that she was moving back in with her parents because nothing was more important than family, she spawned a movement of adult children flocking home to their folks. A new hashtag started trending: #FamilyReunited.

But most intriguing were Cece's two best friends: Vance, whom she called her gay boyfriend, and Katrina, known as the girl with the megawatt smile. Katrina was also famous for her comical facial expressions and ability to find the levity in every situation. The three of them went everywhere together. The way Vance and Katrina formed a protective circle around Cece was incredible. No one got through them. Greta envied their bond. She had her own friends, of course, but not the kind who wanted to spend every waking moment with her. Those three were so close that Katrina and Vance even lived in an apartment in Cece's building, just five floors down. "I don't do anything without them," Cece once said, her gaze focused off in the distance.

When Cece did speak in public, Greta noticed that her answers were cryptic. For a while, her catchphrase was "Let me in," accompanied by a dreamy, searching sort of look. When she first started saying it, the Twitterverse went crazy. Was it sexual innuendo? A secret message to one of her many male admirers? The password to one of the clubs she frequented? *Let me in.* Three simple words that had everyone buzzing. As it turned out, it was the slogan for her new perfume. When the ad came out, the video went viral as everyone had an aha moment.

Greta knew there was no middle ground when it came to Cece. People either seemed to love her or hate her. Most found her endlessly fascinating. She'd mastered the art of looking dreamily mysterious.

For years, Greta's family had received the Vanderhaven Christmas card, but it wasn't until she was eight years old that she'd found out they were related. That year the Vanderhavens were photographed at a circus, with Cece in tights and a spangled bodysuit perched up on the trapeze, and her mother and father below, posing with clowns, a fire-eater, and a juggler. Elephants raised on hind legs framed the gathering on either side. This was before Cece's sister, Brenna, was born, so it had been just the three of them. Greta had picked up the photo from the kitchen table and practically pressed her nose to it, staring at the glamorous little girl in the picture.

"That poor child," her mother said, observing her interest. She was at the kitchen island, chopping vegetables for pasta primavera.

"Who?" Greta still had her eyes on the card, wondering how it would feel to be dressed in such shimmering glory, high up on the trapeze. It had to be wonderful.

"That little girl. Cece. Her mom said they're sending her to boarding school next year because it's just too much trouble to transport her to and from school. Security issues. I can't even imagine." She picked up the cutting board and slid the vegetables into a bowl. "I don't know how a mother could do that. If you went to boarding school next year, I would miss you so much, Greta. I wouldn't be able to stand it."

"You *know* her mom?" Greta had asked incredulously.

She nodded. "Of course I know her. Deborah is my cousin."

The story that came out was that Cece's mom and Greta's mom were close growing up, but then Deborah left Wisconsin and went off to New York to be a model. Within a few weeks, she'd met the extremely wealthy Harry Vanderhaven. They'd seemed like an unlikely couple:

she, a young Midwestern girl; he, a ruthless businessman known to crush anyone in his path, but something clicked. They had a whirlwind romance and quickly married.

Deborah didn't even get a chance to do much modeling, and she never returned to Wisconsin. Greta's mom had tried to keep in touch with her, but after a while, the yearly Christmas cards were their only contact. Greta came to look forward to them every Christmas season. After Cece's younger sister, Brenna, was born, there were four family members, of course, but the cards were just as fantastic. When Brenna was a baby, the scene showed the family unwrapping gifts, opening a box to find Brenna. Another time the family members were depicted in Santa's workshop, helping the elves make toys. One year they all posed in formal wear, Deborah and the girls in flowing red ball gowns, the father in a tux.

When she was young, Greta had mentally inserted herself into each annual photo, trying to imagine what it would be like to live that way. She couldn't even imagine having a life that glamorous.

After the holidays were over, Greta always asked if she could keep the card, and her mom would shrug and say yes. Her mother didn't understand her interest. One year she'd pointed to Brenna and said, "That little girl always has such a sad-puppy look, poor thing." Greta had been too busy looking at Cece to notice, but now that it had been pointed out, she could see that Brenna didn't appear nearly as thrilled as her big sister. Cece gazed adoringly at the camera while Brenna's eyes were shifted to one side, as if looking for someone in a crowd. Or searching for a way out.

Greta's family had a Christmas card photo of their own, but it was not nearly as impressive. It was always a picture of the four of them in front of their decorated artificial tree, a glowing star up top. Her dad had started a tradition where she and her brother, Travis, each held up a sign. Greta's always said, "We're still the Hansens," and her little brother's said, "Merry Christmas and Happy New Year." Friends and family who got their cards seemed to find the signs amusing, so every year, even though Greta thought it was somewhat lame, she played along and held up the sign. It made her father happy.

The internship with the Vanderhavens came about at the suggestion of her university adviser, Mr. Kurtz, who'd recommended a summer internship after graduation. He said, "In some job markets, a business degree from a state university won't get you too far. The experience gained as an intern would set you apart."

"I was going to just look for a job," she said.

He shook his head, regarding Greta sadly. "It's competitive out there. Doing an internship first will give you an edge and might even lead to a job, a better one than you'd get otherwise."

"Okay."

"What area of business were you leaning toward?"

She shook her head. "I'm sort of keeping my options open at this point. All I know for sure is that I'd like to do something that makes the world a better place. You know, not just sales or advertising. And not retail or manufacturing or anything like that." Greta sensed she was losing him, so she spoke more quickly. "Something that helps people. I'd like to make a difference, you know? Maybe work for a nonprofit or something . . ." Her voice trailed off as his expression deepened in disapproval.

"Right out of the gate, you might not be able to be so idealistic, especially when applying for an internship," he said. "The important thing is to get out there and show them what you're made of. Take some initiative, give them your ideas, do something impressive. This is the time to get yourself noticed."

She knew he meant well, but what he didn't know was that Greta wasn't usually the taking-initiative type. She had opinions, of course, but found it hard to assert herself. The one exception concerned team projects at school. When a grade was on the line, she found it easy to take charge, breaking the project into parts, assigning each student a job, and checking back with each of them to make sure they had completed their tasks. In other areas of life, though, she found herself falling back and letting others take the lead. But she knew Mr. Kurtz was right. She'd never get ahead in the business world by standing back in the shadows. She mentally vowed to be less shy and more bold going forward.

"Now is the time to capitalize on your contacts," he said, his face serious.

"My contacts?" she asked.

"Yes, Greta, contacts," he repeated. "You know, influential people in business or leaders of charitable organizations. Surely you've encountered some important people in past jobs, or maybe during your volunteer work?"

She shook her head. Her volunteer work had been at an animal shelter, cleaning cages and walking dogs. Her past jobs had included a brief stint at the front desk of a local Motel 6 and, after that, working the cash register at Kohl's department store. The discount was awesome, but she'd never met anyone noteworthy.

He said, "Surely your parents must have some contacts?"

She reflected and came up with nothing. Greta's mother was a dental hygienist, and her dad taught eighth grade. They came home with lots of interesting stories to tell over the dinner table, but that was about it. "Not so much," she admitted.

"Any friends of the family that could help you out?"

"No."

Mr. Kurtz glanced over her head at the clock that hung above the doorway. He tried again, this time halfheartedly, like he already knew she wouldn't have a good answer. "Any relatives in business?"

And then, Greta remembered. "I'm related to Deborah Vanderhaven on my mother's side."

He perked up then and leaned forward, his eyes bright. "Deborah Vanderhaven? The wife of Harry Vanderhaven, the owner of the Vanderhaven Corporation?"

She nodded. "That's the one."

"Well." He folded his arms, looking pleased. "Why didn't you say that in the first place? Being related to the Vanderhavens is the very definition of having great contacts. Get your mother to put in a good word for you, and set something up for the summer." He grinned. "I would say my work here is done. You're good to go." He beckoned toward the partially open door, and she turned to see another girl waiting in the hallway. She knew then that she'd been dismissed.

It wasn't that easy, though. When she called home and asked for Deborah's contact information, her mother sighed. "Why do you want it?"

Greta explained about the meeting with Mr. Kurtz, making sure to stress the importance of an outstanding internship for securing future postgraduate employment. When she'd finished, there was silence on the other end of the phone. "Mom?"

"Yes, I'm here, honey."

"Do you think this is a bad idea?"

"No, it's fine. I just don't want you to get your hopes up. Deborah and I used to be as close as sisters, but then we drifted apart. I tried to keep in touch, but over the years, her end of it got to be less and less. I have an email address for her, but I haven't used it in ages. I don't know if it's still good."

"Or I could mail my résumé to her," Greta said. "We have their address from the Christmas cards, right?"

Another pause. "The cards have a return address, but it's not where they live," her mother told her. "It's the address to their attorney's office. I guess it's for security reasons."

"Oh."

She continued. "And even if I knew their actual address, they don't get mail delivery to their building."

That was weird. "How do they get their mail?"

"From what I understand, they have a post office box. An assistant from the office picks it up, sorts it, and delivers the personal mail to their apartment."

"Would my cover letter and résumé get through?"

"I don't know, Greta. But you know, life is short. You might as well go for it."

"So you think I have a shot?"

"Honey, you always have a shot, but why don't you try the email first?"

With those words in mind, Greta sent an email of inquiry along with her phone number.

Two hours later, her cell phone rang. She answered it to hear the voice of a very excited Deborah Vanderhaven.

"Little Greta Hansen!" She said this over and over again. "I was so excited to hear from you! Your email was an answer to my prayers! Of course we have an internship for you!"

"I'm so glad to hear that," Greta said, trying to sound professional, even as part of her was reeling from disbelief. She took a deep breath and continued. "I know a lot of the summer intern positions have been filled already . . . "

"Nonsense! You're family! We wouldn't dream of turning you down!"

Greta had always thought Deborah Vanderhaven seemed serious and unapproachable. In photos, Deborah looked stunning for a woman her age, but something about her public image was flat, lacking in personality. It was hard to reconcile that impression with the enthusiastic voice on the phone.

She said, "I appreciate it, Mrs. Vanderhaven—"

"No, no!" she protested. "Not Mrs. Vanderhaven. Call me Deborah! Or is it Aunt Deborah?" Before Greta could answer, she solved the problem herself. "No, we're cousins, so I guess it's just Deborah."

"Thank you, Deborah."

She rattled on some more about how the Vanderhaven Corporation would take good care of Greta, and of course, she would stay at their apartment. "We'll make sure to give you an excellent letter of recommendation too!"

"Just what you'd do for anyone else," Greta said. "I don't need preferential treatment."

Deborah said to give her regards to Greta's mother. "I hope you realize what a special person she is."

"Believe me, I do. She's the best," Greta said sincerely.

"I hope you tell her that."

"I do. All the time."

Then Deborah said she had to wrap up the conversation, but not before she informed Greta that her assistant would be in touch to make all the arrangements. As promised, the assistant, Lexie, called Greta shortly thereafter and set up everything—the date of departure, the ride to the airport, the plane tickets.

"Do you know what I'll be doing?" Greta asked.

"Doing?" Lexie sounded puzzled.

"For my internship. Which area of the company will I be working in?"

Lexie laughed. "I haven't a clue, Greta. No one told me."

"I guess I'll find out when I get there," she said.

"I guess so." Lexie got right back to business. "Michael, the family driver, will be picking you up at the airport," she said. "Look for a dark-haired gentleman holding a sign with your name on it near the baggage claim."

"It won't be Cece and her friends coming to get me?" Greta asked, half hoping.

"Oh, no," Lexie said with a low chuckle. "You don't want Cece picking you up. There would be a stampede."

Greta knew that expecting Cece Vanderhaven to pick her up from the airport was unrealistic, but she had to ask. At least they'd be living together for the summer. It was going to be like a dream come true.

CHAPTER TWO

"Dalton, I can't believe you're going through with this," said his best friend, Will. They were in the waiting area of the Greyhound bus station, and although Dalton's bus wasn't leaving for another few minutes, he wanted to be ready. Emptying his pockets was as symbolic as it was necessary.

"Believe it. This is happening." Dalton stuck his loose cash—twenty-three dollars in assorted bills and a handful of coins—into his jeans pocket, then handed his wallet to Will, along with the keys to his apartment.

"A platinum card," Will said, thumbing through the slots in the wallet. "And your driver's license too. Score! I could pass myself off as Dalton T. Bishop, no problem. You'll be sleeping on the streets while I'm ordering room service at the Waldorf and living the good life."

"The joke will be on you because I put a hold on all my accounts." Dalton looked longingly at his cell phone and said, "I think I will miss you most of all," before handing it over. He tugged on the brim of his baseball cap so it shaded his eyes and did a mental assessment of everything he now owned. He had bus tickets, both today's and for the return; a small amount of cash; a lightweight jacket; an extra T-shirt; a shaving kit with a toothbrush and toothpaste; his ReadyHelp device; a notebook and pen; and his harmonica.

He'd chosen his clothing carefully. He wore an old pair of jeans, some scuffed athletic shoes, and a plain gray T-shirt. Nothing that would make him stand out. Picking up the backpack at his feet, Dalton stuffed everything inside. He'd bought the backpack at a thrift shop for two dollars, happy to find one that looked so weathered and shabby. As soon as he'd spotted the denim iron-on patch on the back and what looked like a bloodstain on the front pocket, he knew it was perfect for his purposes.

Yes, he was ready to officially shed his old life and become someone else for two weeks. Someone less privileged and more aware of how the world treats the disadvantaged. He left his backpack with Will and went to hit the bathroom one last time. While he washed his hands, Dalton took note of what it was like to have unlimited running water and liquid soap. In the days to come, this might be a luxury.

When he returned to the waiting area, Will greeted him with a grin. He said, "Man, you have balls. I couldn't handle going that long without a hot shower and a comfortable bed. You could die out there, and for what? Frankly, the whole thing just seems kind of stupid."

"I know. Just take good care of my car and my stuff," Dalton said, gesturing to the phone and wallet in his friend's hand. "And I'll see you in two weeks."

"I can't believe you're leaving your phone behind. Why don't you just take it and not use it?"

He shook his head. "I know myself, and it would be too tempting. I want the authentic experience. You know me: do it right or not at all." Besides, not having it would keep him from texting his former girlfriend late at night. He'd been blindsided by the breakup, which had come out of nowhere. Even as he assumed everything had been fine, his relationship had been unraveling after she'd met a guy named Drew two months earlier.

His ex-girlfriend made dumping Dalton for Drew sound like the obvious choice. She'd explained it this way: "He's everything I thought you were, except you're not. I mean, you're out of college two years and still not doing anything." She said it as if this were a good reason. Like he'd understand.

"It's not that I'm not doing anything," Dalton had protested. "I just finished my master's, and I'm in a relationship!" At least, he'd thought he was in a relationship.

"He has a life plan, and it includes me," she said. "I know it's sad, but you know as well as I do that we weren't a great combination. Our relationship was just drifting."

"Drifting?" This was a shock. *He* hadn't felt any drifting.

"I'm sorry," she said, not sounding like she meant it. "You just aren't my someone."

Dalton felt like he'd been hit from behind. "Your someone?"

"You know, like when you see a person across a room and just know they're your someone. The one you're meant to be with. Drew is my someone. You're not. I'm sorry. That's just the way it is."

Two years of his life, and she'd said they weren't a great combination. That they were drifting. That Dalton wasn't her someone. He still felt love for her, but it was waning with each passing day.

Becoming homeless would be easy compared to the pain of heartbreak. Two weeks without a phone would prevent him from sending take-me-back texts disguised as friendly platonic updates. Not having his driver's license would enable Dalton to walk away from his own life temporarily and become someone else.

Will said, "There are homeless people who have cell phones. I see them all the time."

"What you're seeing is people with cell phones who aren't at home."

"No, seriously. There are street people with phones."

"Maybe so. But that's not the way I'm playing it."

Will didn't look convinced. "What if you get attacked or break a leg or something? How will you get help?"

"That's what this is for," Dalton said, pulling out the ReadyHelp device and holding it between his fingers. It was designed for the elderly, but he'd researched it and knew that with its lithium battery and built-in GPS, it would serve his purposes just fine. "I'll just push the button and say, 'I've fallen, and I can't get up,' and they'll send help."

A slow grin crossed Will's face. "You're a crazy man, Dalton."

"You know it."

When the announcement came over the loudspeaker saying it was time for his bus to board, they got to their feet. Will pulled him into a forceful man hug, then gave him a firm pat on the back.

"You're going to see me again," Dalton told him, taking a step back. "It's not like I'm going off to war."

"I might come into the city to see you in a few days." The words came out in a hurried rush. "Just to check on you. Is that okay?"

Dalton slung the backpack over his shoulder. He could see his bus through the window. A line of people waited patiently for their turn to climb the steps. "Of course it's okay, but I don't know where I'm going to be. Don't freak out if you can't find me."

"I thought you were going to Times Square?"

"The bus lets off on Forty-Second Street, so I'm starting off in Times Square, but I don't know what's going to happen after that. It wouldn't be much of an adventure if I planned it all out."

"It's not much of an adventure either way." Worry creased Will's forehead.

He and Dalton had been friends since their university days. They had a lot in common. Both had overachieving fathers who didn't know what to make of having sons who weren't wired the same way. Dalton's older brother, Grant, went along with everything their dad had planned, not minding at all. Grant was fine with playing golf, dating the right girls, and working toward taking over the family business in twenty years when their dad retired.

Dalton was the problem. His parents didn't know what to make of him. He joked around too much for their tastes. He was different from his older brother. He thought of himself as a freethinker; his parents saw him as rebellious. After he'd graduated from prep school, he'd chosen a university that didn't meet with their approval. To their credit, they'd paid his tuition but not without a lot of grumbling.

Every step of the way, Dalton heard lectures about his ill-informed decisions and how they would detrimentally affect his entire future. His parents didn't like his major—philosophy—saying it was a waste of time. And when he went to graduate school for social work, they were so embarrassed, they couldn't even tell their friends. You'd think he had gone to rehab. He'd graduated with honors, but even so, his education was still such a sore spot, his father could only shake his head when the subject came up.

So many times Dalton had wished he could please his father, but he couldn't do that and be true to himself. The thought of going to an office every day, poring over spreadsheets and strategizing how to take down competitors, made his stomach turn. His brother excelled in that area, and his parents had assumed both sons would follow that path, but Dalton had veered off course, heading for parts still unknown. He hated being a disappointment. It helped one day when his grandma had taken him aside after a family gathering and said, "Dalton, it's important to live your own life." She'd tapped his chest with one long skinny finger. "Never let other people interfere with your heart's desire. Listen to your intuition. You'll know what's best for you."

Will understood what it was like to stray from family expectations because he had gone through that as well. By being themselves, they were disappointments to everything their old, established families stood for.

Will was the only one who knew about his crazy scheme. Dalton appreciated his concern. He clamped a reassuring hand on his friend's shoulder. "Will, believe me, it's all going to be fine. No one's going to mess with me. Besides, I don't have anything to steal, and I'm going to keep a low profile. Really, what could go wrong?" And then he left to get on the bus, ready to begin.

CHAPTER THREE

LaGuardia Airport was not at all what Greta expected. When she thought of New York City, the things that came to mind were Broadway, culture, and fashion, so she'd expected to walk off the plane and find a modern and sleek airport. In her mind's eye, she'd envisioned abstract sculptures in the terminal and gleaming floors with clearly marked signs overhead, all the better to lead weary travelers to their destinations.

Instead, she found the airport nondescript, as generic as the Milwaukee airport. To make matters worse, there was a line to the women's bathroom. Once she was inside, the room smelled like a dirty diaper.

Even though the airport was a disappointment, there was no place she'd rather have been. She took it all in, marveling at the buzz of anticipation circling the people who were coming and going. The airport was a United Nations of languages. She recognized Spanish, German, and French but was clueless about most of the others. One young couple spoke to each other, their words punctuated by energetic tongue clicks. She tried not to stare but listened as their voices rose and fell, full of passion and enthusiasm. Different from English but so beautiful to hear.

Standing in line at the restroom, Greta inched forward along with everyone else, all patiently waiting their turn. When she was out of the stall and washing her hands, her carry-on at her feet, she accidentally dripped a little liquid soap on the counter. Then she noticed a wadded-up paper towel left on the adjacent sink. Without even thinking about it, she reached over and threw it out, then took a fresh towel to wipe up the mess before cleaning up another puddle on the other side of the basin. When she looked up, a woman was watching, an amused look on her face.

"I just hate to leave things dirty," Greta explained.

The woman smiled. "By any chance, are you from the Midwest?"

Greta straightened up. "Why, yes. I flew in from Wisconsin about twenty minutes ago. How did you know?"

"Just a hunch. Enjoy your time in the city." She leaned toward the mirror to examine her teeth. Finding them satisfactory, she smiled at her reflection in approval.

"Thanks. I will." People in New York were turning out to be very friendly.

Greta made her way toward the baggage claim, going down a ramp that led to a set of stairs. On her right, she passed a few offices, noticing the people who worked behind the glass fronts. At the baggage carousel, she recognized a few people who'd been on her flight, reassuring her she was in the right place.

There was a system to the baggage carousel, a routine people seemed to follow instinctively. Everyone knew to step forward to pull their luggage off and then back up and give others room so they could do the same. When her own tan suitcase came into view, Greta politely and quickly claimed it. That done, she was just about to go look for the driver who'd be meeting her when he found her first.

"Greta? Greta Hansen?" The voice came from behind her.

She swiveled around to see a young guy with deep-set eyes and dark, slicked-back hair. She recognized him as the man who had held the car door open in dozens of photos of Cece coming and going from all her events.

"Yes, are you Michael?" Greta held out her hand, but he didn't take it, just frowned.

"Yes."

"It's very nice to meet you."

He nodded and went to work, pulling out the handle of her suitcase and gesturing for her to hand over her carry-on, which he piggybacked on top. "Follow me," he said with a tilt of his head. "I'm sorry, but there was construction, so I had to park far away."

Greta followed, chatting nervously as they went. She told him she didn't mind walking to the car—she was just grateful he'd come. "My first time in New York!" she said. "I love it already. I think this is going to be a great summer."

Once she was safely inside the back of the car, Michael turned on some music, and she felt comfortable relaxing and taking it all in. Greta watched in wide-eyed wonder when they cut through Central Park, thinking of all the movies and TV shows that had scenes set there. For most of her life, Manhattan had been just a place on a screen, somewhere that other people traveled to for business or to see the Macy's Thanksgiving Day Parade or whatever. Little had she known that one day she'd be spending the summer with one of the most famous families in New York City.

Coming out of the park, Greta took her phone out and began taking pictures every time the car paused or slowed. As she went along, she texted them to Travis and her best friend, Jacey. As usual, her brother didn't answer just yet. Jacey, though, texted back right away, as excited for her as anyone could be. She wanted to know everything about Cece's life and her friends, Vance and Katrina. Greta promised to keep her updated every step of the way.

When the car pulled up to the curb, she recognized the outside of Cece's building. After her phone conversation with Deborah Vanderhaven, she'd done a search and found an article on a decorating site with lots of details about their home. The Vanderhavens lived on Central Park West, occupying the top three floors of one of the most exclusive buildings in Manhattan. Their 14,000-square-foot apartment included eight bedrooms, five bathrooms, two kitchens (a regular one and an eat-in chef's kitchen), a media room, and a rooftop exercise pool. The family had started out living on one floor and wound up buying the two floors below to make one big residence. The article quoted Mrs. Vanderhaven as saying, "It's not as big as it sounds. Sometimes I feel like we could use even more space."

Michael left the engine idling while he got out and came around to her side. Within seconds, he had helped her out and united Greta with her luggage. "And you have reached your destination," he said, gesturing to the door. "I'm going to be leaving to park the car for the night."

She glanced at the entrance, gold double doors stamped in a diamond pattern, guarded by a doorman in a snappy blue uniform. "I just go in?" Somehow it seemed like there should be more to it.

His head bobbed a yes. "Don't worry, you're expected." A look passed between Michael and the doorman, who beckoned for Greta to come closer.

The doorman held the door and asked, "Do you need some assistance with your luggage, miss?"

Oh, so nice of him! "No, thanks," she said, smiling. "I've got it."

"Very good." As if she'd done something admirable.

Inside, she found herself in an opulent entryway resembling the lobby of an upscale hotel. On the right, two women sat behind a glossy counter, and on the far wall was another set of doors identical to the exterior doors. The left wall was adorned with three paintings, all landscapes, each one topped with its own spotlight. Two short columns in between were topped with ferns.

After the two women consulted a list, checked Greta's ID, and got phone confirmation, she was cleared. The younger of the two accompanied her to the elevator and punched in the code that would take her to the Vanderhaven residence. As the elevator rose to the top of the building, it hit Greta that this was it. After so many years of admiring Cece from afar, she was finally going to meet her in person. They were so different. Greta was newly graduated from college and hadn't made her mark yet, while Cece was so successful, someone who made things happen. Cece could teach her so much about how to deal with people in the business world, but more importantly, Greta hoped they'd become friends. It was a lot to hope for, but didn't all dreams start out that way?

CHAPTER FOUR

It was a short walk from the bus to Times Square, but suddenly, Dalton wasn't in a hurry. The next two weeks, he'd be adrift, and although it was by choice, a small part of him was beginning to doubt his plan. In theory, spending two weeks as a homeless person had sounded like a fine idea, but on some level, he must have known it was crazy, because he hadn't told anyone but Will, who readily had agreed to be his emergency contact. "Can't say I understand it," he'd said, "but I'm there for you."

So now Dalton found himself dragging his feet. As it turned out, he was low on just about everything else but had an endless supply of time.

When he originally conceived this idea, he intended to live on the streets for the first week and spend the second week trying out different shelters. He knew the weather might be a challenge. He'd heard it was better to be homeless in the summer than the winter for obvious reasons, but the extreme heat brought its own problems.

The air was especially hot and heavy, radiating off the city streets. Even the breeze felt like it came from an open oven door. For June, it was a bit much, and as the days went on, he suspected it would be even more miserable.

Dalton meandered patiently through the crowd, stepping aside for couples holding hands and slowing to let one elderly woman shuffle ahead of him.

He was usually polite anyway, and it was easy to be gracious when he had no schedule to keep and nowhere to be.

Times Square was just the way he'd always imagined. Even though his home in Connecticut was less than fifty miles away, he'd never walked around Times Square in person, knowing it only from television and movies. He'd been fascinated by the place since he was a little guy. He'd watch the ball drop at the stroke of midnight each New Year's Eve and note the antics of the crowd.

The only times he'd gotten close in real life had been when his family took trips into the city to see shows and catch dinner. No one else was interested in a side trip to Times Square. It was, his father once declared, "the biggest tourist trap in the world." He'd said this from the back seat of the car as their driver navigated around the perimeter. Dalton had been left pressing his nose against the glass, trying to see as much as he could as they drove by.

Now he was there, right in the thick of it. He walked around Times Square for an hour or so, trying to stay close to the buildings so he'd be in the shade. Every now and then, he went into one of the little gift shops to cool off. They all had pretty much the same stuff. T-shirts proclaiming the wearer loved New York, a giant red heart where the word *love* should be. There were snow globes and kitchen magnets and all sorts of other things that would provide proof for tourists to show they'd been to New York.

Times Square, Dalton discovered, was more triangle-shaped than square, and had a set of bleachers on one end, the better to people watch and take pictures.

At one point he stopped to watch a guy play the saxophone, his instrument case open for donations. The musician was good, better than good, playing and moving with a soulful passion. Out of habit, Dalton reached into his pocket for a contribution and then, remembering his circumstances, dropped a few coins instead of giving dollar bills. The saxophone player nodded in appreciation, not missing a note.

He avoided the middle area of the triangle, where people dressed as cartoon characters and action figures corralled tourists into getting their photos taken with them for cash. The Naked Cowboy was there in his white briefs, boots, and cowboy hat, his guitar giving him just a little more coverage. Dalton didn't see any Naked Cowgirls, but there were some topless women with stars painted strategically on their chests. No one seemed to be objecting to the nudity, so he guessed it was allowed.

By dinnertime, after it had cooled off some and the crowds had thinned, he went in search of a member of the very demographic he was trying to impersonate: guys who were homeless. The street musicians with open cases could well be homeless, but the ones he'd seen were casually but neatly attired, so he decided they were probably music students who had to practice anyway and opted to pick up a few dollars at the same time.

He finally spotted a guy sitting cross-legged around the corner, his back resting against a brick storefront. A piece of cardboard propped up at his feet said, **HOMELESS VET. ANY AMOUNT OF MONEY WILL HELP**. Next to the sign was a round plastic container. It held a few coins but nothing major. He didn't look old. Dalton guessed that he was maybe forty or so. He had a rolling cart parked next to him, the kind old ladies use when they walk to the grocery store. A baseball cap covered his head, the rim wet with sweat. His shaggy hair covered his ears, and his beard needed trimming. As Dalton approached, he heard the man quietly saying, "Please? Please?" in kind of a sad voice to those passing by, but everyone kept going. No one even looked his way.

"Mind if I join you?" Dalton asked. He saw the man hesitate and added, "Just for a little bit. I've been walking for ages, and I want to take a load off."

He shrugged. "Suit yourself. It's a free country."

Dalton shook off his backpack and settled down next to him, leaving some space. "Tough crowd, huh?" He watched as people walked past without even a glance. They might as well have been invisible.

"Just the usual," he said with a sigh.

Now Dalton saw him more clearly. He didn't look to be forty after all. Closer to thirty, give or take. It was his weary look—the circles under his eyes, the beaten-down expression, the sad mouth—that made him look older. His features were noble. He had angular cheekbones and the kind of nose one would see on a Greek statue, but there was nothing noble about sitting on a hot sidewalk hoping strangers would give you money.

Dalton could almost hear his dad's voice in his head. He knew what advice he'd give this guy: *Get a job. Get off your lazy butt and work for a living, like the rest of us. No one gets a free pass in life.*

His dad had inherited the family business and a small fortune along with it, which he'd managed to turn into a large business empire and a massive fortune, something of which he was very proud. Rightly so, but he thought that made him an expert on turning nothing into something, when really he'd turned something into more something. Even with Dalton's privileged upbringing, he knew it was a lot harder to start with zero and build from there.

"So you're a homeless vet, right?" As soon as the words were out of his mouth, Dalton regretted saying them. The man looked wounded, as if he thought Dalton was making fun of him. "I'm sorry." He spoke quickly, backpedaling. "I'm new to this, and I said the wrong thing." He stuck out his hand. "Dalton."

He looked at Dalton's hand for a second; then his face relaxed, and he reached over and shook. "Matt. Matt Gower."

"Hi, Matt. Glad to meet you." They sat in silence for a few minutes, watching as a woman pushing a stroller paused to drop some quarters into Matt's container. The toddler in the stroller was sleeping, slumped to one side, his miniature mouth slightly open.

"Thank you, ma'am. Much appreciated," Matt said. She nodded and kept going. After another minute, he turned and asked, "You said you're new to this. New to what?"

"Being homeless."

He barked out a short laugh. "You're not homeless."

"Yes, I am." Dalton patted his backpack. "Everything I have in the world is right in here."

Matt gave him a suspicious sideways glance. "How long you been homeless?"

"Just a few hours," he admitted. "But I'm out here, without much to my name, and there's no place else for me to go, so it's official. I'm homeless."

"Let me guess. Your girlfriend kicked you out."

"No."

"Huh." Matt looked thoughtful now. "Okay, I've got it figured out. You flunked out of college and have no backup plan."

"No, that's not it." *Just the opposite,* Dalton reflected. He had a master's degree in social psychology and had graduated with honors.

"I'll get this. Don't tell me. You won't get a job, and your folks are sick of you sponging off them?"

"No." Dalton shook his head.

Matt mulled over the remaining possibilities for a minute and finally said, "Then it has to be drugs or drinking."

"No. I don't do drugs, and I'm not a big drinker."

"Okay, I give up. Why are you homeless?"

"It's a long story, but basically, my father and I had a difference of opinion, and I've got something to prove to him."

"Never heard that one before. Care to elaborate?"

"I'd rather not get into it," Dalton said. "Just trust me on this. We don't get along. It's like we're from different planets."

"You're mad now, but after a few days in the heat, no comfortable bed to sleep in, you'll be thinking differently. Then you'll go back and patch things up with your dad." Matt spoke with certainty, like he'd seen this kind of thing before.

"Believe me, that's not going to happen," Dalton said.

Matt nodded, accepting, and changed the subject. "Got anything to eat in that bag?"

Even though Dalton knew he hadn't packed any food, he made a show of unzipping the backpack and looking inside. "Nope, I . . ." He stopped, seeing something new at the bottom, then reached in and pulled out two packages of beef jerky. One of them had a yellow sticky note attached. The scrawled words were all Will: *Try Not To Starve To Death*. Dalton thought back. The only opportunity Will had to put the jerky into the backpack would have been when Dalton was in the bathroom at the bus station. Sneaky. "Just some beef jerky. You want some?"

Matt's face brightened as he took one of the bags. "Really? I can have the whole thing?"

"Sure. I've got two." Dalton opened his bag, and they both began to eat. Matt had a full bottle of water on the pavement next to him. He opened it and offered Dalton the first swig, which Dalton gratefully accepted. Jerky made a guy thirsty.

"So where did you serve?" Dalton asked.

"Afghanistan."

"That must have been tough."

"It's still tough," Matt said.

"What was it like over there?"

Matt glared. "It's not something I want to talk about."

"I'm sorry."

They sat in silence for a good fifteen minutes. Matt said, "I didn't mean to be rude. I just don't talk about it."

"I get it. I shouldn't have asked."

"It's okay. Everyone asks. It's just, you know, too painful to talk about, and it makes things worse to dwell on it."

Dalton nodded.

Another few minutes went by, the two men sitting quietly side by side, the passing pedestrians oblivious to the tension. Matt said, "It was bad enough the first time, but I keep reliving it. It's like it followed me home."

"Flashbacks?" Dalton kept his gaze ahead toward the street.

"Yeah," Matt said, and slowly the words came out. He didn't talk about what happened in Afghanistan but revealed bits and pieces about his life after he'd returned to the States. He'd had panic attacks and long nights without sleep. The nights when he did sleep were filled with nightmares. During the day, he'd had episodes where he experienced the horrors of war all over again, not just remembering it but living it, the smells and sounds and adrenaline rushes. The certainty that he was about to die. Dalton had read about all these things, but reading about it and hearing it from someone who lived it were entirely different things. "No one understands," Matt said sadly. "No one."

"I can't say I understand because I wasn't there," Dalton said. "But I'm sorry you went through it." What he wanted to say was that he cared. He really cared and wished he could help in some way. He almost said that very thing but stopped himself, thinking it was too personal too soon.

"I'll never be the same person I was, and that pisses me off," Matt said. "And it affects everything. Right after I came home, I thought I was doing okay, but then I'd do some random thing, and it would remind me I wasn't quite right. I'd go to the grocery store, and it was so bright and colorful, and there were so many choices. Everywhere you looked. So. Many. Choices. There weren't just apples—there were all these different kinds of apples, stacked up all over the place. How can a person even choose? It was overwhelming, you know?"

Dalton nodded, even though he didn't quite know. He'd learned from his volunteer work that recognizing other people's pain was important.

"And then I went to my nephew's birthday party. It was a backyard thing, piñata, cake, tons of presents, the usual, but it all seemed like too much. So many presents, so much food, so many people talking and laughing. I kept thinking about the kids back in Afghanistan and what their lives are like. There's so much pain and death out in the world. It's everywhere, and the people here have no clue."

"But you do," Dalton said, his voice soft.

"Yeah, but I wish I didn't. I'm a wreck. And really, what does any of this matter?" He gestured to the people walking past: a group of Asian teenagers in big sunglasses, an elderly couple laughing, a businesswoman dressed in office attire except for her athletic shoes. "It's all a struggle. I can't even go into the middle of Times Square because the crowds are too unpredictable, and being out in the open scares the hell out of me. I feel calmer around the corner, with my back against a wall." He patted the brick wall behind them.

"Safer?" Dalton suggested.

"Yeah, a little bit safer, but I never quite feel safe. Not really. Thunderstorms make me insane. The first Fourth of July I was home, I took tranquilizers so I'd sleep through it, but I had nightmares the whole night and couldn't get myself to wake up because of the pills. During the day, I always have this heavy feeling, like something really bad is about to happen, and I can't stop it."

"It sounds horrible."

"It is." Matt took a long pull from the water. He screwed the cap back onto the bottle. "Really horrible. One time, right after I got home, I went to a strip mall by myself. I was happy because it went pretty well. I bought the thing I came for, some Tylenol PM at Walgreens, and I talked to the cashier like normal and everything. I was heading out to the parking lot when a car engine started up, real loud like it had a bad muffler, and I just froze. I was back there, like, literally back there." Dalton knew *back there* meant Afghanistan. "I was between two cars, and I dropped down and took cover and couldn't move. Could not move an inch. My heart was pounding so loud, I could feel it in my ears, and I could taste dust. I had to call a friend to come pick me up. I couldn't function for days."

"I've heard," Dalton said carefully, "that there are effective therapies for PTSD now."

"That's what they say."

"You don't believe it?"

He shook his head. "Maybe it works for some. I don't know."

"Why not try it?"

Matt gave him a look like he was out of his mind. "It's not that I don't want to get better. It just takes so much to get there." He waved his hand out toward the street.

"To get where?"

"The place where I'd have to go for this so-called magic therapy. I don't even know where I'd start. The VA, I guess, but before I can get help, I'd have to make phone calls and fill out paperwork and talk to people and get appointments and then find a way to get to the appointments. There are all these steps, and if you even mess up once, you have to start over."

As he spoke, the truth of it sank in for Dalton. When just going about your day was exhausting, there wasn't much left over for anything else. He said, "And it's all too much?"

Matt nodded. "Too much. I've already said more to you than I've told anyone besides Ellie, and I feel like I've been wrung out. Arranging to get treatment would take more out of me than I can do. It would be like asking a paralyzed man to climb Mount Everest."

"They should make it easier to get into a program."

His mouth twitched, as if to say, *what can you do?* "There are more than a hundred thousand homeless veterans. They're probably doing the best they can."

And that was it. Matt wasn't looking for anyone else to solve his problem. He wasn't blaming the military for his current circumstances. He was just trying to get through life, miserable and alone. And there were more than a hundred thousand out there just like him. The idea was mind blowing.

They talked for another hour or so, with Dalton doing most of the asking. He wanted to know how Matt got to this point. Didn't he have family and friends? Someone had to have a couch he could crash on, right? Anything would be better than living on the streets, begging for change. Matt haltingly answered his questions. His family was a total mess, he said, citing alcoholism and abuse as the reasons he enlisted in the first place. His sister was okay, but she was married and had little kids, so she couldn't help. And his friends? Well, they'd helped at the start, when he first returned, but eventually, they grew impatient with him. "They wanted the old Matt," he said. "I think I scared them, the way I freaked out, not being able to handle even the smallest things. I would snap sometimes when things weren't going my way." He stared ahead as if remembering. "I could feel that I was out of control, but I couldn't stop it. Once, I had a meltdown at a party, and I could see their eyes just looking . . . It's too much for most people to handle. My problems are too big." He blinked and looked down.

"So there's no one you can turn to? There must be people who miss you."

He didn't say anything for the longest time, just stared ahead like he was in a trance. Finally, the corners of his mouth turned up into a smile. "There was this one girl."

Ah, there was always a girl. "Yes?"

"She's really special." He leaned to one side and pulled a wallet out of his back pocket, then carefully took out a photo and handed it to Dalton. "Careful. This photo got me through some hard times."

The photo was of a dark-haired woman, her head tilted up to the camera, an amused smile on her face. "She's beautiful," Dalton said. He turned it over and saw the name *Ellie Fronk* written on the back.

"Yeah. She was the greatest. *Is* the greatest," Matt said, correcting himself.

"You're in love with her." Without even thinking, Dalton blurted out the words. From the look on Matt's face, he'd gotten it right. Dalton gave him back the photo, and Matt tucked it carefully into his wallet.

"Yep." His smile faded. "She waited for me and everything, but when I got back, I wasn't the same. She tried to understand—I'll give her that—but there's no fixing me. She deserves better. I can tell you that much."

"So what happened? She broke up with you?"

"No, nothing like that. Ellie tried so hard to help me, but I was a total mess and wasn't getting better. One day she came home with tickets to a Broadway show she got from someone at work, and she was all excited about us going. I tried not to show her what a wreck I was. I even got most of the way through the play, but I had a panic attack during this one part, and I had to get out of there. I told her I was going to the bathroom and just bolted right out of the theater, and I've been out here on the streets ever since. A million times I've thought of letting her know what happened, but I just can't."

"How come?"

"Too ashamed, I guess. She's better off without me. Ellie deserves better."

"When did this happen?"

"A few months ago. I saw her once, right here in Manhattan, walking with her sister. I followed them for a little bit, but I didn't have the nerve to talk to them."

"You could still call her."

He shook his head. "No. What would I say? I mean, I just left. Who does that? I don't even understand it myself."

Dalton tried to be empathetic, but it was difficult. It was noble of Matt to want to shield his girlfriend from his troubles, and yet with her, he had a chance. What good could possibly happen out here on the streets? They sat in complete silence for a long time after that. Lots of people walked past, but only a few gave money. Matt was happy for every dime. Panhandling took a lot more effort than Dalton had realized. When the sun started to go down, Matt struggled to his feet. "Time to find a place for the night. Take care, Dalton."

"Wait a minute." He rose from the pavement. "I'm new to all this. Do you have any tips on where to go to sleep?"

"Nope," he said, walking away. "I fly solo. You're on your own."

Dalton watched him heading determinedly down Eighth Avenue, pulling his two-wheeled cart behind him. During their talk, he'd mentioned a general distrust of homeless shelters, saying you had to be careful. Not all of them were clean, and sometimes other people stole your stuff. He'd gone only a few times, when the weather was extreme. Matt was also worried about social workers. They meant well, but one he'd encountered had been pushy about wanting to get him into some kind of group home. Dalton wasn't sure what that was all about, but Matt was sure the woman got some kind of bonus for recruiting veterans. "No one's getting rich on my problems," he said, which struck Dalton as kind of paranoid, but really, what did he know? He was a guy from Connecticut, and he was here to learn.

So Dalton doubted Matt was heading to a shelter. *Where else do the homeless sleep in a big city like this?* he wondered. *The subway? A back alley behind a dumpster?* He was curious. As Matt grew smaller and smaller off in the distance, Dalton made a sudden decision. He was going to follow him.

CHAPTER FIVE

Greta stepped off the elevator, taking a deep breath to calm the nervous butterflies inside. She wanted to present herself as calm, cool, and professional. She had landed a dream job and wanted to make a good first impression.

Just ahead was an entry area with a gold embossed door that presumably led into the Vanderhaven apartment. The ceilings above, she noticed, were tall and edged with ornate crown molding. Next to the door, a vase of flowers sat on a white table trimmed in gold. An oval gilded mirror hung above it. Stalling for time because she was nervous, she went to give the flowers a quick sniff.

When she caught sight of herself in the mirror, she checked her teeth, then got out a comb to smooth some flyaway strands. She was still fussing with her hair when she heard a whirring noise. She looked up to see a camera swing her way, stopping when it was pointing at her face.

Greta tucked her comb back into her bag and went straight to the door. Before she could knock, it swung open. She'd been hoping it would be Cece and her two best friends, but having Deborah Vanderhaven greet her was a pretty close second. She looked as fabulous in person as she did in photos. Today she wore a periwinkle-blue skirt and matching blazer over a white blouse with short little boots that Greta didn't think were an obvious choice, but the combination totally worked. Her style was big city, but her greeting was from one Wisconsin relative to another.

"Greta!" she exclaimed, ushering her into their home. "Greta Hansen! I'm so happy you're here."

She gave Greta a big hug, enveloping her in a scent that Greta knew as her signature fragrance. Greta's mother had once gotten a sample vial at an upscale department store on a trip to Chicago and said it was heaven for the nose. Cece's perfume, Let Me In, they had decided, was not as good. Close, but not quite.

When she pulled back, Greta said, "I'm really excited to be here. I can't thank you enough for setting up the internship and letting me stay with you."

"Of course!" she said. "We're delighted you could join us." She slipped an arm around Greta's shoulders and walked out of the foyer and into a sitting area. Greta looked back at her suitcase, sitting forlornly on the Oriental rug.

Seeing her glance, Mrs. Vanderhaven said, "Just the one bag?" as if it weren't quite enough.

"It's a big suitcase. I was able to fit a lot in." She'd debated bringing two pieces of luggage but decided against it, thinking she'd be buying new clothes in New York.

She nodded. "Just leave your suitcase there for now. I'm eager to talk to you."

"Of course, Mrs. Vanderhaven."

"No, no!" She laughed and waved her hand. "Please. Call me Deborah."

Greta took a seat on a tall upholstered chair and made a mental note of everything she saw in the room, memorizing details for her late-night phone call to Jacey. Her mom, too, would want to hear everything. Staring across the room at Deborah Vanderhaven, Greta was reminded of a modern-day Jacqueline Kennedy Onassis. Classic elegance. Not anything like her mom, who sometimes went grocery shopping after gardening, not realizing her T-shirt was streaked with dirt.

Deborah sat opposite her, crossed her legs at the ankles, and began. "I know I've already told you this, but your email couldn't have come at a better time. I am overjoyed that you are going to be staying with us."

"Thank you. I'm happy to be here."

Deborah was silent, as if weighing her next thoughts. After a moment, she said, "I know I can trust you to use the utmost discretion, but I want to make sure you know, right from the start, that you are not to share anything that goes on in this household with anyone. No photos, no stories, no details about our lives. I am particularly talking about anything to do with Cece or Brenna."

"Of course. I never would," Greta said, readily agreeing even as her heart sank. This changed everything. So much for sharing details with Jacey. She'd promised her a play-by-play of the whole exciting summer, especially her first meeting with Cece and friends, but now she'd have to keep it more general.

"All of that will be covered in the nondisclosure agreement in your contract, but you won't be seeing that until tomorrow, and I wanted to tell you first thing."

"I didn't know there'd be a contract." Were there always contracts when interning for companies? She suddenly realized she didn't know much about what she was getting herself into.

Deborah smiled. "Nothing to worry about. Just a formality. You understand." She sighed as if burdened. "The attorneys who safeguard us are very thorough. It's a mixed blessing. I just wanted to tell you myself so you don't feel ambushed tomorrow. I'll be at the airport by then, and I won't be around to answer any questions you might have."

"You're going on a trip?"

Deborah brightened. "Oh, yes. We always go to Paris for a few weeks over the summer. Business mixed with pleasure," she said. "It's our tradition. We've done it for ages now."

Now that Deborah mentioned it, Greta did remember seeing a lot of pictures of Mr. and Mrs. Vanderhaven in Europe during the summertime. But she didn't know they went every year. For a few weeks? That seemed like a long time. "Do the girls go too?"

"Oh, no, just me and Harry. Brenna would be dreadfully bored, and Cece has her own things to attend to."

As if on cue, Brenna bounded into the room wearing pajamas, a stuffed monkey clutched under her arm. She went straight for her mother, who held out her arms to pull her into a hug. "Come here, my baby." Deborah gave her a kiss and then scooted over in her seat to make room for Brenna to sit next to her.

"Nanny said to come say good night," Brenna said and, suddenly realizing Greta was in the room, gave her cousin a shy sideways glance. She was a cute little girl with chestnut-brown hair and big dark eyes.

"You're just in time to meet your cousin Greta. She flew in from Wisconsin to spend the summer with us. You remember me telling you she'd be coming here to stay with us?"

Brenna nodded.

"Go ahead, you don't need to be afraid. Say hello."

"Hello, Greta." Her voice was whispery and sweet.

"Hi, Brenna. I'm glad to meet you. I hope we get a chance to spend some time together."

She smiled. "Okay."

"Now off you go," her mother said, giving her a boost off the seat and planting one last kiss on her cheek. "Daddy and I are leaving very early in the morning, so we won't see you before we go, but if you're good and don't cry, Nanny will give you a present at lunchtime."

Brenna's face crumpled. "But I don't want you to go away."

"We've been over this before." Deborah's tone was firm. "I know you don't like it when we're gone, but this trip is very important for Daddy's business. It'll just be for a little bit, and Nanny will be with you the entire time." She cupped Brenna's chin. "Be a brave girl for Mommy, and I'll be back before you know it." She whispered something in her daughter's ear, and Brenna slowly nodded. "Okay, then. Off you go."

Brenna trudged out of the room, pausing at the doorway to give a little wave. "Good night, Greta."

"Good night, Brenna."

"My Velcro child. She has a bit of separation anxiety," Deborah said with a sigh. "Now where were we?"

"You were going to tell me about my internship?"

"Oh, yes! As you may know, the Vanderhaven Corporation is the parent company of many, many other companies and divisions. There were any number of positions we could have given you, but after several meetings and much discussion, we've decided that you will serve as an intern with Cece's own company."

"I'll be interning at Firstborn Daughter, Inc.?" *Whoa.* It was like the universe had heard her deepest secret wish and granted it. It seemed too good to be true. "For the whole summer?"

"Every minute that you're here. I think you'll find it to be fun but a definite challenge." She raised her eyebrows questioningly. "What do you think?"

"I'm thrilled," Greta assured her. "And willing to do whatever needs to be done."

Deborah smiled. "I have no doubt of that, Greta. You are your mother's daughter, after all."

"What exactly will I be doing? When do I start? Where is the office?" Greta couldn't help herself; the questions just poured out one after another.

Deborah held up a hand. "Your duties will be determined by Katrina and Vance and will vary from day to day. The main objective is to keep Cece's image polished to a fine sheen. Firstborn Daughter, Inc. is an extension of Cece herself. The fragrance, the clothing, the cosmetics—all of it has become such a great source of revenue because the young women who buy the products want to be like Cece. Anything that takes away from her image will be devastating to the brand."

"I see." Greta cocked her head to one side. "So what exactly will I be doing?"

"Protecting the brand as if your life depended on it," she said, as if that explained things.

"So I'll be helping with . . . ?"

Deborah tented her fingers together thoughtfully. "I don't have time to get into the particulars. Katrina and Vance will brief you first thing tomorrow. Until then, you are not to talk to anyone about our family or our apartment. Absolutely no photos. If photos are leaked to the media and we trace them back to you, it will be very bad." She frowned. "We don't want to take legal action against a relative, but you know how attorneys are. I'd hate to see it come to that."

Greta had never had any encounters with attorneys, but she got the general idea. "No photos. Got it."

"The household staff will have off while we're gone, but Nanny will be here, and a cleaning crew will come twice a week. Groceries will be delivered and laundry picked up every third day and delivered the next. And Michael will be available to drive. Katrina knows how to reach him. The binder in your bedroom will give you all the details."

"Okay." Greta felt like she had been plunked down in another culture and hadn't quite caught on yet.

Deborah stood up. "I'm sorry to wrap this up so quickly. Early flight, you know," she said apologetically. She waited for Greta to get her suitcase and gave her a quick tour of their apartment, pointing out rooms as she strode past, the heels of her boots clicking on the marble floors. The first floor contained what she called all the common areas. None of them looked common to Greta, who surmised that the term applied to usage. They bypassed the second floor, which contained the family's private quarters as well as Nanny's bedroom.

"Does she live here?" Greta asked.

"Sometimes," Deborah said, climbing the stairs to the third floor. "Brenna likes to have her close by." She pointed out an elevator that she said the family rarely used. "We believe in climbing stairs," she said, as if this were the definitive answer to a philosophical debate. Greta smiled weakly as she followed, trying not to clunk the wheels of her suitcase against the steps.

On the third floor, Deborah walked Greta to the door of the guest room that would be her home for the summer. "I think you'll find you have everything you need," she said. "And tomorrow Katrina and Vance will fill you in." She gave her a quick hug, and then Greta was on her own.

Once she closed the door and got a good look, a feeling of awe came over her. The room was like a luxury hotel suite, with a comfortable queen-size bed covered with half a dozen pillows. A big-screen TV was across from the bed, a desk sat in the corner, and brocade curtains covered an alcove to the right. When she pushed them back, she got a view of the city. "Amazing," she whispered, taking it all in. The apartment was so high that the sky hovered right above her, the stars just out of reach.

Exploring, she found expensive shampoos and conditioners—all Cece's brand—in the bathroom, along with plush towels and a shower the size of a pony stall.

A small refrigerator was stocked with a variety of bottled water and other beverages. She recognized the brand names as being from companies the Vanderhavens owned. She grabbed a water and got out the nutrition bars she'd packed in her suitcase.

After she was finished eating, she washed up at the sink and got in her jammies, then settled back on the bed with her phone. Her first call was to her mother. Going against her promise to Cece's mom, Greta told her everything about the house and her cousin, right down to how the place was decorated and what Deborah was wearing. She swore her to secrecy and knew she wouldn't share, not even a word.

"And what about Harry and Cece?" Mom asked. "What are they like?"

"I didn't see them," Greta said. "I'm not even sure if they're home."

"Is Deborah's place like those houses we see in the Mansion section?" Greta's family had subscribed to the *Wall Street Journal* for years, and the Friday edition featured a section that highlighted the homes of the rich and famous. Her mother had always marveled at how the wealthy lived with their extra kitchens and butler pantries, tennis courts and indoor pools, libraries and media rooms and workout spaces, all of it fabulous and luxurious and large. Once, when Greta had said it seemed like a lot to keep track of, her mother had laughed and said, "They have people to take care of that. And a manager to take care of the people."

Now she was asking how the Vanderhavens' apartment compared to the other lavish homes. "Yes. It's gorgeous," Greta said. "I feel like I'm staying at the Ritz or something." Not that she'd ever stayed at the Ritz. "The bedroom they put me in is half the size of our house."

"Don't get too used to it. Soon enough you'll be back home and slumming again." Greta could hear the smile in her mother's voice.

After they exchanged goodbyes, Greta texted Jacey. She didn't reveal much, just that she had arrived, had met Cece's mom and sister, and would find out more tomorrow. She started to type that she'd be interning for Firstborn Daughter, Inc., then deleted the words and instead wrote that she'd be meeting Cece, Katrina, and Vance the next day. The idea of the nondisclosure agreement in her contract loomed like a dark cloud overhead. She didn't want to get in trouble before she even got started.

After settling into bed, she set her alarm for six thirty, thinking that would give her plenty of time for showering and dressing so she'd be ready for breakfast by eight. Deborah Vanderhaven had said she should plan to meet everyone in the kitchen for a breakfast meeting. She'd rushed over so much information that Greta wasn't sure whom *everyone* would be or what the meeting would cover. She'd just have to find out in the morning.

CHAPTER SIX

Dalton followed Matt. At one point, when he'd gotten too close, he stopped to buy a bottle of water from a newsstand to create some space. He took a few swigs before tucking it away in his backpack, then continued on, trying to stay out of Matt's line of vision. Matt had confessed to having some pretty serious emotional responses over things that most people would think were nothing. But the truth was that Dalton wasn't afraid he'd get violent; he just didn't want Matt to think he'd betrayed his trust. The guy had enough problems. Dalton didn't want to contribute to them.

They were moving away from Times Square. The urban landscape here changed, with fewer touristy stores and more hotels, restaurants, and office buildings. Dalton started to recognize bits and pieces from previous visits to the city. When they passed Carnegie Hall, he had a clear idea of where they were and where Matt was heading.

Central Park.

Dalton knew a thing or two about Central Park, having studied it ahead of time. The park was two and a half miles long and half a mile wide, 843 acres in all. Technically, it was closed from one o'clock until six o'clock in the morning, but from his research, Dalton knew plenty of homeless people slept there. And lots of wildlife too: raccoons, squirrels, rats, and mice, to name a few. None of which he'd want to encounter after dark, or anytime really. He'd heard there used to be coyotes, but his guess was that if there were any currently living in the park, they'd shy away from people. Rodents, though? Maybe he'd seen too many horror movies, but he could imagine them crawling over a sleeping person. The idea made him shudder.

They were on a paved path now, and Matt had slowed his pace, as if getting closer to his destination. Dalton got a little bolder, getting so near that if Matt turned around, he would certainly spot him. But he hadn't turned around yet.

Two guys came running past, one of them all in white with a sweatband around his head. Matt kept on, not even seeming to notice them.

When he approached a hot dog stand, the woman working it called to him by name. "Hey, Matt!" she said, waving her arm back and forth. He moved toward her, and Dalton plopped down onto a nearby bench, pulling his baseball cap over his eyes.

He couldn't help but hear the exchange between them, the woman telling him she was closing for the day and asking if he wanted a hot dog. "I'd have to throw it out anyway." She wore a green baseball cap and apron.

"That's so nice of you," Matt said, his voice grateful and enthused. "Yeah, yeah. That'd be great."

She asked if he wanted sauerkraut or condiments, and he said yes to all of it. When she handed it over, he said, "What a treat. Thank you, Trisha."

"Thank you for your service to our country. I hope things get better for you."

"They already have, thanks to you." He gave her a nod and set off, taking bites from the hot dog as he walked.

He went deeper into the park, so Dalton did too, but while Matt was on the path, he walked on the adjacent grass. When Matt stopped, Dalton darted behind a tree. This turned out to be good timing, because

Matt did a complete turn, checking to see if anyone was watching, then went off the path in the opposite direction.

Following him without being detected was getting trickier. For a second, Dalton debated walking away, but the truth of it was that he had no place to go and had gotten this far already. It would be a shame not to see this thing through.

So he continued, keeping as far back as he could without losing Matt completely. They were far from the path now, no people in sight, the terrain rising and sloping. Matt circled around boulders that looked like they'd been there since time began. Lucky for Dalton, the wheels on Matt's cart made a lot of noise as they banged against the ground. Another good thing? The man was determined to get where he was going and concentrating only on what was ahead of him. Dalton crouched down behind rocks and darted behind trees, wondering when this would end.

Just when Dalton was ready to give up and turn back, Matt stopped by a big bush located in front of an outcropping of rock. He pulled the cart to one side of the bush, dropped to his knees, and crawled back behind the shrubbery until he was out of sight. A few seconds later, his hand shot out and pulled the cart toward him until that, too, was no longer in view. *What the what?* He'd disappeared.

Dalton stood there for a good fifteen minutes, waiting to make sure Matt wasn't coming out, then slowly made his way forward to see where he'd gone. The wind had picked up, making a little noise as the breeze went through the trees, masking the sound of his soft-soled shoes on the grass. When he finally got to the bush, he circled slowly around it, trying not to breathe. The rock outcropping was as large as a minivan and sloped downward toward the overgrown bush. Peering between the rock and the greenery, he saw Matt's cart lying on its side. There was a large indentation in the base of the rock, a small cave, just large enough for a person to curl up inside of it, which is what Matt was doing. Fortunately for Dalton, his face was covered with what looked like a lightweight blanket. Or maybe a tablecloth? Dalton squinted, trying to see. Hard to say, but whatever it was, it would serve as nighttime protection from bugs.

Dalton sneaked away in the opposite direction, thinking about what he'd seen. Matt had come up with an ingenious spot for safe sleeping. Inside the cavity of the rock, he was out of sight. He had coverage from rain, and the cart parked in front of the opening served as protection from animals. The cart was good as a barrier, but it was close enough that if someone tried to take it, he was only an arm's reach away. His possessions in the cart were in plastic bags, so there was no worry of anything he owned getting wet or dirty.

Dalton had heard of the homeless washing up and brushing their teeth in the fountains in Central Park during the times they knew the park personnel wouldn't be around. If you had to be homeless, it could be worse. Not that sleeping in the park was a good long-term solution, but at least it kept a body going.

Now he needed to find his own place to sleep. He walked for a long time but was unable to find anything similar to Matt's perfect little cave. Matt must have thought he'd hit the big time when he found that spot. No wonder he didn't want anyone tagging along. Dalton kept searching. Everything looked fine for a Sunday afternoon walk, but nothing resembled a place to sleep. Finally, he came out to a clearing and was back on a path. It was dark by then, and he was tired of walking. He found the nearest park bench and, using his backpack as a pillow, settled down to sleep.

CHAPTER SEVEN

In the morning, Greta went downstairs, eager to get started. When she rounded the corner into the kitchen, she spotted Brenna sitting at the counter. An older woman faced her, elbows propped on the counter, her hands cupping her chin. She was speaking to Brenna in a low and encouraging voice.

Greta held back for a second, feeling like an intruder. It was silly to be anxious. She'd already met Brenna, who was a sweet little girl, and there was nothing scary about the woman with her. So why was her heart palpitating? She had to get over this. What had Mr. Kurtz said? Yes, now she remembered. *Take some initiative.* Shaking off her nerves, she walked into the room. "Good morning."

The woman looked startled, then recovered quickly with a smile. "You must be the cousin Brenna was telling me about." Some people gave off a warm, loving glow, and that's what Greta felt now. The woman had curly dark hair threaded with gray, high cheekbones, and flawless skin. She had just a few lines around her eyes. It was hard to judge her age, but Greta got the sense she might be as old as sixty.

"Yes." Greta strode forward, her hand outstretched. The woman met her halfway and shook her hand. "I'm Greta Hansen. Here for the summer. Just got in last night."

"Welcome!" she said. "I'm Brenna's nanny. You can call me Nanny if you want; everyone else does."

"Because that's who you are," Brenna said, stirring the milk in her cereal bowl. Only a few pieces of cereal remained, and the milk had a sugary hue.

"Because that's what I *do*." Nanny gave Brenna's hair an affectionate pat and turned back to Greta, saying, "If you need anything or have any questions about the household, feel free to ask. If I can help, I'd be happy to." She leaned back against the counter, and Greta noticed how stylishly she was dressed. Gray pinstriped pants and a button-down shirt with a chunky, shiny necklace and matching earrings. Even the staff was impeccably attired.

"Thank you. I'm supposed to meet Cece and Vance and Katrina in the kitchen for a breakfast meeting. I know I'm kind of early, but am I in the right place?" Greta remembered hearing that the Vanderhavens had two kitchens and hoped she'd found the right one.

Nanny nodded. "You are. I imagine they'll be here any minute. Do you want a cup of coffee or some juice while you wait? Maybe both?"

A minute later, Greta was seated at the large kitchen table, a cup of coffee and a small orange juice in front of her. It was odd to be waited on. She'd offered to get it herself, but Nanny just waved away her efforts, gently instructing her to sit. "I'm waiting for Brenna to finish anyway. It will give me something to do."

After making sure Greta had her beverages, Nanny declared Brenna finished, saying, "We have to get going, or you'll be late for your violin lesson."

They left the room with Nanny steering Brenna out the door by her shoulders. Right before they disappeared from sight, Brenna stopped in the doorway like she had the night before, turned, and said, "Bye, Greta. See you later," and gave her a little finger wave. She was so cute, Greta could have scooped her up and put her in her pocket. She'd always wanted a little sister. At least for the summer, she could experience a secondhand sister relationship.

She looked around the huge kitchen, everything shiny and pretty. The floor consisted of short pieces of wood stained different colors and interlaid like puzzle pieces into an intricate pattern. The refrigerator was cleverly hidden with doors that matched the cabinets. The counters were white stone with flecks of silver. Astoundingly enough, there was nothing on the counters except the coffee maker. Remembering her own family's house with the chip bags on top of the fridge; the phones charging on the countertop; and the toaster, microwave, and dish-drying rack all taking up space between the appliances, she wondered where the Vanderhavens put their stuff.

She heard Vance and Katrina before she saw them, recognizing their voices as they came down the hall. In the video clips, they were always jubilant, cheering Cece on in her endeavors. The voices she heard now were bickering, annoyed.

As they walked into the room and spotted her, there was a shift; she saw Katrina's face morph from aggravated to cheerful in the split second she walked through the doorway. "Greta?" she said. "Greta Hansen?"

Funny that everyone addressed her that way. She'd heard her first and last names verbally combined more times on this trip than she had ever before in her life. "That's me."

They introduced themselves, even though it wasn't necessary. She would have known them anywhere. As Greta started to get up to shake their hands, Vance very nicely told her to stay put. He carried a large box, the kind she associated with doughnuts, but when he set it down on the table and started taking out the contents, she saw it actually contained individual containers of cut fruit along with dozens of miniature muffins. Katrina, who'd had several file folders clutched to her chest when she walked through the door, began shuffling through them.

Greta felt like she was seeing a video clip come to life. She'd seen it all: *Katrina and Vance surprise Cece with a picnic feast! Katrina, Vance, and Cece take an impromptu trip to San Francisco in Cece's private jet! Vance covers Katrina's eyes right before Cece comes out wearing a stunning custom evening gown. Katrina squeals with delight!*

Without their being aware of it, Greta Hansen had been part of their lives all along, an invisible friend laughing along with them, cheering them on, sharing the good days and the bad. Following Cece's life was the one guilty pleasure she'd been unable to shake from her childhood and teen years, a fascination bordering on obsession. Greta felt like she knew everything about them, but of course, it was completely one sided. Even though she was related to Cece, they didn't know her at all.

Which reminded her: Where was Cece? Before she could ask, Katrina began talking nonstop, telling her how they didn't know she was coming until the last minute and how her presence changed everything. *Everything.* She and Vance had been up all night, she said, regrouping. "That's why I look like hell," she said, pointing to her eyes, which confusingly looked just fine.

"Greta, help yourself," Vance said, indicating the food.

"Thanks." She took two tiny muffins and a cup of cubed cantaloupe. "When will Cece get here?"

Katrina shrugged. "Whenever she wants to would be my guess. We stopped by her room on our way in to wake her up, and she was already in the shower, so we took that as a good sign."

Vance went and got coffees for both of them. "We barely slept at all," he said, returning to the table. "We had to come up with your backstory and leak some teasers on social media so it wouldn't come out of left field. It's not as easy as you'd think."

"Backstory?" The word came out muffled because Greta had popped a mini-muffin into her mouth and was able to open her lips only a little bit.

Katrina shook her head. "Deborah could have given us more notice. She just threw this cousin thing at us and then took off for

Paris. Typical." She took a plastic fork and speared a grape. "We had to come up with a story to explain your sudden presence. And it had to be fantastic and dramatic and yet completely plausible. With social media, everything is out there, so we couldn't contradict anything publicly known about you. It can be tricky, but I think we pulled it off."

"I'm not sure I understand," Greta said.

"It can be a whirlwind around here," Vance said sympathetically. "I'll tell you what we tell Cece: just follow our cues, and you'll be fine."

"First of all," Katrina said, pulling a sheet of paper out of one of the files, "you'll need to sign this nondisclosure agreement, which prohibits you from taking photos or disclosing information. Put your initials in the space provided after each paragraph, then sign on the second page."

Greta had just started to read it when Vance added, "It's the same as the copy in your binder in your room."

Greta looked up. "Deborah mentioned a binder, but I never saw it." She racked her brain, trying to think of how her room had been laid out. So much had happened since she'd arrived. Could she have missed something that important?

They exchanged a glance. "You didn't see the binder? I put it right on the desk in your room," Katrina said.

"I never saw it. But it might be that I just didn't notice it. I got in kind of late, and I had to call my mom . . . "

"Okay," Katrina said abruptly. "Basically, it says not to share any information or images to the outside world, especially to social media. Besides being grounds for dismissal, you can be sued, and believe me, the Vanderhavens have a legal team like you wouldn't believe. No one wins against them."

"You're kind of scaring me here, Katrina. Deborah said this contract was just a formality. Do you really think they would sue me?"

She gave a slight nod. "Deborah wouldn't, but there's no telling with Cece's dad. He's a ball-breaker. Harry Vanderhaven is all about winning, and if he thinks you're not on his team, then you're the enemy, and you'd better watch your back."

"Really?" Greta said, alarmed.

Katrina nodded. "You didn't hear it from me, but he can be downright mean. In business, he steamrolls over anyone who stands in his way, and he's the same at home. Believe me, he runs a tight ship. I've seen him make a maid cry for missing a spot when dusting. And where his daughters are concerned? It's *all* personal."

Seeing Greta's worried look, Vance joined in. "You have nothing to worry about, Greta. As long as you don't make anything public, you'll be fine."

"Okay." Greta exhaled slowly, then went over the paperwork again, scanning the terms. Nothing stood out as being objectionable. She was being paid as much in a month as she'd have made in a year working full-time at the department store. Not only that, but this internship would look good on her résumé. The contract was in effect for the summer, but the nondisclosure terms extended for all time, presumably to prevent her from writing a tell-all book years down the road. She would never do such a thing, but they didn't know that, of course.

She initialed where specified, then dated and signed her name on the last line. "All set," Greta said, pushing the document back across the table.

Katrina gave it a once-over, double-checking what she'd done, then stuck it into a folder. "Congratulations. You're now officially an indentured servant working for Firstborn Daughter, Inc."

"We're a pretty exclusive group. Be prepared: this is the kind of job that sucks the life out of you, but at least we're paid well," Vance said, taking a sip of his coffee.

Greta set her spoon down. "Wait a minute. You guys are paid?"

Vance and Katrina exchanged a look again; Katrina's eyes widened. "Oops," she said. "Guess we weren't supposed to let that one out."

They leaned together and whispered to each other for a minute, glancing her way every now and then as if assessing her trustworthiness. Just when Greta was about to ask if they wanted a moment alone, they seemed to come to a decision. The next thing she knew, they were swearing her to secrecy and revealing all the details of their association with Firstborn Daughter, Inc.

Greta listened, rapt, almost in disbelief, as her whole perception of Cece's life unraveled before her. Vance and Katrina had been hired by the Vanderhaven Corporation to be Cece's best friends, a part they'd played magnificently, Vance said, for the last three years. Everything she had ever seen on social media—the impromptu pillow fights, the jet-setting across the country, the all-night clubbing—had been carefully planned and orchestrated. That time a drunk accosted Cece, and Vance punched him in the face? Rehearsed a dozen times before it actually happened. The song they wrote one night when the three of them stayed up to watch the rise of the thunder moon? Composed ahead of time by someone in the music business. The fashions Cece came up with after sketching some random doodles? They were created by top designers who didn't get name credit but received percentages of sales in exchange for their work.

When they finished, Greta stared at them, stunned. "So none of it is real? You aren't even friends with Cece?" Her voice was small, broken.

"No, no, no!" Vance said. "We totally love Cece. It would be hard not to."

"Yeah, Cece's great," Katrina agreed. "The lifestyle is wearing, though, and it's tough always having to be on." She made finger quotes around the last word.

Vance added, "It's hard not being my authentic self, and having everyone else, all my family and friends back home, think that this is who I am. I mean, I love Cece, but it's not easy."

"So when you go to the Firstborn Daughter office—"

Vance held up his hand. "There isn't an office. I mean, there's an address, and someone works there answering the phone and forwarding the mail, but everything else is done through Cece's dad's office. We do all the planning here. We're responsible for scripting all the adventures you see on YouTube and on Cece's social media accounts."

"So how did you get the job?"

Simple, they explained. They were both actors and had been recent college graduates when they'd answered a call for an audition for a secret project.

"I got called back, like, four times," Vance said.

"Me too. They gave me these crazy scripts. Every time it was something different," Katrina said. "One time I was a jealous lover. Another time I had to act like a happy drunk."

"I had that one too!" Vance said. "Did you get the one where you won the lottery?"

Katrina shook her head. "No. But I do remember that I had to improvise being locked out of my apartment after partying all night."

"So when did you find out what the job was?" Greta asked, still processing the fact that Cece's best friends had auditioned for the part.

"Not until after we signed the contract," Vance said. "We knew it was a multiyear gig that paid a lot of money and we'd get living expenses comped. I had no problem signing the secrecy clauses. I figured I was going to be on Broadway with some big-name actors who wanted their privacy protected."

Katrina reached over and squeezed his arm. "Remember waiting at the attorney's office and finally hearing what we signed up for? The look on your face was unreal."

"Yeah, I was pretty shaken up. If I had known, I never would have agreed to it. So much for my acting career," he said ruefully. There was a thoughtful silence, Greta reeling from finding out the truth, Katrina and Vance exhausted from telling it. It was a lot to process. She sensed that on their part, it was a relief to be able to tell someone. If they couldn't even tell their family and friends the truth, it must have been killing them.

"So now you know," Katrina said. "I'm guessing we weren't supposed to tell you. We'd assumed Deborah filled you in already."

"No, I didn't know any of this."

"You have to keep this to yourself. *No one can know.* We could get sued; you could get sued. Promise me you won't breathe a word."

"I promise."

Vance leaned over the table, his face serious. "And most importantly, you can't tell Cece we're paid actors. If she knew, she'd be crushed."

Wow. This put a new twist on things. "Cece doesn't know?" Greta asked.

"No," Vance said firmly. "She has no idea, and that's the way her parents want it. If Cece found out—"

A voice from behind Vance floated across the room. "If I found out what?" They looked up to see Cece dressed in a silk bathrobe, her hair still damp from the shower, a puzzled look on her face.

CHAPTER EIGHT

Dalton woke up at dawn to the sound of birds chirping. His backpack was jammed between his head and the back of the bench, and his cheek was pressed against the slats of the seat. He sat up and rubbed his face, sure that he looked every bit like a homeless person.

When he'd dreamed up this project, he'd imagined homelessness to be a form of urban camping, but the first night had taught him it wasn't anything like that at all. It was more like being locked out of your house and having to sleep on the lawn.

Bugs had buzzed around his ears and eyes as he'd tried to go to sleep, so he'd gotten out his jacket and covered his face with it. Not the ideal fix, because it made him feel like he was suffocating. The bench, which had started out not being too bad, became intolerable as the night wore on. People, he reflected, were not meant to sleep outdoors on wooden slats. Besides feeling cramped and sore, he'd also felt exposed and vulnerable, realizing that his backpack could be easily snatched. No wonder Matt had crawled into a crevice and hidden his cart behind a bush. When you own so little, he realized, your possessions become all the more precious. Partway through the night, he'd stuck his arm through the loop of the backpack and lain on top of it to make it theft-proof.

It wasn't even fully light yet, and the park was beginning to wake up. Two female joggers came past, yoga-mom types. They eyed Dalton warily. He called out, "Good morning," but they didn't respond. If anything, they made a show of not responding. He knew then that he was no longer Dalton Bishop, a tall, not-too-bad-looking guy from a privileged family. In the space of less than a day, he'd morphed into Random Homeless Dude, a guy who slept on a park bench. In almost no time at all, his social standing had plummeted to zero.

With nothing better to do, he got up and stretched his legs, stuffed his jacket into the backpack, and tried to rub the slat marks off his cheek. Using a guy's prerogative, he peed in the woods, then set off to find a fountain or bathroom where he could wash up. He found a fountain first, but it was already in use by an older couple. The man was rough looking, his age hard to guess, somewhere between fifty and a hundred and twenty. He was brushing his teeth, the foam frothing at his mouth. He leaned over and spit as Dalton walked past. The woman, his wife maybe, was scooping water to her face. Seeing him stare, she gave him a hard look in return.

"Good morning," Dalton said.

"Hmmpf," she replied, her nose in the air.

Twice that morning, he'd tried a friendly greeting, and twice he'd struck out. He kept walking until he found a men's room, where he washed up and brushed his teeth. He skipped shaving, figuring those days were over for the time being. After combing his hair, he took a long look in the mirror. Not too bad, even if he did feel like hell. It was humid in the bathroom, and his clothes clung to him. What he wouldn't give for a hot shower, with fresh clothing to follow. And he was hungry, really hungry. He still had money, so getting something to eat wouldn't be a problem this morning, but what about a few days from now?

The idea of being dirty, hot, and hungry without a way out made Dalton a little panicky. He'd always prided himself on being self-sufficient, but it turned out he was more spoiled than he'd known.

It was consoling to think that if he came close to starving, he did have a backup plan. Will was on standby and would come into the city on a moment's notice. Dalton could always call him if he could borrow a phone. And if not, his ReadyHelp device would connect him, since Will was listed as Dalton's emergency contact. But he shouldn't be thinking of quitting already. He'd been homeless for less than a day. He couldn't give up so easily.

Dalton left the park and headed back to Times Square. Along the way, he stopped at a street vendor and got himself a hot pretzel, then found a place to sit. The pretzel was good—hot, salty, and stretchy, like they should be. Combined with the remainder of the water in his bottle, it made a halfway decent breakfast.

Times Square, day two. As early as it was, the tourists were in full force. Some of the storefronts were just opening, their owners lifting the metal grilles from inside, the sound of the doors rising like ball bearings rolling on a track. He glanced down the side street where he'd met Matt the night before but didn't see him. He decided to venture out and explore the city.

When Dalton stumbled upon Bryant Park, he found a whole different crowd than he'd seen earlier. Times Square had been tourist central, with guests from all over the world snapping pictures of themselves with the giant lit-up displays behind them. The kind of people willing to fork over five bucks for a picture with a guy dressed up as SpongeBob.

At Bryant Park, a large grassy area in the middle created a carpet for couples and young families, while café tables and chairs dotted the perimeter. On the grass, two boys tossed a football back and forth. On the far end stood a line of banquet tables, staffed by teenage girls who were leaning over the table, talking to younger children. From where Dalton stood, it looked like they were showing them how to do a craft project.

He found an empty table and sat down, glad it wasn't too hot yet and that there was a slight breeze. People watching—boys playing football and the pedestrians going past—occupied his time. He had nowhere to be and nothing scheduled. It was nice. So many times in the last few hours, he had wanted to reach for his phone. He hadn't realized what a compulsion it was until he didn't have it anymore.

As nice as it was sitting in the park, and it was pleasant enough, it was also sort of monotonous. And lonely. If he'd been with someone, they'd have a lot to discuss, but there was no one else. He was starting to envy the tooth-brushing couple at the water fountain. At least they had each other. The absence of everyday comforts was turning out to be the least of his problems.

After an hour or so, he got up to let someone else have the table. Continuing down the block and around the corner, he found himself in front of the New York Public Library, the main one on Fifth Avenue, the one that was in the first *Ghostbusters* movie. He recognized the big row of steps going up to the entrance, which was flanked by massive columns. Down at street level, stone lions stood guard on either side of the base of the stairs.

The library was famous, and he'd been close to it countless times before but had never been inside. He grinned. Today he was trying new things. He bounded up the stairs, following a group of people flowing through the entrance. He stopped at the table just inside the door to let a security officer search his backpack. "Is there an admission fee?" he asked, knowing that if the answer was yes, he'd be heading back out the door.

The officer gave him an odd look. "This is the library. It's free."

"Cool." After getting his bag inspected, he zipped the top shut and slung it over his shoulder.

The library turned out to be the perfect place to kill time. It was air-conditioned and gorgeous inside, with lots of benches for sitting. With its murals and awesome architecture, the library struck him as being the Sistine Chapel of Manhattan. He came across a visitor film that played every thirty minutes and sat through it twice, then went off in search of Charles Dickens's writing desk, which was located in a locked room. He could see the desk through the glass door front, but it was off-limits to the public. From there, he went to the children's library and saw, in a glass case, Winnie-the-Pooh and four of his friends: Eeyore, Tigger, Kanga, and Piglet, the actual stuffed animals owned by Christopher Robin, the son of the author A. A. Milne, who had written the stories of Winnie-the-Pooh and the Hundred Acre Wood.

He found the display to be a bit of a letdown. The stuffed animals were small and not very colorful. Sort of antique-looking, like you'd find in an old person's attic. Tigger in particular was disappointing, not looking at all bouncy. None of it was what he expected. Still, it was interesting.

When he got hungry, he went to the library's café and blew eight dollars getting a sandwich and beverage. It was an impulse buy and cost more than he could spare. He suspected that later he'd regret spending so much money, but at the moment, it hit the spot.

For a good part of the day, he'd forgotten he was homeless. Instead, he felt like a tourist, taking in all this beautiful building had to offer. His family had been to New York dozens of times, and yet they'd never visited the library. He couldn't imagine why. It was incredible.

The library closed at quarter to six. By then, the crowd had thinned down considerably, so when a staff member politely informed him he had to leave, Dalton headed out. It had been a pretty good day.

At the bottom of the stairs, it hit him that he had no place to go. He stood for a moment watching the cars and taxis heading down the street in front of him, all the people inside them, he speculated, heading for home.

Home. As much an emotional space as a physical building. In his real life, he had an apartment of his own and a family home, where despite his black-sheep status he was always welcome. He felt unmoored not having a place to go back to, and he wasn't even officially homeless. It was an experiment, just that, and one he could end at any time, but he wasn't a quitter and wouldn't give up after one night. There was more for him to learn.

Like a magnet drawn to metal, he felt himself being pulled back to Times Square. Having a destination cheered him up, and he began to walk with purpose. He would, he decided, get something to eat, then wander around a little bit to look for Matt Gower. After that, he'd try to drum up some money if he could. He wasn't at rock bottom yet, but his resources were getting lower, and the idea of not having enough money to eat was a scary one. After hanging out in Times Square for the early part of the evening, he planned to leave while it was still light and head to the park to look for a better sleeping spot. That bench had been far from ideal, but it had taught him that he could have done a better job packing. A thin blanket would have provided coverage from bugs and a barrier from the night air. In a pinch, it could be draped over a bush and made into a tent. If it was waterproof on one side, all the better. He'd heard of a young designer who'd created a coat that unfolded for purposes such as these. Something like that would have been invaluable.

Times Square was just as crowded and loud as the day before. On one corner, a Peruvian trio played, two guys on pan flutes and one on drums. Dalton kept walking. On the other side of Times Square, a kid wearing a knit skullcap danced to the loud thumping of a boom box. Bystanders clapped in time as he spun and flipped to the music. Dalton continued on. Performers dressed up as Disney characters, action figures, and other random entertainers called out as he went by. "You take picture with me, yes?" asked Spider-Man.

"No, thanks."

He went into the Times Square McDonald's. It wasn't his first choice, but he knew the menu. It was cheap, quick, and tasty. The line was long, and it was humid indoors, but twenty minutes later, he was fed for the night.

He returned to the brick wall he'd shared with Matt, slid down to sit, and got out his harmonica. With his baseball cap in front of his crossed legs, he was in business. This was, he decided, a good spot, after all. It was off the beaten path but still had enough people going by that someone was bound to throw some money his way. In exchange, he was prepared to entertain them with the musical musings of his Hohner harmonica. He knew only two songs: "When the Saints Go Marching In" and "Row, Row, Row Your Boat." He'd learned these two songs at summer camp by rote memorization when he was ten, and weirdly enough, the knowledge had stuck with him.

His limited repertoire didn't matter to the people walking past because all they heard was what he was playing at the time. A few looked down and smiled as they went by, but it took a good twenty minutes before he saw any money, and that was change, a few quarters flung into his cap by an older woman in a hurry. He would have thanked her, but she was out of earshot by the time he could get the words out.

He kept going, totally getting into it, conducting with one hand while holding the harmonica to his mouth with the other. When he saw a pair of men's hiking boots stop directly in front of him, he looked up to see a scowling guy with cropped hair staring down. The man had his arms folded disapprovingly in front of his sleeveless T-shirt. Dalton was at the "merrily, merrily, merrily" part of the song and stopped. "Can I help you?"

"Are you crippled?" he asked angrily.

"Me? No."

"Do you have a debilitating physical condition, some disease that doesn't allow you to function properly?"

"No."

"Are you mentally ill?"

Dalton could see where this was going. He shifted uncomfortably on the pavement. "Not technically."

"Then why don't you get a damn job like the rest of us? A healthy young guy like you begging for money. You should be ashamed of yourself." Having smugly made his point, he strode off and didn't look back.

"Thank you, sir. You have a good evening too!" Dalton yelled at his back as he kept going. From the hunch of his shoulders, it was clear he'd heard him, but he didn't bother to respond. Dalton felt rattled by the man's anger. Rattled and ashamed. Even knowing he was participating in a social experiment of his own choosing didn't help.

It's not like he didn't know that some people felt this way. This man was just a rougher version of his father. It was different, though, hearing someone talk about the homeless in general versus having that kind of contempt aimed right at him. Even though he'd done nothing wrong, he felt shame sweep over him. It didn't get more personal than that.

In an attempt to shake it off, he turned back to the harmonica. For some inexplicable reason, business picked up after that. It might have been that the people who came by were more generous, or maybe he just looked a whole lot sadder, but the money flowed in for the last three songs. One group of Asian tourists was exceedingly generous. They wanted him to stand up and pose for pictures with them, which he did. By the excited way they went on and on, he speculated that they thought he was someone else. Someone important. A celebrity maybe? He wasn't sure, but whatever. In all, he made seventeen dollars and thirty-six cents. And got heckled only once. Pretty good for his first time panhandling.

Later in the park, he filled his plastic water bottle with water from one of the restrooms, then used the facilities and washed up. This was his life now: trying to stay hydrated and fed, avoiding bugs and predators, keeping his possessions safe, and searching for a fairly comfortable place to sleep. Tomorrow he'd seek out other homeless people and try to get a read on their situations.

CHAPTER NINE

Cece looked small and plain. Standing there with wet hair and no makeup, she looked more like a teenager than an adult woman. The troubled look on her face was not an expression Greta recognized from the videos. Cece asked again, "If I found out what?"

Katrina stood up and threw her arms out wide, one of them pointing straight at Greta. "If you found out that Greta's here!"

Vance joined in. "We were going to make it a surprise and have Greta show up at the door, but you got here too quickly."

"Greta's here?" She turned her head and did a double take, then smiled.

Greta got up from the table, ready to thank her for the internship, but before she could say a word, Cece had thrown her arms around her, giving her a tight hug. The two were nearly the same height, their heads so closely aligned that their ears nearly touched. "Oh, Greta, I'm so glad you're finally here," she whispered.

Finally here? Greta found this puzzling since she'd arrived as quickly as she could on a flight Deborah's assistant had booked. It's not like she could have come any earlier. Maybe it was just an expression. "Thank you. I'm glad to be here." Greta started to say what an honor it was to be allowed to intern for Firstborn Daughter, Inc. and how it would make her résumé stand out in a big way when Katrina broke in.

"I hate to interrupt," she said, "but we have a full schedule, and we're already behind."

Cece's face fell. "Can't we just forget about the schedule? I'd love to have the day to spend with Greta." Her words tamped down the energy in the room.

"I think we'd all love a day off," Vance said with a laugh. "If we could forget the schedule, we would, Cece. But hair and makeup will be here in an hour, and you still have to eat. We have to go over the setup and learn our lines, because the film crew comes at twelve thirty. A lot of other people are involved besides us. We can't let them down."

A film crew? Hair and makeup? Greta had no idea what was going on, but her first day on the job was sounding way more involved than she'd anticipated.

Cece sighed dramatically. "I hate this. I just hate this. Why don't I ever get to decide?"

"Cece, if you'd just—" Katrina tried to speak.

"It's exhausting!"

Vance rushed in to put an arm around Cece's shoulders and began to speak soothingly. "Now, Cece, mornings are always tough, but we'll get through it together, right?"

"I know, but . . . "

"Come on, Cece," he said playfully. "I know it's hard to get started, but after we get warmed up, we have a lot of fun, don't we? Don't we?"

She nodded. He walked her to the other side of the room and kept talking, his face next to hers, voice low. Cece's shoulders dropped, relaxing as he spoke. She didn't have the personality Greta had expected from seeing her videos. Was she overtired? Hungover? Impossible to know. One good thing, Greta reflected: Cece seemed genuinely happy to see her. Maybe with time they'd become friends. Actual friends, not like the kind her parents hired.

Katrina whispered to Greta, "It's amazing the way he can always get her to calm down. I call him the Cece Whisperer."

"Because Vance is Cece's gay boyfriend," Greta said.

"What?"

"Hashtag gay boyfriend," Greta clarified, referencing what she'd seen on social media.

"Oh, yeah."

Within a minute or two, Cece came back smiling and joined everyone else at the kitchen table. Once Cece began eating, Katrina laid out what they'd be doing that morning. "Vance and I stayed up almost all night coming up with your backstory, Greta, and I think you'll love what we came up with." She had an over-the-top smile that made Greta think loving it was her only option. "We're playing up the cousin aspect of the relationship between you and Cece and doing a kind of compare-and-contrast thing."

Vance said, "Sort of like that kids' story *The Country Mouse and the City Mouse.*"

"I don't think I know that one," Greta said.

"Don't worry about it. It's not critical for you to know it."

"Why do I need a backstory?"

Katrina looked a little exasperated, but Vance jumped in to explain. "All of Cece's social media accounts are carefully orchestrated. What her followers are seeing are not just random bits of her life but videos and stills designed to enhance the brand. For instance, when Cece's clothing line won that 'Made in America' award, we could have just announced it and shown a picture of the plaque, but that would have been boring, so instead we had her tour one of the manufacturing facilities—"

"I remember that!" Greta said, recalling the time the three had visited the factory that manufactured Cece's clothing line. They'd handed out thank-you cards with $500 tucked inside to each of the employees. "The people working at the machines couldn't believe you guys were there. They had to shut down the line, and then they all gave Cece a standing ovation and clapped for like five minutes. The one guy said because he had that job, he finally had health insurance that would pay for his daughter's surgery. Oh, man, that one made me cry."

"That's what I'm talking about," Vance said approvingly. "We want to create an emotional response. Making a connection is always our goal."

"Wait a minute. So none of it is real?" Greta asked, stunned. First, she'd found out that Vance and Katrina had auditioned to be Cece's friends. Now she was coming to the realization that everything she knew about Cece's life was a sham, a fabrication made to sell perfume and clothing.

"We try to tie it in to Cece's life as much as possible. Every now and then, we include her parents and Brenna to drive home that she's a part of the Vanderhaven family empire, but for the most part, we emphasize the single-girl-in-the-city aspect. A majority of the clips and photos are filmed here, so that part is real. We're really in Cece's kitchen or bedroom or whatever. When we're at an event or a club, we have to set it up ahead of time so we can get permission to film there and get photo releases from whoever winds up being in the shot. It gets more involved, especially if we're in a club and there are a lot of people in the background."

"What about when you guys had a bet to see which one of you could bake the best Christmas cookies?" That one had been Greta's personal favorite. Vance and Katrina had a cookie Bake-Off while Cece served as the judge. As it turned out, it hadn't been much of a contest. Vance had done an absolutely awesome job. His cookies had looked fantastic while Katrina's gingerbread men had been a disaster—undercooked, misshapen, and droopy. The expression on Katrina's face when she pulled her cookies out of the oven became a meme Greta had seen hundreds of times, captioned with "When even your cookies hate you." She'd watched that particular clip whenever she felt a little down, and it made her laugh every single time.

Vance laughed. "Our favorite bakery whipped up my cookies. I told them not to make them too perfect, and they did an incredible job. In exchange for their silence, we featured their business on Valentine's Day."

Greta kept glancing Cece's way to see her take on all of this, but she just nibbled on some fruit, not participating in the conversation at all.

Katrina added, "After the Valentine Day's episode, their sales went up something like four hundred percent. A total win for everyone."

Greta felt a catch in her chest. Finding out none of it was real felt like a betrayal. "But you said you were an expert baker because you used to help your mom make Christmas cookies."

"That part's true," he said with a nod. "Family tradition. My sisters and I always gathered around the kitchen table making cutout cookies and decorating them. We did our share of eating them too."

Katrina riffled through her folders and passed out paperwork to each of them. Glancing over it, Greta saw what looked like a script, complete with stage directions and dialogue for each of them. The scene began with a knock on the door. When Cece opened it, Greta would be on the other side, crying. And it went from there with five pages of dialogue.

Greta looked at Katrina. "I don't get it. What is this?"

"What we're shooting today. Generally, we film ten or fifteen minutes and then edit it into smaller bits. The shorter clips are released on social media sites as teasers for the longer version. We wait to release that one to the YouTube channel. By the time it comes out, her followers are dying to see the whole thing."

"I understand that it's a script," Greta said, slightly exasperated. "But why is the script saying that I just showed up without any notice? I would never do that. And this thing about me crying that my boyfriend, Nate, dumped me? That's not true. Why can't I just be coming to visit and to do an internship?"

"That's your backstory," Vance said. "If we said you were coming to do an internship, that would be way too boring, so we dreamed up this awesome entrance for you."

"It will be a great opportunity for you to spread your wings, dramatically speaking," Katrina said. "And when you start off in such a low place, that gives us room to have a great character arc."

"A character arc?" Greta understood what a character arc was; she just didn't know how it applied to her.

"You know," Katrina said, "a character arc. You show up devastated from the breakup with your boyfriend. You're also down on your luck, down to your last dollar. Then Cece takes you in, gives you a makeover and some great advice, and totally turns your life around."

Cece suddenly glanced up, interested. "I love doing makeovers. And Greta is so pretty already, it wouldn't take much."

"Now we're talking," Vance said with a grin. "When Cece's on board, it always turns out great. You're gonna love this, Greta, and so will Cece's followers. They'll be so excited watching as you're transformed from Greta's Midwestern cousin from dairy farm country to a glamorous New Yorker seeing all the sights. It's a great angle."

Greta said, "But I don't live on a dairy farm. My family lives in a house in the suburbs right off the interstate. We can drive to Milwaukee in, like, thirty minutes."

"We're taking some liberties, it's true, but if it makes you feel better, we won't show a farm and say you live there. We'll imply that you're used to a more rural life. Vance and I saw that Highway 83 runs from your subdivision past farm fields on the way to the shopping complex and movie theater, and we figured we'd work in some of that footage to show how different your life is from Cece's here in Manhattan," Katrina said. "Not a lie, just an inference."

Greta mulled it over for a few seconds. "I guess I'm okay with that, but me getting dumped by my boyfriend? There's no way I want to play it that way." For that matter, how did they even know about Nate? She'd never posted anything about the breakup, although she had changed her relationship status to single and stopped mentioning him. They'd gone out for only a few months. At first, he'd seemed like a great guy. Lots of fun, not too needy, said all the right things. After a while, she'd started to notice times when he seemed bossy and full of himself. When he commented on his female cousin's fifty-pound weight gain after two years of marriage and said, in complete seriousness, that he thought it was grounds for divorce, Greta had gained total clarity. Gaining weight was grounds for divorce? What a superficial jerk. He was, she decided, not even someone she'd want as a friend, much less as a boyfriend.

When she told him the relationship was over and why, he laughed. "If speaking my mind is a reason to dump me, you're going to be alone your whole life." It had bruised her feelings at the time and made her wonder too—was he right? She hadn't really had any successful long-term relationships with men. Why was that? *Too picky,* some said. She was being unrealistic. *No one is perfect,* they reminded her.

As she watched friends become happy couples, she sometimes wondered if she *would* be alone her whole life. She imagined decades going by, living alone, traveling by herself, no one to talk to at the end of the workday. The thought made her sad.

But what was wrong with holding out for the perfect match? It seemed to her that making a commitment to a man she wasn't ideally suited for would be even worse. Maybe she was being overly romantic, but if she couldn't have perfect, what was the point?

She'd been insulted when Nate told her she was going to be single her whole life, and hurt too, but beyond that, there wasn't much in the way of breakup drama. Soon both of them had moved on. She saw him out at a bar a few months later and said hi as she walked past. He smiled and returned the greeting. Not a big deal.

Greta felt compelled to share her side of things. "Just for the record, I broke up with Nate. And there was no drama. At all. I don't think he even cared that much."

Katrina said, "Greta, will you come in the other room with me for a moment? Just for a minute." Before she could answer, Katrina got up from her chair and leaned over and said to Cece, "I'm going to show Greta where her marks are for the scene, okay? We'll be right back."

"Okay," Cece said. "Don't be gone too long."

Greta got up and followed her wordlessly to the front door. Once there, she said, "So where are my marks?"

"We mark the floor with tape to show where you should be at different times during filming," Katrina said impatiently. "That doesn't matter. We'll go over it later. I brought you out here because we need to talk."

She leaned in, her face serious. "You just signed a contract agreeing to this, Greta, so suck it up and do it the way we wrote it, okay?" Her words were harsh, but her expression was pleading. "If you don't, it'll just be harder for the rest of us. We have a lot riding on this particular episode. It's going to be included in the package that's being shopped around for Cece's reality show."

"Cece's getting her own reality show?"

Katrina nodded. "There's been a lot of interest. With Cece's following, she's already a major celebrity, and we need to capitalize on that while we can. We've been putting together a montage of clips that will knock their socks off. Originally, we were going to call it *Visiting with the Vanderhavens*, but now we're leaning toward *Oh, That Cece!* What do you think?"

"You could go either way, I guess."

"It's going to be huge. I mean, like, colossal. And with you in the cousin role, you've found yourself a new, very high-paying job." She pointed a finger. "Greta Hansen, you're going to be a star."

Katrina was talking as if she was going to be living here permanently. Greta had a sudden need to set her straight. "Oh, no, I'm just here for the summer."

"You can say goodbye to that. If the Vanderhavens want you on board, they'll make you an offer, and they'll make sure it's one you won't refuse. You'll have more fame and money than you ever dreamed of, but you'll find out pretty quickly it's not what it's cracked up to be." She sighed. "Vance and I have been wanting to walk away for ages now."

"So why don't you?"

"There's some weird clause in each of our contracts that says we can't vacate our positions until a replacement has been provided for."

"What does that mean?"

"There's a lot more legal language than that, but basically, it means that publicly we're Cece's best friends for the purposes of her brand, and until they cast different best friends, we're obligated to fulfill the roles. And they won't cast different best friends. We've already asked," she said, in answer to the questioning look on Greta's face. "Apparently, we're doing such a fabulous job, it would be difficult to replace us. And Cece is so secluded that we're about the only people she comes into contact with on a regular basis, so Vance and I are locked into this thing forever. We've hired an attorney to go over that contract line by line, and he couldn't find any loopholes. Believe me, if I had a time machine, I'd go back and stop myself from signing the damn thing."

Greta was starting to get a sick feeling. "Is my contract set up like that?" She thought back to how quickly she'd scanned it before signing. She should have read it more thoroughly.

"No, yours has an end date. Lucky you."

Greta exhaled in relief. "That's good."

"Yeah, that's good for now, but be careful if they offer an extension, because there will be something in there that will let them decide how long they want you here, instead of the other way around. It's easy to get blinded by the money and not notice all the rest of the stuff in the contract." Katrina grimaced. "By the way, the thing about the reality show is top secret. Don't breathe a word of it to anyone."

"Except Cece?"

"No, not even Cece. *Especially* not Cece. Getting her psyched up to do these short clips is torture. I can only imagine how she'll react to having to do full episodes on a regular basis. It's going to be a nightmare."

"I won't say anything, I promise," Greta said. "Can I ask you a question?"

"Sure."

"What's going on with Cece today?"

Katrina looked puzzled. "What do you mean?"

"She's different from what I expected."

"How so?"

"In the videos, she's always kind of bubbly, laughing all the time. And then sometimes she's sort of flirty and mysterious, but this morning, she seems . . . " She stopped to think of how to phrase it.

"Blah?"

"No, not blah. Sick, maybe? Not really with it." What she wanted to say was that Cece acted like someone who had just come out of a coma, didn't like what she saw, and wanted to go back again. "Is she using anything?"

"Like drugs, you mean?" Katrina shook her head. "No, she's not on drugs. What you're seeing is Cece the way she usually is. We work with her so that on film, we get the reaction we need and then splice it in accordingly into the clip. It's all carefully curated to present the correct image. That's why you'll never see Cece on a talk show or interviewed by anyone outside of our control. She doesn't do impromptu very well. Vance and I have to do a lot of hand-holding with her to get the end result just right. Mostly Vance, because she responds better to him, and he has more patience."

Greta simply said, "Oh."

"It's exhausting, is what it is." She said this as if she'd been asked to define the situation.

"I see." But Greta didn't really see at all. Was Cece as lackluster as she appeared? She was starting to think that so much of what she knew of Cece Vanderhaven's life was a facade, a grand illusion designed to impress, much like the family's yearly Christmas cards.

Katrina started to whisper, pouring her heart out in a way that made Greta uncomfortable. She and Vance had the same therapist. "He's a Jungian," she said, and the conversation spun off from there. From the way she talked, everyone in the Vanderhaven circle had a therapist. That it was a given, like going to the barber or getting your car's oil changed. "Originally, we went to the same guy Cece did, and he was fine, but we were worried about him telling the Vanderhavens what we were discussing, so we switched therapists."

"But I thought there was some kind of patient-confidentiality thing?"

"Supposedly, yes. But everything's for sale. You know that." She leaned in. "Vance and I have grappled with how to be team players while still keeping an emotional and spiritual balance. It's so hard, Greta, so, so hard. It's, like, we're trying to establish some space for ourselves, and the Vanderhavens keep pulling us back in." She went on to talk about sleepless nights and drinking too much to lessen the stress.

"It sounds terrible," Greta said, nodding sympathetically.

Katrina exhaled in relief. "No one else would understand," she said. "It's a very specific kind of stress. Everyone thinks we have this fabulous life."

"You're entitled to feel the way you do." Greta meant it. Who was to say Katrina's feelings weren't valid? Other people not understanding didn't negate her experience. In the context of her life, the stress was real. It's easy to speculate that others have it better, but the prince traded places with the pauper, and both of them found out it wasn't so easy on the other side.

Katrina pulled her into a hug and, when they pulled apart, wiped a tear from her eye. "Thanks, Greta. You're a great listener. Don't repeat any of this to Cece, okay? I wouldn't hurt her for the world."

"I promise I won't say a word."

Walking back into the kitchen, they encountered Vance and Cece, right where they'd left them. Cece said, "Greta, did you see your marks?"

"My marks?" She'd completely forgotten their pretense for leaving the room.

"I just explained to Greta how it works," Katrina said. "This is all new to Greta, so we're going to have to be very patient with her today. We're counting on you to help, Cece."

Cece brightened. "Of course I'll help Greta!"

When Vance's phone pinged, he took a look and said to Katrina, "We've got the crowd lined up. I planned for a medium turnout."

The rest of the morning was a flurry of activity. A team of people, eight in all, walked into the apartment, two of them pulling a rolling rack of clothes and another wheeling in what looked like a portable barber chair complete with a remote to raise or lower the chair height. The makeup artist had a case of cosmetics the size of a large toolbox. Katrina and Vance went through the clothes on the rack, choosing outfits for the shoot.

Greta sat watching as they took turns getting their hair and makeup done. Katrina's and Vance's times in the chair went quickly, but Cece's turn went on and on. She squirmed at one point and said, "How much longer?"

"Not too much longer," the makeup guy said. "And when I finish, you will be magnificent!"

When he was done and he turned the chair around, Cece did look magnificent, as beautiful as in her cosmetics ads.

"How do I look?" she asked, tipping her chin up.

Greta said, "Absolutely gorgeous." It was the truth. Cece had gone from being merely pretty to stunning. Her hair hung in sleek waves over her shoulders. It was glossy, catching the light in all the right ways. Greta had watched the transformation as it happened and still was amazed by the end result. She couldn't wait to see what they could do for her.

When the team began to pack up their stuff, Greta said to Katrina, "Wait a minute! What about me?"

"Not today," she said briskly. "We're doing a character arc, remember? You'll start out frumpy like you are now and gradually, with Cece's help, get transformed into a beautiful swan." She gave her arm a squeeze. "Can you wait?"

"I guess so."

After most of the hair and makeup team left, they sat at the kitchen table and ran through their lines. As Cece and Greta read, Vance made adjustments to the dialogue, and each of them marked the changes accordingly. Greta frowned. So much of what they had her saying was contrary to her personality. She would never show up at someone's house sobbing that her life was over because some guy had dumped her. When she objected, Katrina reminded her that this wasn't her per se, but a character named Greta. "Like an alternate-world Greta Hansen. Think of it as being like a part in a movie."

Greta folded her arms. "I know I'm playing a role, but the people who know me will take it as the truth. It's embarrassing."

Katrina said, "If you want, we can change the boyfriend's name. Would that help?"

"Yes." It did help.

"It's like playing pretend," Cece chimed in. "Like we did when we were kids?" As if they'd grown up together. The idea made Greta smile. Eventually, she caved in, agreeing to play it the way it had been written.

Filming the short scene took more than an hour and was way more involved than Greta would have imagined. A young woman held up cue cards with Cece's lines, and some guy in headphones held a boom microphone above their heads. They had to do it over and over again, Greta bursting through the door and throwing herself into Cece's arms, while Katrina and Vance rushed in from the other room to see what the ruckus was. They had to film from Greta's vantage point going through the door, and then from Cece's of Greta coming toward her. One time she pushed through the door so quickly that the edge caught Cece on the shoulder. Greta was horrified, but Cece just burst out laughing. It was good to see her take it so well because most of the time she looked miserable, asking how much longer this was going to take and if they could be done already. Greta knew how she felt. Making everything look spontaneous and exciting was taxing.

Once they had watched all the footage on a laptop and determined they had enough to work with, Vance told the camera crew they could go. As the team packed up their equipment, Vance and Katrina went into a huddle, deciding how to edit the footage and how they'd release it. Cece was not part of that conversation.

"Finally!" Cece said, collapsing into a nearby chair. "I thought we'd never finish."

"It did seem to take a long time," Greta agreed.

"Right?" She perked up. "I have to do it every day too."

"Not every day, Cece," Katrina corrected. "Four times a week."

"It seems like every day," she said, sighing. "They always say just a little more, and then I do a little more, and then there's more after that. It goes on and on."

"So you don't like what you do?" Greta asked. In her imaginings back home, she'd had a million questions for Cece. She'd wanted to know how she'd created a multimillion-dollar company by the time she was twenty-three, how it felt to be from such a prestigious family, what goals she had for future ventures. But those were yesterday's questions; today none of them seemed relevant. "I mean, you get to go to all the exclusive clubs and design new fashions and be in commercials."

"Sometimes it's fun," Cece said. "I love dancing, and I like when we visit kids in hospitals." She slung her leg over the arm of the chair and leaned back. "Katrina, do we have any hospital visits scheduled?"

"Not anytime soon," Katrina said.

"You see?" Cece said to Greta. "I'm always locked into their schedule. I almost never get to choose what I want to do."

"You'll like what we're doing tomorrow," Katrina said. "We're going to lunch at Bellemont, so the public can get a good look at Greta." She addressed the next part to Greta, explaining that the Bellemont was a restaurant owned by the Vanderhavens. "It's got that industrial vintage decor. The menu is upscale pub food. You'll like it."

"Sounds great."

Cece asked, "Can Brenna come with us to the restaurant?"

"No, Cece, not this time."

"Brenna never gets to come," Cece said sadly to Greta. "I keep asking, but she's not allowed." Millions of fans followed Cece's every move, all of them thinking she had this dream life, and here she couldn't even invite her own sister along for lunch. How sad not to be able to make those kinds of decisions.

"Maybe she can come another day," Vance said, never taking his eyes off the laptop. "Or maybe this—how about you and Greta take Brenna to Serendipity for ice cream next week? I'll find somewhere to slip it into the schedule."

"Yes," Cece said. "That would be great."

Vance grinned. "I'll make a note of it. In the meantime, we can look forward to tomorrow's lunch at Bellemont."

CHAPTER TEN

On the second morning of Dalton's homelessness experiment, he was awakened by someone nudging his foot with the tip of a shoe. The night before he'd found a similar setup to Matt's, minus the little rock cave, and so he'd spent the night lying between a large boulder and a row of bushes. He'd used his backpack as a pillow and tried unsuccessfully to convince himself he was in a safe and comfortable spot. He'd fallen asleep secure in the notion he was completely hidden, but sometime during the night, he must have shifted in his sleep, because now his exposed feet sticking out in the open had attracted the attention of what he would find out later was a nice police officer.

"Sir, sir, are you okay?"

What? Dalton's eyes flicked open. It felt as if he'd just drifted off to sleep, but judging by the first bit of daylight through the branches, it was early morning. He rubbed his eyes, his mind still cloudy.

"Sir, are you injured or ill?"

He managed to get out an answer. "I'm okay." His voice sounded thick from dry mouth.

"Come out of there now."

Dalton wasn't entirely sure who was talking, but the man's authoritative tone made him think not listening was not an option. "Just a minute."

"Sir, you need to come out now. I want to see your hands."

Dalton scooted out on his butt, branches scraping against his face as he went. "I'm coming out. I don't have any weapons." He scrambled to his feet, arms raised, the backpack dangling off one arm.

The police officer was a big guy, so tall and bulky he loomed over Dalton. Still, Dalton wasn't worried. He'd heard of the homeless being arrested for petty crimes, but for the most part, the police just told them to move along. "Good morning, officer," he said.

"Too much to drink, son?" He had aviator sunglasses perched on the top of his head and an amused expression Dalton found reassuring.

"No, sir, I'm just out of money and trying to figure out my living arrangements."

"The park isn't a good option," he said, shaking his head. "It's family friendly during the day, but it's not safe at night. Not to mention it's against the law."

"Okay."

"I don't want to find you here again," he said.

"No, sir. I won't do it again." Not in that particular spot, anyway.

"There are lots of services available in the area. If you're by yourself, you can apply at the intake center on East Thirtieth Street, and they'll let you know about shelter availability for men. They might also know how you'd go about getting a referral for treatment for substance abuse and alcohol addiction."

"Thanks, I'll check it out," Dalton said, brushing a leaf off the front of his shirt and wondering what it was about his appearance that indicated he was addicted to drugs or alcohol. It had to be because he was sleeping on the ground in Central Park.

"There's a public restroom that way, if you want to clean up," the officer said. "You probably want to wash your face. And you have a twig in your hair." He pointed.

Dalton ran his fingers through his hair. "Good idea. About the restroom, I mean."

"Good luck to you, son. I hope things get better for you." And then he strode off without even issuing a ticket. All he'd done was give him some good advice. Dalton made a mental note to give the NYPD a five-star Yelp review when this whole experiment was over.

Crossing the park, Dalton found the restroom, removed the foliage from his hair, and took care of the rest of his morning routine. His bathroom at home, with its privacy and actual shower, suddenly seemed ultra-luxurious. He'd always taken it for granted.

After finishing up at the bathroom, he went in search of something to quell his growling stomach. He stopped at a juice truck a few blocks from the park to get a tall carrot juice. It was five dollars, which was outrageous, but he justified the cost because it was nutritious and filling. Sipping as he walked, he maneuvered around others on the sidewalk who were not paying attention. Really not paying attention. It struck him as odd that no one made way for him. He was starting to wonder if he was invisible.

Besides being ignored on the sidewalks, he'd also noticed that in the last two days he'd gotten zero attention from the opposite sex. It wasn't like he thought he was that great. He didn't expect attention, but getting checked out, especially by groups of giggling teenage girls, was not uncommon for him. It seemed like his grubby homeless appearance had turned off the switch that controlled whatever sex appeal he'd once had.

As a test, he smiled at two young women who looked like college students. One looked right through him, and the other gave him something that resembled a pity smile.

A pity smile?

Unbelievable that Dalton T. Bishop, once a catch, had been demoted to the kind of guy girls felt sorry for. The realization of this hurt more than sleeping on the ground.

He wandered around, passing stores where he couldn't afford to shop and restaurants that probably wouldn't seat him even if he'd had the money. He was aware of his own body odor and knew if he could smell it, others could too, if they got close enough. He stopped in at Saint Patrick's Cathedral just to get out of the heat and immediately knew he was in the right place. Inside, it was cavernous and cool. No sooner was he inside than he felt a sense of awe and wonder. The arches, the pillars, and the stained glass invited you to look upward. You couldn't stand in that space and not think about God and heaven.

A calm came over him.

He surveyed the space and all the people there—all different ages, races, and nationalities. There was no service going on at the moment, but it still felt like the house of God. Some folks were busy lighting candles, others prayed in the pews, and still more milled about looking at the statues and architecture. There was this hushed reverence. Being inside that cathedral, one would think that maybe all of humanity could get along, that war and poverty could be eliminated, and that children everywhere could be fed and educated.

He sat in one of the pews for a while, praying for a little bit, something he didn't generally do, but it seemed right to do it here. He prayed that these two weeks would end in success. With Matt still on his mind, Dalton prayed that his new acquaintance's life would improve and that he'd be able to heal from the horrors he'd experienced. He added a request that all the homeless in the world would find food, shelter, and a sense of security, and then added another prayer for his family and friends.

He glanced upward and suddenly remembered what his former girlfriend had said. *You just aren't my someone.* Oh, man, that had hurt. Funny that it came to him just now. He hadn't been thinking about her at all.

Feeling almost foolish, he added one more prayer. *Please let me find my someone.* He imagined the prayer rising up with all the others, heading to their destination. Dalton wasn't sure if self-serving prayers carried the same weight as those intended for other people, but it didn't hurt to try.

He sat for a bit and puzzled on the fact that although his family came to the city on a fairly regular basis, they'd never once set foot inside this cathedral. Dalton was finding that the city of New York was so much more than great restaurants and Broadway shows. A person could spend a month here doing something different every single day and not even scratch the surface. Of course, that person would need money to do it right.

Getting up, he walked around and was lost in thought, standing in front of a statue of Mary holding a dying Jesus in her arms, when a young woman tapped him on the shoulder. "Excuse me, would you mind taking a picture of us?" Before he could answer, she handed him her cell phone. After going without, it seemed like a miracle to have a cell phone right in his hand. So many times since he'd landed in Manhattan, his hand had itched with the desire to check his phone, the lack of it taunting him like a phantom limb. He looked at her phone and had a random insane urge to take off running and keep the phone for himself. But the moment passed, and so did the impulse.

"No problem," Dalton said, while she and her friend linked arms.

"Make sure to get a lot of the cathedral in the background," she whispered. "We already took selfies. We want a few of us where you can see where we are."

He took a few shots and handed the phone back. She and her friend looked at the images and nodded in approval. "It's for our grandfather," she explained. "He was supposed to come with us, but he's in the hospital. I told him we'd light a candle for him. I know he'll love to see a picture of us here."

"I hope he'll be okay." Dalton could see now that they looked similar: petite build, big brown eyes, and dark hair. One had her hair pulled back into a ponytail; the other's hair was braided. They looked close enough to be cousins or sisters.

"It's his heart," she whispered loudly. "They replaced a valve, and he's doing great. He needs time to recover, but he says he feels better already. We were all so worried, but he looks better every day."

The other girl spoke up. "He always says you can't kill a Fronk; you can only slow them down."

Fronk? Every hair on the back of Dalton's neck stood up. He'd seen that name for the first time just recently, and it was a name a person would find hard to forget. "What did you say? Did you say you can't kill a Fronk?"

"That's our last name. Fronk," the first young woman explained. "We're sisters."

"Like Ellie Fronk?"

The girl with the ponytail looked startled. Well, actually, she appeared slightly freaked out. Her whole body stiffened, and her eyes widened. "How do you know my name?" she asked, her tone decidedly less friendly.

Dalton said, "*You're* Ellie Fronk?" They stared at each other, both stunned. "Ellie?" His mouth dropped open as she gave a slight nod. What were the odds that in a city this large, he'd run into Matt's former girlfriend? It was crazy.

Her sister edged closer, protectively. "How do you know my sister's name? Have you been following us?"

"No, no, I promise you, it's nothing like that. It's just that I just met someone you know, and he was just talking about you, so it's weird that we met like this."

Ellie said, "Someone was talking about me?"

Dalton nodded. "He showed me your picture, and it had your name on the back."

"Who showed you my picture?" Ellie still looked shocked, but there was something else there now. Curiosity? Hope?

"A guy named Matt. Matt Gower?"

Ellie didn't faint, but for a second, he thought she might. She reached out to grip her sister's arm but kept her eyes on Dalton. "You talked to Matt recently?"

"Yes."

"When was this? When did you see him?"

"The day before yesterday."

Ellie's sister motioned for the three of them to go to the back of the cathedral, where they could talk more easily. "You have to forgive my sister," she said. "She's been through a lot. Matt went missing a few months ago, and she almost lost her mind worrying. She filed a missing person's report, went around to all his friends, put up flyers. It's been months. Ellie was sure he was dead."

Dalton repeated everything Matt had told him, including how he didn't want to be a burden to Ellie. That part bothered her.

"He didn't want to be a burden? That doesn't sound like something Matt would think. He knew how much I loved him. He was never a burden." She turned to her sister. "What do you think, Mia?"

So now he knew her sister's name was Mia. Mia Fronk.

"Can you prove that you talked to Matt?" Mia asked. "How do we know that you aren't some weirdo who saw the flyers and followed us just to mess with us?"

"Why would anyone do that? That's just mean." Her sister still looked at him expectantly, so he tried to think of some proof. "He talked about some kid's birthday party with a piñata, and how all the presents seemed like too much, kind of excessive compared to how the people in Afghanistan live. And how the grocery store here had too many choices. He said something about all the different kinds of apples." Dalton could tell by the look on her face she was coming around. "And one time, he was at Walgreens buying Tylenol." He stopped to clarify. "Tylenol PM, I think he said. And a loud noise in the parking lot freaked him out so much that he couldn't move and had to call a friend to pick him up."

Ellie said, "He talked to Matt. No one else would have known all that." She turned to him. "I'm surprised he told you those things. He wasn't that open with anyone but me."

"Sometimes it's easier to talk to strangers."

"I love Matt. I would have done anything for him," she said sadly. "It killed me to see him suffering. I wanted to help him."

"He didn't think anyone understood what he was going through. He said you'd be better off without him." Matt's words gave Dalton some insight into his despair, even as he couldn't make sense of his actions.

"Can you take me to where you saw him?" she asked. "I have to find him."

He thought for a second. "Sure, I could do that."

The three of them piled into a cab, and ten minutes later they were near Times Square, at the place Dalton had first met Matt. "He was sitting right there," he said, indicating the space where the sidewalk met the side of the building. "With a cardboard sign that said *Homeless Vet* and something underneath it about any amount helping."

"He was *begging*?" Ellie's eyes widened in dismay. "Oh God, I think I feel sick."

Her sister dug a water bottle out of her purse and pressed it into her hands. "You haven't eaten anything today; you're probably hungry. Just drink some water."

Ellie nodded and took a few swigs before handing it back to her sister. "Where else could he be? Did he mention if he hung out anywhere else?"

"No. He just said he avoided the crazy crowds of Times Square. He liked this spot because it was quieter and seemed safer."

"That sounds about right."

She held her hand over her eyes, looking up and down the street. "Do you think if I come here every day, I'll see him?"

"I don't know." Dalton shook his head. He wished he could be of more help. She seemed so hopeful. "Maybe."

"You can't come every day," her sister said, objecting. "What about your job?"

"I'll use up my vacation time. I'll call in sick. I don't know. I'll think of something."

"I do know of another place he goes to in Central Park," Dalton said. "He went there one night to sleep."

"Matt sleeps in the park," Ellie said in disbelief. "He sleeps in the park when he could be next to me."

"I don't think it's like that," he said. "He didn't leave to get away from you. He left because he was having a panic attack and not coping well."

"Does he sleep there on a regular basis?" she asked.

Another question to which he didn't know the answer. "I can show you where it is," he said, trying to be helpful.

Another cab ride and a long walk later, and they were in the approximate spot where he'd seen Matt disappear behind some bushes for the night. But only the approximate area. The problem was, Dalton couldn't find the exact location. The park was so big and the terrain so similar that there were a lot of bushes adjacent to rock formations. It was embarrassing how many times he checked before admitting to the sisters he wasn't exactly sure. "It was around here," he said. "I'm sorry, but I can't find the exact spot."

"How did you know about it to begin with?" Ellie asked.

"We both happened to be heading this way right before sundown. He was walking ahead of me, and when I saw him duck behind the bush, I looked and saw him curled up there, sheltered by the rock. He'd covered his face by then, so I don't think he saw me." He'd been pretty open with them so far, but he drew the line when it came to admitting he'd followed Matt. That had *serial killer* written all over it.

"I'm coming back," Ellie said decisively. "Every day and every night until I find him. And I'm notifying the NYPD that he's been spotted here so they can keep an eye out for him too. They couldn't do much before, but now that I have some recent leads, that has to help, right?"

A slight breeze rustled the branches overhead. Nearby, a bird squawked. They were less than half a mile from a path frequented by runners and strolling tourists, but here it was just the three of them, looking for someone who wasn't there. "I would think so," Dalton said. "I hope you find him. He's a good guy, just going through something."

"I will find him," Ellie said. "For the first time in ages, I have hope. I can't thank you enough."

"You're welcome. I wish we had found him."

"This is kind of embarrassing . . . " Ellie toed the grass for a split second and then finished her thought. "But I just realized that I don't know your name."

"Dalton. Dalton Bishop."

"Thank you, Dalton Bishop. I would like to buy you lunch." She held a hand up. "I will be offended if you say no. I really want to do this."

Always the gentleman, Dalton accepted her kind offer, and the trio walked down one of the avenues and turned onto a side street to go to a pizzeria the sisters swore had some of the best pizza in New York, if not the world. Just hearing the word *pizza* made Dalton's stomach contract and twist. Even if it turned out to be cardboard covered with cheese and pepperoni, he'd eat his share and be grateful for it.

As they walked, Mia kept up the conversation, telling him about their grandfather and what a great guy he was. She said that their grandmother had died about a year ago, and he wished he had gone with her. "Not that he has a death wish," she said. "It's just that he misses her so much."

"We all do," Ellie added wistfully. She'd been silent since they'd left the park, her eyes flitting back and forth, assessing everyone in the immediate area as they went. Dalton knew what she was doing: looking for Matt. He was somewhere in Manhattan, mixed in with more than a million other people. Finding one person among so many was a daunting task, but Dalton had randomly run into him and then accidentally met Ellie and her sister, which seemed to prove anything was possible.

Mia said, "Grandpa makes a point to do something in Grandma's honor every day. Something nice for someone else. A good deed for Grace, is what he calls it. He said he wants to do her proud."

"That's nice." Dalton had a feeling he'd like their grandfather. "If everyone did that, the world would be a better place."

When they arrived at the pizzeria, he held the door open for the sisters, then followed them inside. The incredible smell alone could make a hungry man crazy. Behind the counter, they could see into the kitchen area, where a man with a red bandanna wrapped around his head pulled a pizza out of a brick oven. Dalton could almost taste it.

They ordered at the register, grabbed their soft drinks, and took a table by the window. The girls sat opposite Dalton, leaving the spot next to him available for his backpack. This pizza restaurant was the kind of place Dalton and his friends had frequented in his younger years. The flooring was made up of black and white checkerboard tiles, and the tabletops were red laminate. Each table was topped with a caddy holding Parmesan cheese, salt and pepper, and paper napkins. Nothing fancy, but somehow perfect in its own way.

"This is so nice of you." Dalton took a sip of his root beer. "Not necessary at all, but I do appreciate it." The carrot juice he'd had earlier was only a faint memory now. "I apologize for my sweaty condition. I know I'm in need of a shower. I'm sure you've noticed that I stink."

Thankfully, both of them waved away his concerns. "I didn't notice," Mia said very kindly. "It's hot out, and I think we're all perspiring." She went on to talk about the respect they had for blue-collar workers and all the construction taking place in the city. "Every time we come, there's more scaffolding and jackhammering going on. It's like they're constantly rebuilding it."

Dalton was politely agreeing when he realized, *Oh, man, they think I'm a construction worker!* On the one hand, it was a letdown to realize he wasn't convincing as a homeless person, but in this case, he was kind of glad. It eliminated the need to lie about why he was living on the streets while still explaining his unpleasant odor.

By the time the pan of pizza was in front of them and they'd taken their first bites, a small crowd had formed on the sidewalk across the street, gathering around a black limousine that had pulled up to the curb. "What's happening over there?" Ellie wondered.

"I don't know." Mia craned her neck to look around her sister. "Those guys look like bodyguards. I think someone important is going into Bellemont."

Dalton took a bite, savoring the cheese that was layered thickly over the seasoned tomato sauce. If this wasn't the best pizza in the world, it came close. As he ate, he followed the girls' gaze through the window to the other side of the road. Celebrities were pretty common in New York, but it was still exciting to spot one. Once his parents had sat behind some well-known chef from the Food Network at a Broadway musical, and it had delighted his mom more than the actual show. Two weeks later, she was still talking about it. "He looked so much smaller than I imagined," she said. "I kept wanting to lean over and touch his ear." Dalton didn't even ask what that was all about.

Now they watched as a burly guy opened the back door of the limo, then held his arm out to shield the occupants from the few stray tourists who clustered around, their phones held up, ready to document the event. In the restaurant where they sat, the piped-in sounds of Dean Martin singing "That's Amore" became the soundtrack to the commotion outside while Ellie and Mia provided the director's cut commentary.

A man exited the car first, a young guy with swooped-back hair, cut long on top and shaved close on the sides. "I know who that is!" Mia exclaimed. "It's Vance!"

"Who?" Dalton asked.

"Vance," Ellie repeated. "You know, Cece Vanderhaven's friend Vance. Hashtag gay boyfriend?"

The name was familiar. Not the hashtag part with the gay boyfriend, but the last name. Vanderhaven. Dalton's father had done some big deals with a Mr. Harry Vanderhaven, and Dalton had met the man once very briefly at his dad's office. All the administrative assistants working that day were in awe of him, fighting over who would bring in the coffee, admiring his coat (which one of them had taken, supposedly to hang), and trying on his gloves. Dalton didn't think much work got done that day. He really didn't understand why people idolized the rich. It was different if they became rich by doing something clever—inventing something or building something—but just by inheriting wealth or having investments accrue over time? It seemed pretty random, but then again, he knew a lot of people who were extremely well off, and he'd also met a fair amount of people who were struggling to get by from one month to the next. If he had to estimate, he'd guess there were approximately the same percentage of jerks in each group. People were people.

"Whoa, that's Katrina!" Mia said, her face pressed close to the glass. "I am obsessed with her, like, completely obsessed. She's so funny. I love when things don't go well and she makes that face."

"When she scrunches up her nose?" Ellie said. "Yeah, that always cracks me up too."

The woman they were talking about paused by the car to let the bystanders film her, then stopped to sign something for a little girl in pigtails. She called out to the crowd, and in response, there was a roar of approval.

"That Katrina is nice to everyone," Ellie said. "She's so down to earth."

"Right?" her sister said. "I feel like I know her."

Dalton watched as Katrina took a step back and did a little game-show flourish toward the car. A second later, out came a woman whose very presence made the crowd go wild while her security detail closed ranks to protect her. Videographers on both sides of the street filmed the scene with bulky cameras that rested on their shoulders. Professionals. They'd obviously known this was going to be happening. The street, too, was now curiously absent of any other cars, as if someone had arranged to have traffic rerouted.

"Oh, man, it's Cece Vanderhaven!" Mia said with a squeal. At some point, she'd gotten her phone out and was now taking pictures through the glass. "I'm posting these for sure. My friend Taylor is going to be so jealous. She's been stalking Cece online for the longest time. She's got a lot of her clothes, and I think she's got her entire jewelry line too."

Dalton had to admit that Cece Vanderhaven made a big entrance. Her clothing, for one thing. She wore a red dress with a wide skirt, pinstripe stockings, and red shoes. "Her shoes are totally perfect," Mia said in approval, still clicking photos. Cece stopped, her hand still on the car door. As the security people hustled her away from the car and toward the restaurant, she occasionally reached through their protective circle to touch fingers with an admirer or pat a child on the head.

When Cece and friends, accompanied by the security team, were on the sidewalk heading into the restaurant, the car door swung open again, but this time no one seemed to notice. A young woman stepped out hesitantly, like she wasn't sure about what to do next.

"Who's that?" Mia asked.

Ellie shook her head. "I've never seen her before. She must be an assistant or something."

The woman gingerly shut the car door, took a step, then stopped as if frozen in place. Dalton sat up and leaned toward the window, wanting a closer look. Something about her captured his attention. He watched as she tucked her hair behind her ear and concentrated, her lips moving, head nodding slightly. Suddenly, he knew what she was doing. Counting down. He mentally joined her. *Seven, six, five, four, three, two, one.* After she'd reached the end, she exhaled and straightened up, her posture one of resolve. When she glanced toward the pizzeria, Dalton gave her a thumbs-up. Meeting his gaze, she grinned, returning the thumbs-up gesture before heading off, going around the car and melting into the crowd.

"Did you know her?" Ellie asked, her eyes widening in amazement.

"No," Dalton said. "I never saw her before."

"Huh," Ellie said, her expression thoughtful. "She sure looked like she knew you."

CHAPTER ELEVEN

The plan was simple enough. Vance had jokingly said even a child could do it, which had made Greta so nervous, it had completely ratcheted up the pressure. Once she'd memorized his instructions, it was the timing that worried her the most.

Greta was told to wait while Vance, Katrina, and Cece left the vehicle. "We'll be exiting on the street side," Vance said. He continued on, saying that once they had walked around the limo and were on the sidewalk, she was to get out, count down slowly from ten, and then follow them into the restaurant. "You'll most likely have to fight through the crowd," he said. "Just go into the entryway of the restaurant and give the person at the front desk your name, and they'll bring you back to the table."

Greta had peppered them with questions. Why get out on the street side? Why not just take the quickest path from the car to the building, and exit the car on the passenger side? That way they'd be on the sidewalk first thing. "Believe me, we have our reasons for everything," Katrina said. "The road will be blocked off, so we don't have to worry about traffic, and we'll be leaving the car on the driver's side so that both cameras get good footage. It also prolongs the entrance." Prolonging the entrance made it more dramatic, she explained. And having Greta join the table after they'd been seated would make her stand out. "Everyone is going to wonder who you are, which is exactly the way we want it." Every public step of Cece's life was planned, strategized, and implemented accordingly.

Vance took over the conversation from there, putting his hand on Greta's shoulder in a friendly way. "You'll leave the car after the rest of us, so it will look almost like we forgot about you. Get out, mentally count down from ten, and then close the car door and follow us in. Got it?" He leaned toward her with a smile, his teeth so perfect and white, they were distracting.

"Yes." Greta nodded. Vance had said they wanted today's footage to show how she didn't quite fit in yet. At the end of her character arc, she'd be transformed, resembling the rest of them in style and confidence. Bit by bit, they'd let the hair, makeup, and wardrobe people do their magic. Then, at that point, they'd create a montage of Greta's transformation from awkward nerd to self-assured fashion-savvy woman. But first, they needed her to be awkward.

Funny, but she didn't really feel like an awkward nerd. She'd always considered herself to be kind of pretty and of average weight and height. It was only in New York that she felt the need to lose some weight and make more effort with her appearance. Standards of beauty, she reflected, only became standard because somebody had deemed them so. She'd once read the autobiography of a silent film actress who'd said that back in the 1920s, women were considered beautiful if they had eyes bigger than their mouths. That was the look then, but it wasn't the yardstick for attractiveness now. Chinese women had their feet bound because tiny feet were revered, and in ancient Greece, a unibrow was considered beautiful. When you looked back, it was all so random.

"You're going to do great," Vance said, sensing her uncertainty. Even if he didn't mean it, Greta still found it encouraging. She could do the lacking-in-confidence part with no problem at all. Hopefully, she would grow along with her fictitious character so that she ended up being as sophisticated as they wanted her to be.

When they pulled up in front of the restaurant, a small crowd had already formed on the sidewalk. "It's like they knew we were coming," Greta said, peering through the glass.

"They did," Vance said. "We posted our lunch plans before we left. Some of them are hired actors."

After the limousine came to a stop, the crowd pressed against the windows. The fans' faces were distorted, fun-house–mirror versions of their actual selves. "You're perfectly safe," Cece assured her. "I know it seems scary, but most of them just want pictures." Even so, Greta was glad when the security detail arrived and herded the fans away from the car.

After the driver let them know it was clear to get out, they left in order: Vance, then Katrina, and finally Cece. Before Cece left, she gave Greta one last hug. "Oh, Greta," she said, eyes shining. "I love that you're here this summer."

After the three of them were on the other side of the car, Greta got out, closed the door, and began counting down. With all the attention focused on Cece, Vance, and Katrina, no one in the crowd noticed her. As she counted, her gaze shifted from one end of the street to the other, finally landing on a pizza place across the street.

Through the front window, she saw a guy sitting at a table across from two girls. She felt him watching her, and as she finished counting down—*three, two, one*—she noticed in amazement that his head was nodding slightly in time. It looked like his lips were moving, saying the numbers along with her. He couldn't have known she was counting, but somehow, he did. Making fun of her? No, she didn't think so.

When she finished counting, she made a point to turn his way. In response, he flashed a grin and gave her a thumbs-up. She smiled and returned the gesture.

When Greta got to the crowd pulsing just outside the front door, one of the security guys broke rank to escort her through the crush and into the restaurant, then abruptly left once she was in front of the host stand. Two men stood behind the elevated desk. "Hi, I'm Greta Hansen, here to join the Vanderhaven party?"

From the look on his face, they'd been briefed and expected her. This outing was turning out to be an eye-opener. She'd watched Cece's videos for years, always assuming they were impromptu, fun clips of her cousin's actual life. If she'd given it any thought at all, she would have guessed it was scripted. How did they manage to get shots from all angles, for one thing? And they were always perfectly attired, even when they wore jammies and watched movies in Cece's gigantic bed. Why didn't that ever strike her as odd? Probably because she wanted it to be true.

Greta consoled herself with the notion that even if most of this was fake, Cece's reaction to her arrival had to be genuine. Cece really had been delighted that Greta had come to stay for the summer.

The host escorted her to the table and pulled out a chair next to Cece. As she sat, he said, "We're glad you could join us today at Bellemont, Ms. Hansen."

Cece leaned over and squeezed her arm. "This is my cousin, Greta," she told the host. "Here for the summer."

"How lovely to be officially introduced," he said, with a slight bow. "I do hope you'll enjoy your stay in New York."

"Thank you."

Wine had been ordered for the table ahead of time, and the server poured her a glass as well. Vance and Katrina made small talk, joking and laughing as they went, and Cece went along with it, smiling when appropriate. The group was on their second glass of wine when two fans, women in their early thirties, approached the table, asking if they could get a picture with Cece.

"Of course!" Cece said. Now she was in her element, asking their names and where they were from. Both of them were New Yorkers. This was a business lunch for them. "How lucky that we happened to be here at the same time!" Cece exclaimed, as if it were her luck and not the other way around.

The first woman crouched down to Cece's level and took a selfie of the two of them. Several selfies. Her friend recorded the whole exchange with her phone. The surrounding tables stopped talking to watch.

"Let me see!" Cece said, and the woman showed her the images on her phone. "Nice," she murmured at the sight of one, and then, "Oh, that's a good one of you. Great smile." You'd have thought that she and this woman were good friends. Greta took a sip of wine and looked on, seeing the pleasure in Cece's face at making these women so happy. In the background, silverware clinked on dishes, and jazz music softly played.

"Can I post this online?" the woman asked.

"Certainly," Cece said. "I'll watch for it."

"Thank you!"

"Do you want to take Greta's picture?" Cece asked, motioning toward her cousin.

"No, that's okay . . . " She started to object, but Cece kept going, her words drowning out her objection.

"Greta is my cousin. She's here visiting from Wisconsin!" Cece's voice rang with enthusiasm.

Greta felt a warm wine flush of love toward Cece for wanting to pull her into the spotlight. She remembered a conversation she'd had with Jacey when she'd first gotten the internship. Jacey had warned her that Cece was probably a snobby bitch, but luckily, she'd been completely wrong.

"Do you mind?" the woman asked, holding her phone up.

"Not at all."

She crouched next to her. Greta smiled as the phone made faint clicking noises.

Cece kept talking. "I've wanted to meet Greta for the longest time, and I'm so excited that she's finally here."

"Sounds like you have some competition," the woman teased Vance and Katrina. "Before you know it, Greta is going to be Cece's best friend."

"We'd be fine with that," Vance said with a smile. "Right, Katrina?"

Katrina made her goofy face, the one with the wrinkled nose, and lifted her shoulders as if to say, *What are you gonna do?* "I'm good with it. Whatever makes Cece happy, that's all we care about."

The woman who was recording video asked, "So what do you say, Cece? Is Greta your new best friend?"

"Yes," Cece said, giving Greta a warm smile. "Absolutely. Greta is my new best friend."

The woman filming said, "So what do the old best friends have to say about that?"

Vance grinned. "We'll gladly step aside to let the cousins have their day in the sun. It's only fair. Katrina and I have had a good run, and if we need to be replaced by someone, I can't think of anyone better than Greta. Cece, we approve."

"Here, here," Katrina said, lifting her glass in solidarity.

Vance lifted his glass as well, looking straight at the woman who was filming. "I'd like to make a toast to Greta Hansen, our replacement and Cece's new best friend. I couldn't have chosen better myself."

"To Greta Hansen," Cece said, her face flushed with happiness. "My cousin and my new best friend."

CHAPTER TWELVE

Dalton knew he'd never met that girl, but something happened when they locked eyes for that brief moment. He felt that click, that connection, that intangible thing that happens when someone comes along, and at first sight, there's that flash of recognition.

He'd had a similar thing happen when he'd met his friend Will freshman year. It was the first day at the university, and their RA had organized a get-acquainted hall meeting. All the freshmen were checking each other out and walking around introducing themselves, while Will leaned back against a wall, his arms folded across his chest. He had a look of complete indifference, like he'd rather be somewhere else. Anywhere else. When a few of the girls started giggling and tossing popcorn at each other, Will caught Dalton's eye and shook his head as if the two of them were the adults, amused by the antics of children. Like they were already friends, and he knew Dalton was thinking the same thing he was.

As it turned out, Will didn't think he was above anyone else. He just hated organized group events. People on their floor found out that he was a good guy, smart and funny. Later on, he said Dalton had seemed familiar too. They were complete strangers who knew each other at first sight.

It was like that times a hundred when Dalton had spotted the young woman across the street. He'd watched as Cece Vanderhaven and her friends left the limousine, looking all glam like they were going to be sitting in the front row at a fashion show. Not this woman, though. She wasn't dressed trendy at all. Instead, she wore a dress with a short-sleeved sweater over it, making her look like every kid's favorite kindergarten teacher. The other three each had a head of hair that looked like they'd just stepped out of a salon. Her hair hung loosely over her shoulders, one side tucked behind her ear. The way she got out of the limo, so unsure, made her seem all the more endearing.

He recognized something in this young woman. Her hesitance showed a tender vulnerability. It made him want to take her hand and tell her everything was going to be fine.

Or maybe she could take his hand and do the same for him.

Ellie and Mia kept talking about Cece and her friends long after the limo pulled away and the crowd dispersed. It was Vance this and Katrina that. They knew everything about Cece's life. It was kind of amazing, really. Dalton kept eating his pizza and nodding sociably. When an employee came and offered to refill his root beer, he gratefully accepted.

After a while, Ellie pushed her plate away and said, "Dalton, it's so weird that we ran into you right after you'd met Matt."

"Yeah, that was a major coincidence."

Mia said, "It happened because we were in Saint Patrick's Cathedral. The whole thing was orchestrated from above." She pointed up at the ceiling tiles and nudged her sister. "Maybe Grandma is behind it."

"That's like something she would do," Ellie said.

"I'm glad I could help," Dalton said. "And thank you for the pizza. It hit the spot. Do either of you want that last piece?" They did not, and so it was his.

Twenty minutes later, standing outside on the sidewalk, they said their goodbyes. Ellie and Mia were heading to the hospital to visit their grandfather. Ellie would return to the city after that to keep looking for Matt. Besides searching on her own, she planned to show his photo to local businesses. "If you give me your phone, I can put my number in your contacts," Ellie said. "Then if you spot Matt, you can call me right away."

Ahem. "I don't have my phone on me. Forgot it at home."

"Let me write down my number." Ellie dug through her purse until she found a pen and scrap of paper. She jotted down her name and the number. "If you lose it, Matt knows it by heart. You can just ask him."

Dalton stared down at the numbers written in blue ink. "I won't lose it." He put the number in the front pocket of his backpack and zippered it shut.

They were still in front of the pizzeria when a taxi pulled up and an elderly couple got out. "Perfect timing," Mia said. Ellie grabbed his shoulders as if she were about to give him a hug, thought better of it, and just gave his arms a quick squeeze. "Did you want to share a cab?"

"No, I'm good," Dalton said. "I'll be walking." And then they were done. The two sisters climbed into the cab. He gave a wave as the cab pulled away and smiled when he saw Ellie's hand flutter through the open window.

Once again, he lacked a purpose. He had nothing to do and nowhere to be. So much of being without a home meant that he was also without a job, family, and friends. Not only that, but he lacked access and money to do the kinds of activities he loved. Basically, he was without all the things that made up what he thought of as his life. Each day had been stripped down to the basics: food, water, and shelter. Well, it could be worse. He had a stomach full of pizza and had spent time with some nice people. A good turn of events.

He stared for a minute at the Bellemont and then impulsively trotted across the street and walked through the door into the restaurant. Inside, it was like another world. Dim lighting, the sounds of soft techno music pulsing from every direction. He couldn't help but notice that the air-conditioning was about a million times better than in the pizza place. Dalton felt his lungs swell in happiness. Once inside, he knew why he'd felt compelled to go there. He wanted to get a closer look at that girl.

"Can I help you?" a man asked from behind the desk.

"I'm just looking for a friend." Dalton gave him a friendly smile, the one that usually worked on almost everyone, but not this time. The man's face was as impassive as a statue's.

"I assure you, your friend is not here."

"Maybe I can take a quick look?" He smiled again. This time, he was rewarded with a glare. *What a grouch.*

"I'm sorry, but you must leave immediately. We have a strict dress code, and you are not in compliance."

Apparently his unshowered state and gross-looking backpack weren't passing muster. "I understand," Dalton said. "I'll come by another time. Thanks."

CHAPTER THIRTEEN

Her first two days had been incredible! Greta mentally ticked off all the things that had happened in the space of about forty-eight hours. First of all, she'd been filmed by a professional crew for footage that hundreds of thousands of people would see. Then, she'd viewed New York by limousine; gone to a classy restaurant with Cece, Katrina, and Vance; and gotten to eat something called steak Gatsby. If all that wasn't enough, Cece Vanderhaven, whom she'd idolized from afar, absolutely adored her! Greta wasn't sure what she had done to earn her affection, but it was clear to everyone she was the new favorite.

She was riding so high on positive endorphins that even a look from a scruffy, good-looking guy eating in the pizza place across the street gave her an electrical jolt. It had happened in an instant. Like a camera going in for a close-up, their eyes had locked, and when he'd smiled at her—*bam!* She felt like there was nothing she couldn't do. This girl was on fire.

The rest of the summer could only get better.

During the limo ride back to Cece's, everyone was talking about Greta and how well she did. Vance and Katrina were so excited, they could barely contain themselves. The back of the vehicle had an L-shaped seat configuration, so there was plenty of space for all of them to stretch out, but they wanted to stay crammed together, each one taking turns hugging her.

Vance said, "I had my doubts about working you into the schedule, Greta, but I have to admit, you're the best thing that ever happened to Cece's World." He and Katrina high-fived each other and beamed with delight.

"You were epic," Cece told her, blowing a kiss. "Everything went so well."

"Unbelievably well," Katrina said, fist pumping in the air. "You're officially my new favorite person, Greta."

"Oh, thank you," she said, trying to be modest. "I just did my best."

"Your best rocks," Vance said. "Your best is the kind of best that changes lives."

"Well, I'm not sure I was *that* good." Greta felt herself blush; she wasn't used to such over-the-top compliments. Her stay in New York was turning out to be exceptional. "That's nice of you to say, though."

When they got back to Cece's place, Vance opened a bottle of champagne, and they all toasted: "To Greta Hansen!" Glasses clinked, and there was drinking and laughing and so many smiles. It was crazy the way they piled on the praise. Greta was the answer to their prayers. The new star of Cece's World. A natural at promotion. Cece kept saying Greta was fabulous, the best cousin ever. That she had waited so long to meet her, and now they'd be friends for life.

Greta almost turned down the champagne because she'd thought she wouldn't care for it. She came to find out that what she didn't like was cheap champagne. The good stuff went down just fine.

After a dinner of Chinese delivery, Katrina and Vance called it a night. Vance leaned over to give Cece a kiss on the cheek. "You know I love you, right, Cece?"

"Of course," she said, her fingers trailing over his cheek. "I love you too, Vance."

"And that will never change, no matter what, right?"

Cece smiled in agreement and gave Katrina a goodbye hug as well.

After they left, Nanny and Brenna joined them and asked if they were interested in playing Jenga. "I'd love to," Cece said. "Greta, are you in?"

"Sure, why not?" They sat around the dining room table, playing Jenga like anyone else, famous or not.

Brenna seemed less pensive tonight, happy to be playing a game with her big sister. In between moves, Cece told them how well the day had gone. "Greta was epic. Absolutely epic!" she said. "Everyone loved her!"

"Oh, I don't know about that," Greta said bashfully.

After the second game, Nanny opted out, so Greta did too, watching the two sisters tease each other and laugh as they played. When Nanny got up to go into the kitchen, she waited a few minutes, then excused herself and followed her.

She walked in to find Nanny cleaning up from dinner. Earlier, they'd put their plates and silverware in the sink and the glasses on the counter. When Greta had started to rinse them off, Katrina had stopped her, saying, "Don't worry about it, Greta. Someone will be along to take care of the washing."

Greta could see that with most of the staff gone, that someone was Nanny. "Can I help?" she asked, startling her.

"I've got it, thanks." Nanny rinsed the dishes and then opened the dishwasher to place each one inside. She hummed a little as she worked. When she realized Greta was still in the room, she paused and asked, "Is there something I can help you find?"

"No, I was just wondering . . ." Something had nagged at her since she'd first met Cece that morning. Something about her cousin just seemed off.

"Wondering what?" Nanny asked, wiping her hands on a dishtowel.

"I don't want you to take this the wrong way, or say anything to Cece because I wouldn't want her to think badly of me. I'd never want to hurt her feelings." She paused, wondering how to say this without coming off the wrong way, then decided there was no diplomatic way to ask this kind of question.

"Yes?" Nanny prompted.

"Cece is wonderful. Really warm and caring, but she's not how I thought she'd be. Something about her . . ."

"Seems different from what you expected?" Nanny finished.

In the other room, Cece and Brenna giggled, the kind of right-from-the-gut laughter done with only people you love and trust.

"Sort of," Greta said, although there was nothing *sort of* about it. Cece had acted completely different from the video clips she'd seen online.

"You're wondering why that is."

"Yes. I mean, she's terrific. Just not what I expected. I'm not trying to be critical. I'm just wondering about the difference between her public persona and how she is in private."

"It's okay," Nanny said. "I know what you're saying. Cece is a lovely girl and a wonderful person, but she's not the same as she was before."

"Before?"

Nanny craned her neck, listening to the laughter in the next room before answering. "No one in the family talks about it, so I'd appreciate your keeping this in confidence."

"Of course."

"Just between us, about four years ago, Brenna and Cece were in the family pool, the one up on the roof." She pointed upward, and Greta nodded, remembering having read about it. "They don't use it anymore, not since the accident."

"The accident?"

"I had off that day, but the rest of the staff was here, and Mrs. Vanderhaven was home. She didn't think anything of letting the girls go swimming on their own. Cece was nineteen at the time and an excellent swimmer, and she was very protective of her little sister. Always has been since the day she was born. Brenna was only four, but she'd had swimming lessons and was pretty good in the water. Besides, she was wearing those water wings, the inflatable ones, the kind that slide up your upper arms?" She indicated, gripping her own arm where a water wing would sit.

"I know the kind."

She leaned back against the counter and sighed. "No one knows for sure what happened. All they know is that Brenna came running down the stairs, screaming. No one understood a word she was saying. She was hysterical. One of the maids followed her back up to the pool, and they found Cece floating facedown."

Oh my. Even knowing that Cece was alive and fine and laughing in the next room, Greta found the story harrowing. Poor Brenna—having to go for help all on her own. "So what happened?"

"They pulled her out of the pool. Someone did CPR, and they called 911."

"I never heard anything about this." If this had made the news, she would have remembered. She'd been on high alert for all things Vanderhaven for years.

"No, it was all kept very hush-hush. The doctors and nurses knew to keep it confidential. The Vanderhavens have donated a lot of money to that hospital," Nanny explained. "Cece only spent one night at the hospital. They never did find out what caused her to become unconscious. They ruled out a stroke. She had no history of seizures. They just couldn't figure it out. To this day, it's a mystery."

"Wow, how awful."

Nanny nodded in agreement. "Physically, she was declared to be in perfect health and released. The only issue that seemed troubling was that she couldn't remember what had happened in the pool, and Brenna couldn't explain it either. But that didn't seem important compared to Cece's life. The whole household was overjoyed when Cece came home. We'd all been sick with worry. The household staff loves these two girls like you wouldn't believe. You'd think they'd be spoiled brats, but that's not the case at all."

"So she was fine when she came home."

She nodded. "Fine enough. Just quiet, or at least that's what we thought. But after a while, everyone started to notice things. She'd been going to the university but had to drop out because she lost interest. She wasn't the same after that. She's impulsive now and just blurts things out. Her personality is different. I actually love the way she is, but it upsets her parents that she's not as career-oriented as she was before. We were all instructed not to talk about it, so you didn't hear about it from me."

"I understand."

Nanny said, "It was shortly after the accident that Cece's World was born. Her parents created the company to give her something to focus on and so she'd have her own source of revenue. It made her happy at first. They'd bring all the designs around, and she'd get to pick which ones would have her label on them. She got to narrow down the fragrances and pick the one that would be her signature perfume."

"Let Me In," Greta said, recalling the name.

"That's the one." She nodded. "Cece enjoyed all the hubbub. She liked reading the comments on her posts and getting hair and makeup done for filming and trying on all the new clothes. It was all so much fun at first, but it's going on three years now, and she's gotten very tired of it. Katrina and Vance do a good job of getting her to go along with everything they need her to do, but frankly, it breaks my heart when she begs not to have to do a scene, and they whisk her off for a shoot. I feel like telling them to just leave her alone." In the other room, the laughter had died down, and now the sisters were talking in hushed tones. Every now and then, they heard Brenna giggle. Nanny sighed. "It's not up to me, of course. I just work here."

"Cece and Brenna seem like they get along well."

"There is a strong bond there," Nanny said. "You'd think with the age difference, there wouldn't be, that these two girls wouldn't have much in common, but if anything, it's just the opposite. I think it's because their parents are gone so much. They can't count on Mom and Dad, but they know they have each other."

They couldn't count on their mom and dad? That was just too sad and so unlike Greta's family. She and her brother both knew that no matter what happened or where they were, their parents were just a phone call away. And even if there were hundreds of miles between them, her mom and dad would move heaven and earth to get to them if need be.

"Anyway," Nanny said, wrapping up the conversation, "the rest of us love Cece the way she is, but her parents don't want to let it get out, so you'll need to keep this to yourself."

"I will. I promise."

"Not a word to anyone. Don't tell a friend or a family member. Especially not your mother. Deborah would be mortified if her cousin knew. She likes the perfect front."

"Okay," Greta said, but secretly, she knew she'd tell her mother someday, probably after she returned home. How could she not?

CHAPTER FOURTEEN

Dalton spent the day in search of homeless people. It wasn't too hard to track them down. He found them in the train station and the subways, the parks, and the back alleys. And Times Square, of course. Few were quite as willing to talk to him as Matt. Meeting him first thing meant he either got lucky or else his gift of beef jerky was an effective tool in opening up a channel of communication.

The ones who were most willing to talk to him were men, all of them down on their luck. Some of them were hopeful things would get better. As one grizzled old man said, "It can't get any worse, so it's gotta get better." He was the most optimistic. A lot of them felt beaten down. They were surviving but not living.

During their talks, some of the same things came up over and over again. They'd gotten to this point after losing a job. Or because of an addiction to drugs or alcohol. Or by aging out of foster care and having nowhere else to go. Some had health problems or mental illnesses that made it difficult to find jobs or impossible to keep working. He kept hearing how they stayed afloat for a while but eventually became bankrupt, both financially and emotionally. And after that, they had nothing left to give. No energy left. They wandered like ghosts as other people looked past them, disregarding their very existence.

Several of them mentioned that they sometimes stayed in shelters, but only when necessary. Some didn't like the rules; others said they didn't think they were safe for them or their possessions. Funny thing: homeless people didn't necessarily like to hang out with other random homeless people. "There are a lot of pissed-off people out there," said one man.

One young guy named Trey had lived in an apartment in Brooklyn with his father. After his dad died unexpectedly, Trey couldn't pay the rent. One day he'd come home to find the locks changed. "How did that make you feel?" Dalton asked, sounding like the kind of armchair psychologist he normally didn't care for. He wasn't asking just to fill the silence. He honestly wanted to know.

He shrugged. "I didn't pay any rent for months, so I couldn't say too much. The man needed his money. I didn't have it. Lucky thing I left the window unlocked, so I could go up the fire escape and get my stuff out." Trey had stayed with friends on and off, but one by one, his drinking made him unwelcome. "Being sober hasn't worked out for me," he said. "I keep going back to the bottle. I'll probably have one in my hand when they find my dead body."

He looked too young to have his fate decided for him. "Do you want to quit?"

Trey smirked. "Yeah, sure. I also want a mansion and a hot girlfriend and a million dollars. Sign me up for all of it."

Midday, Dalton went to a park and spotted a couple who looked friendly and open to conversation. He found out that their names were Diego and Lauren, and that both were nineteen. They told him they'd met in foster care. When he first saw them, they were sitting under a tree, a tattered suitcase next to them. In front of Diego was a cardboard box lined with a plastic bag. The plastic bag was filled with ice and water bottles, which he was selling for two dollars each. Dalton started the conversation by becoming a customer. "I'll take one of those," he said, even though this purchase wasn't technically in his budget.

Diego took out a bottle and traded it for his money. "Here you go, sir."

"Thanks. Mind if I sit for a minute?"

"Suit yourself."

Since he'd just given them two dollars, they decided he was okay. He heard their story and how they coped. This water business provided them with enough money to eat and even sometimes extra for things like toiletries. But they wanted something better. They knew how middle-class America lived, and they wanted it for themselves. A safe apartment, a fridge full of food, a bed to sleep in, and dinner together every evening at their very own kitchen table. "That's not asking for too much, is it?" Lauren asked softly.

"No, it's not too much to ask. But most people work full-time to get those things."

"I would work full-time," Diego said, resting his hand on his girlfriend's knee. "I totally would. I'd work more than full-time if they'd let me." Lauren nodded in agreement.

"So—and I'm not saying this to be a smart-ass; I really want to know—what's stopping you?"

He shrugged. "Who would hire me? Lots of people are looking for jobs. Why would they pick me? Look at me. I don't have the right clothes. I need a haircut. I have no home address to put on an application, only an email. I have a record for shoplifting. Believe me, I was screwed in life before I even got here."

Twenty feet away, two guys who looked like college students threw a Frisbee back and forth. One guy tossed it so it spiraled above his friend's head. The other guy leaped into the air like he had springs for feet. He snatched it, hanging in midair for a split second, with only space around him, the sky above and the grass below. It was a sight to behold.

"Great catch," Lauren said, shielding her eyes with the flat of her hand.

Dalton had one last question for Diego, and it was the question that had started his two-week homeless experiment. "What would help? What would turn things around for you so you could get off the streets and into the life you want?"

He gazed off in the distance. Just when Dalton thought he wasn't going to answer, he narrowed his eyes and said, "I need someone and something I can count on to pull me through."

Dalton picked at a blade of grass. "Like at a shelter? Consistent rules you can count on?"

"No, no." His brow furrowed. "Not like a shelter at all. Shelters are just places to put people. They don't differentiate. The crazy ones get mixed in with the ones who just need some help, a hand up."

"So you'd like a different kind of shelter? Or some kind of program that's set up just for you?"

"I don't want someone telling me what to do," Diego said. He gestured, indicating himself and Lauren. "We're not stupid. We know what we want, and we know how we screwed up in the past. We own it. The help we need is in going forward."

"Right. I think I get it."

He wasn't done, though, and now he leaned toward Dalton, his finger wagging. "The problem with the shelters and the programs is that everything is compartmentalized. You got one set of people running the food program and one group doing the addiction counseling and other people that help you look for housing. They try to put a human face on it. They call us *guests* or *clients*." He finger-quoted the two words. "But it's all a farce. No one knows you, and no one has enough time, and if you stop showing up, no one's going to wonder what happened to you. They just move on to the next sad person."

A woman holding a little boy's hand stopped in front of them, two dollars held out to Diego. He handed her a bottle. "Here you go, ma'am."

"Thank you." She gestured to her child. "Can my son take some ice?"

"Of course."

The little boy, maybe four years old, surveyed the ice as if trying to decide, then plunged his hand in and pulled out a fistful. "Whoa!" he said, water dripping off his arm.

"Pretty cold, huh?" Diego laughed.

The woman thanked them, and they walked off, the boy still clutching his handful of ice. The whole scene struck Dalton as being so normal. A couple sitting on a blanket selling water in the park, interacting with a customer in a friendly way. Except for their appearance, they were just like other kids he'd met in college.

With a jolt, he realized that although he'd prided himself on being compassionate, he'd thought on some level that the homeless were not quite as smart as other people. Hearing Diego use words like *compartmentalized* and *differentiate* made him realize how mistaken he'd been. Diego had expressed what was wrong with the system in a concise and informed way and given Dalton more insight than all the articles he'd read.

Diego was right in that one size didn't fit all. Social workers and those who worked in the shelters and programs for the homeless were, from what he saw, well meaning and hardworking. But the problem was overwhelming, and each client had different problems, some of them not readily apparent. They tried. Most of them did the best they could with the resources they had.

Even with all the good they did, there were failures too. Folks they tried to help went back to a life of drugs or crime, despite their best efforts. No wonder there was so much burnout in the field.

As the afternoon wore on, Diego and Lauren sold all their water inventory. "You did well," Dalton commented.

"We usually do," Lauren said. "We used to have a shopping cart, and we'd go to the bus stops where the tourists were waiting in line. Standing in the sun makes people hot and thirsty. One day we made three hundred bucks. We kept restocking and going back. It was crazy."

"You don't do that anymore?"

"Nah," she said. "Someone stole our cart when we were sleeping. Diego woke up and took off after him, but when he caught up to the guy, the jerk's friend knocked him down and punched him, like, eight times. Gave him a black eye."

"I totally could have taken both of them if I'd been more awake," Diego said, as if this story were an affront to his manhood. "They caught me off guard."

At dinnertime, they told him about a soup kitchen nearby where the food wasn't all that bad. "The people who run it are so nice," Lauren said.

They weren't going, because they said they had other plans. *Other plans?* Dalton was curious but didn't ask. "Thanks for letting me hang out with you this afternoon," he said. "Would you mind giving me your email address? If I come across any job opportunities, I'll let you know." Diego jotted it down and handed it to him, and then Dalton was on his way, off to have his very first meal in a soup kitchen. This experience was turning out to be different from what he'd expected, but whatever it was, it wasn't boring.

CHAPTER FIFTEEN

Greta had finished a call to her mom and was plugging her phone into the charger when there was a loud rapping on her bedroom door. The unexpectedness of it made her jump. The clock read just past eleven o'clock, and she had only the small bedside lamp on, which made it all the more eerie. "Yes?" she called out.

"It's Katrina."

She crossed the room and opened the door, hoping the lack of light helped her appearance. Her pajamas were comfortable but worn, and her freshly washed face revealed blotchy skin and dark under-eye circles. Katrina had a manila envelope clutched to her chest and a funny look on her face. Greta asked, "Is everything okay?"

"Can I come in?" she whispered.

"Of course." Greta let her in, then closed the door quietly behind her.

"I just wanted to let you know that Vance and I are leaving."

"Leaving? Where are you going?"

"That's the great part," she said, and then a sudden grin broke out like she couldn't help herself. "We don't know yet. All we know is that we're heading to the airport and flying far, far away."

"When will you be back?"

"Never, if we can help it." She thrust the envelope into Greta's hands. "We're leaving you in charge."

"I don't get it." Greta wasn't playing dumb; she really didn't get it. "Does Cece know about this?"

"No one knows but our attorney. And you, of course. Vance and I, we can't thank you enough, Greta. There was only the one loophole, and it didn't look like that was *ever* going to happen. We thought we were stuck in this job forever. Then little Greta Hansen from Wisconsin comes along with her Jesus sandals and knockoff purse, and the next thing we know, Cece's saying you're her favorite and her very best friend." Her eyes widened. "And I'm like, yes! Thank God that woman in the restaurant made a video. It's already out there going viral."

As Katrina spelled it out, the pieces came together for Greta. She put a hand to her forehead and said, "Oh, I get it. I'm the best friend replacement. Which means you're now released from your contract."

"That's right! We are free. Our attorney said this satisfies the clause in the contract." She grabbed Greta's shoulders and pulled her in for a hug. "If I live to be a hundred, I can honestly say I'll never forget you, Greta Hansen. Thank you, thank you, thank you! Vance and I will be watching to see how this all plays out from wherever we are."

She was crushing Greta. They were a sandwich with the manila envelope in the middle. Greta said, "Are you going to tell Cece before you go?"

Katrina pulled away before answering. "We thought about waiting a day or two so we could tell her ourselves and get her used to the idea, but honestly, Greta? We're afraid she'll try to talk us out of it, and that would make it even harder. This way will be like pulling off a Band-Aid. Painful, but over quickly." She glanced at the floor. "We really do love Cece and don't want to hurt her. We just need to live our own lives, you know?"

"I know, but she's going to be so upset."

"I know." She sighed. "Unfortunately, that's unavoidable. But we have a letter for her in the envelope that explains everything. You can give it to her tomorrow. The keys to our apartment are in there too.

It also has the next few weeks' schedule and everything else you need. Vance and I covered every detail, so you'll be able to take over for us."

A wave of panic came over Greta. "I don't think I can do this."

"You'll be fine," she said, sounding assured, but Greta wasn't convinced. Really, how much did Katrina know about her? They'd known each other for such a short time. Katrina had no idea how long it took Greta to catch on to things that had more than two steps. Another problem? She was a big-time daydreamer. Sometimes she got so lost in thought that she drove past her exit on the expressway. How could someone so spacey be trusted to take over Firstborn Daughter, Inc.?

"You'll do fine," Katrina repeated. "Just read through the information in the envelope. I'm not sure exactly where we'll be, but you can try texting us if you have a question. And Nanny can help in a pinch. That woman's a saint. Seriously, a saint, and she knows everything about this family. I don't know what they pay her, but it's not enough."

An unfamiliar ping came from behind Katrina. "Just a minute." She took her cell phone out of her back pocket and stared at the screen. "It's Vance. He got us a cab, and he's wondering what's taking me so long. I have to go."

"No, no, wait!" Greta grabbed her arm. "I can't be in charge. I don't even know what's happening tomorrow."

"It's okay, Greta, no one expects perfection. Besides, tomorrow's easy. Cece has a formal dinner, a fund-raiser for one of her debutante friends. It's called the Forgotten Man Ball. It's supposed to be this thing where the high-society ladies bring some guy they want to thank, someone who normally wouldn't go to one of these affairs. You know, like the family house manager or the doorman. We set it up so she'll be taking Michael."

"The driver?"

"That's the one. I'm not going to lie to you, I wasn't looking forward to this Forgotten Man Ball thing. Dinner and then dancing, all of it very formal. I thought it sounded completely lame, and to make it even worse, Michael is a pain in the ass. Vance and I were scheduled to go as a pair, but now we're off the hook." She practically sang the last few words. "You'll have to go as a single, but I think it will be fine. You probably won't have to mess with paparazzi or getting mobbed by fans. It's a private event, so you only have to worry about the exposure you and Cece will get from the car to the banquet hall and then back again."

So many words flew in Greta's direction that only a few registered in her brain. "I don't get it," she said, feeling her anxiety level rising. "This is way beyond me. I don't know how to do any of this."

"It's all in the envelope," Katrina repeated. "Vance and I are sorry to leave you hanging like this, but Cece has taken a liking to you, and I can tell you'll do great. We're giving you the baton; just run with it."

"The baton?"

"Metaphorically speaking." She smiled. "Just breathe, okay? Take it day by day, hour by hour. Read all the information, and if you still don't understand something, ask Nanny or shoot us a text." The phone in her hand pinged again, and when she glanced at the screen, her face lit up with joy. Greta had seen hundreds of images of her on social media but had never seen her smile that big. "I'm sorry, Greta, but I have to go."

The thing was, she didn't sound sorry at all.

CHAPTER SIXTEEN

At the soup kitchen, Dalton had a more than adequate meal, which turned out not to be soup at all but a kind of stew ladled over rice, served with canned peaches and a cold cup of water. The joy of eating at a table with other people made up for the long wait in line.

All too soon, it was over, and he was on the streets again.

If there were a guidebook for being homeless in New York, sleeping under a bridge would be listed as a must-do, so of course he had to do just that. It wasn't hard to find one. There were lots of bridges in the city. He located one in Central Park and settled down in an unoccupied spot on one end for his night's sleep. The concrete above him was almost like a ceiling, or so he tried to tell himself. He was still more exposed than he wanted to be, but with his money and harmonica in his pocket and his ReadyHelp device hanging around his neck, there wasn't much to steal. True, there was a chance of being randomly attacked, but he was a pretty big guy and wasn't too worried. His last concern—getting picked up by the police for whatever and getting jailed for a night—sounded less like a problem and more like checking into the Comfort Inn.

He looped his arm through the strap of his backpack and positioned it to be a pillow. Comfortable? Not really. But he remembered all the stories he'd heard from folks who'd had their possessions stolen while they slept. There was no way he was letting that happen.

CHAPTER SEVENTEEN

Greta tossed and turned all night, worrying about how she was supposed to take over Katrina's and Vance's jobs, positions they'd had and refined over the course of years. She'd read over everything in the envelope multiple times. They'd been thorough, listing schedules and contact information, along with little personal notes telling her the best way to prod Cece along when she dug her heels in and didn't want to do something. They made her sound like an overtired toddler rather than an adult woman living a life she didn't choose.

Katrina and Vance did the film editing themselves, but only because they preferred to have control. A note in the envelope said a woman named Nina who was part of the camera crew could do the editing for her. Vance had written: *Be very specific about what you want, though, because Nina tends to add her own embellishments.* What did he mean by *embellishments*? Greta had no idea.

Greta yearned to call her mom, but even though it was an hour earlier in Wisconsin, she knew her mother would already be sound asleep. She pulled out her own Vanderhaven contract, seeing what would happen if she up and quit. Every cell in her body wanted to shake off this responsibility and go home to her family. The contract didn't spell out the repercussions for leaving before the end of the summer, but she knew they couldn't be good.

After about fifteen minutes, she made a decision. She would stay. For one thing, she'd signed a contract, but even if that weren't the case, quitting when things got hard wasn't the way she operated. It would be humiliating to go home now.

Besides, how could she leave Cece? She'd just lost Katrina and Vance. Greta didn't want to abandon her during a crisis.

Luckily, the next day was Saturday with nothing scheduled during the day, so that gave her time to figure things out. Saturday evening, as Katrina had mentioned, was the Forgotten Man Ball. Greta read in the notes that the event was organized by one of Cece's fellow debutantes. She vaguely remembered hearing that Cece had been a debutante, but she was a little shaky on what the position entailed, so she googled to find out more and came across an article mentioning Cece by name. At seventeen, Cece had been one of forty-six young women to come out that season at the International Debutante Ball held at the Waldorf Astoria hotel. There was a photo of Cece wearing a white strapless gown and long white gloves. She looked stunning, like a movie star from the 1930s. The article said the point of the ball was to make connections, something that apparently worked, because here it was six years later, and Cece was invited to the Forgotten Man Ball, hosted by someone named Leah Ann Miller. Or maybe it was Leah Ann who'd made the connection, seeing as how she was getting the very famous Cece Vanderhaven to come to her shindig.

All this thinking and googling and worrying kept Greta from sleeping much, so when she caught sight of the morning sun peeking through the edges of the window blinds, it was both good and bad. Bad because she hadn't slept much, but good because she could give up on trying and just start her day. After showering and getting dressed, she headed downstairs, taking the envelope with her. In the kitchen, she found Nanny and Brenna eating breakfast.

"Good morning!" Nanny's tone was chipper. Even Brenna smiled her way. After the game of Jenga the night before, they'd become friends.

Greta sidled up to the counter, still clutching the envelope to her chest. "I'm not so sure it *is* a good morning," she said. "Did you know that Katrina and Vance left last night?"

Nanny's brow furrowed. "Left? For where?" Brenna stopped eating her cereal and looked at Greta quizzically.

"I'm not sure, but I don't think they're coming back anytime soon." Greta leaned against the counter and gave them the quick version of the story, being careful not to mention the contract. It was a fair bet that Nanny knew Vance and Katrina were friends for pay, but it was unlikely that Brenna did. Like Cece, she probably just thought they were the regular kind of friends, the kind who hung around with you because they enjoyed being in your company. Nothing legally binding.

When she finished speaking, Brenna blurted out, "I'm glad they're gone. They were mean to Cece."

"How were they mean to Cece?" Greta asked.

Brenna looked up at her, her big brown eyes wide and expressive. "They always made her do things she didn't want to do. One time they made her cry."

Nanny said, "They weren't trying to be mean, Brenna. Cece has chores she has to do for her business, and they were just helping her get things done."

"Now Cece doesn't have to do it anymore." Brenna stirred the milk in her bowl. "She can stay home and play with me."

A nice thought, but not that practical. Greta directed her next question to Nanny. "They sort of left me in charge, but I just got here, and I don't know too much about any of this. Can we call Mr. and Mrs. Vanderhaven? If they hear what happened, they'll cut their trip short and come home, right?"

Nanny sighed. "You'd think so, wouldn't you?"

"They won't?"

"Not a chance."

Okay . . . "Doesn't Cece have a manager or assistant or something? There has to be someone who can do this better than me."

Nanny said, "Brenna, you seem to be finished with that cereal. Why don't you clean up your place and go on upstairs to get dressed? If you want, you can peek in on Cece. If she's awake, tell her to come down, and I'll make her an omelet."

"Okay." She slid off her stool and carried her bowl, the spoon still in it, over to the sink, then half walked, half skipped out of the room.

When she was gone, Greta said, "I take it you wanted to talk without Brenna here."

"That's exactly right." Nanny walked around to the other side of the counter, grabbed a dishcloth, and wiped up the spot where Brenna had been sitting. "Mr. and Mrs. Vanderhaven won't come back for something like this. And Cece doesn't have a manager or an assistant. Vance and Katrina handled everything—and with good reason. The fewer people who know that Cece's personality doesn't match what's on the screen, the better, as far as the Vanderhavens are concerned." She folded the cloth and laid it across the sink divider.

"So you're saying I'm on my own."

"Not entirely. I'll help however I can, and of course the crew, the hair and makeup people, and the security detail will be the same. You'll be working off the schedule that was already set up. Cece really seems to like you. I think you'll do fine."

Why did everyone say that to her? "What if Cece takes a break until her parents come back? I can make some calls and cancel her events, say she has the flu . . . "

Nanny shook her head. "That would be a bad idea anytime, but especially now. They've been building up to the reality show deal for a long time, and it's just short of being finalized." It seemed to Greta that everyone knew about the pending reality show except for Cece, the one who mattered most. "If that doesn't go through, Mr. Vanderhaven is going to be livid."

"What happens then? He's going to kill me?" Greta tried to say it in jest, but it didn't come out that way.

Nanny gave her a sympathetic smile. "It's okay, Greta." She came around the counter and gave her a hug. "Just breathe. You'll get through this. Follow the schedule, and take it as it goes. The important thing is to act like you're having fun, because that's the best way to keep Cece on board."

"Doesn't it seem like Cece should have some say in all of this?" Greta said. "If she hates doing it, why do her parents force it on her?"

"I've wondered that very thing many times myself. Unfortunately, it's not up to either of us."

When Cece came down for breakfast, Greta was reading over the information Vance and Katrina had left one more time, looking for a way out, searching for the name of a grown-up who could take charge, but there was no one. Still in her bathrobe, Cece floated into the kitchen as gracefully as a swan crossing a pond. She had some indefinable something, a sweetness and grace that shone from within. That part of the public persona was true, anyway.

Without makeup and with her hair slightly mussed, she looked seventeen, maybe eighteen at the most, and much less glamorous. Still really pretty, but not head-turning. Amazing what a difference it made to look beneath the ornamentation. Like cake without the icing.

She gave Nanny and Greta each a good morning hug and enthusiastically said yes to Nanny's offer of an omelet before taking a stool at the counter. Before Greta could say anything, Cece said, "Brenna said Katrina and Vance are gone, and you're in charge now."

"Unfortunately, yes," she said. "I'm sorry."

"Don't feel bad. It's not your fault," Cece said, patting her arm.

Greta said, "I'm going to try my hardest, but I don't know what I'm doing, so I hope you'll be patient with me."

Cece said, "You're going to be wonderful. I just know it." She tossed her head. "If you want to know the truth, I was tired of Vance and

Katrina and their endless schedule. 'Do this, Cece. Do that. No, you can't stay home. Get in the car. Wave. Smile.' I couldn't even get out of the car without them telling me how to do it. I had to swing my legs out first, very slowly." Her eyes got wide. "And then slowly get out. Like a sloth, Vance always said. *Do it like a sloth.* And then I always had to turn my head and wink and wave. I got so tired of it, I wanted to scream."

"It sounds exhausting," Greta said, sympathizing.

"You would never treat me that way, would you, Greta?"

She reached over to squeeze Greta's hand and smiled. A second earlier, Greta had intended to explain that there were going to be some things they had to do whether they wanted to or not. That there was a schedule, an itinerary of events, places where Cece was expected to be—but it would be fine. They'd get through it. It had to be done, like it or not.

But seeing the trust in her eyes, Greta just couldn't force the words out. If Vance and Katrina felt like they'd been freed from prison, why not Cece? "Of course not," she said. "We'll only do what you want to do." She made a silent wish to the universe that Cece would want to do all the things listed on the itinerary, but even if she didn't, so what? Did her parents expect Greta to force Cece to do something against her will? Doing that went against her very nature. The Hansens were efficient, but they were not cruel people. Her mother said it was always better to be kind.

"We're going to have so much fun!" Cece said, her spirits lifted. As she ate the omelet Nanny made for her, she chattered on about all the places in New York she wanted Greta to see. She ate so slowly that eventually Nanny and Brenna left to shop for a new swimsuit for Brenna, promising they'd be back in a few hours. Greta had a moment of panic when Nanny told her this, feeling like the babysitter who hadn't been properly briefed, but they exchanged phone numbers, which helped.

As Cece ate her second piece of jelly toast, Greta decided to jump in and go over the day's events. She pulled out the sheet of paper with information about the Forgotten Man Ball, along with the four tickets, which she spread out in front of them. "We have the day free to do whatever we want!" Greta said, trying to make her voice sound gleeful. "And then tonight . . . " She paused for dramatic effect. "We get to get dressed up and go to this dinner-and-dance thing called the Forgotten Man Ball with Michael, your driver. He's going to be your forgotten man."

"Not doing it," Cece said between chews. "Not with Michael."

Greta tried again. "But the hair and makeup people are coming at four, and the security detail is scheduled for the drive there. Everyone is expecting you." Even to her ears, the words sounded hollow. She kept going. "Leah Ann Miller is hosting it. It's a fund-raiser for"—she looked at the sheet—"the Museum of Modern Art. Very cool, right?"

"I like the Museum of Modern Art," Cece conceded. "But I don't know that name. Leah . . . what was the rest?"

"Leah Ann Miller. She was a debutante the year you came out. One of the forty-six debutantes that were at the Waldorf Astoria. Remember?"

Cece shrugged. So much for making valuable connections. Greta had to admit forty-six was a lot of debutantes. Cece couldn't be expected to know all those young women. And years had passed since the event had taken place.

Greta took a deep breath and came out with it. "Look, Cece, I know you'd rather not go to this dinner thing tonight, and I totally get it. Honest, I do. But Katrina and Vance left me in charge, and I'll get in a lot of trouble with your dad if you don't go. Could you just go to this one thing, just for me?" If she could get her to go even to one thing, she wouldn't be a complete failure.

The corners of Cece's mouth turned down, and she looked glum. "Why does it have to be Michael?"

Greta mulled this over and decided if her main objection was Michael, she could work with that. "Trust me, I didn't pick Michael;

someone else did. The fund-raiser is called the Forgotten Man Ball because the young women are supposed to invite a man who doesn't normally get to go to black-tie events." Greta glanced down at the four tickets on the counter. They were printed on cream-colored card stock and embossed in black and gold. A black-tie event. Totally glam. The tickets were fancier than most wedding invitations. Turning them over, she saw a scan code. "Just kind of brainstorming here, but how about you and I go without him? We could mix it up a bit. I could go as your date instead and be the forgotten woman. You can tell everyone that I'm your cousin from Wisconsin, and I was dying to go. How's that? Believe me, I never go to black-tie events, so that fulfills one of the requirements."

"But there are four tickets," she said, pointing. "That means they'll be expecting four people."

"Oh." It was hard to negate that one, and here Greta had thought she'd come up with a solution. Apparently not. "Okay, then. How about we take Nanny and Brenna? Then we'd have four people."

"Kids can't go," Cece said. "And it's called the Forgotten Man Ball, Greta. *Man.*" She repeated it for emphasis. "They'll expect me to bring a man."

"That's kind of sexist, don't you think?"

She shrugged. "I wasn't the one who set it up that way. No one asked my opinion."

No one had asked Greta's opinion either, but now it was her problem. She'd been in New York for two nights, and already her internship wasn't a real internship and nothing about Cece and her friends was the way she'd imagined. If that weren't enough, this morning she'd suddenly been promoted against her will. And now she had to find two dates for tonight's event or she would fail her very first challenge.

The upside? New York was full of men. How hard could it be?

CHAPTER EIGHTEEN

Dalton didn't sleep very deeply, aware of the constant drone of voices off in the distance and a slight shuffling noise nearby. He wasn't sure if it was animals or people. Was he dreaming? He didn't think so. Toward morning he got a whiff of smoke and woke up thinking something was on fire. He opened his eyes to see a scrawny middle-aged guy sitting eight feet away, a cigarette dangling off his lips.

When he sat up, the guy glanced his way. "Morning, princess," he said. "Sleep well?"

"Not so much." Dalton rubbed his eyes. "What time is it?"

"Early." He took a drag and then exhaled a puff of smoke.

"Yeah, I got that much on my own." Dalton squinted. The sun had already risen over the horizon. It couldn't be that early. He did a quick inventory of his pockets and backpack and found everything accounted for. To the smoker, he said, "Have a good day," and then he was off to find a bathroom.

Washing his face, he thought about something his father used to say: "When you're young, you have time but not enough money, and when you're older, you have money but not enough time." Dalton always found that saying puzzling. His father's family was wealthy, so he'd always had money. From the time he was born, he'd never had to worry about anything. Schooling, medical bills, vacations, dinners at the nicest restaurants—Dalton and his family never thought twice about doing anything. Now that he gave it some thought, he found it impressive that his dad was never content to coast on his family's accomplishments. He wanted his own success, and he wanted that for Dalton and his brother too. His worst fear was having a son who was a leech, one who lived a life of luxury and not one of substance. He didn't understand that Dalton's refusal to follow the family path wasn't due to laziness or feeling privileged. Dalton just had different ideas of what a purposeful life looked like.

Brushing his teeth in the men's bathroom, Dalton thought about his dad's quote and how true it was for him. He now had all the time in the world but not nearly enough money. Dad had been right, after all.

Dalton had only one pressing item on his agenda today: a visit to a hot dog vendor.

It didn't take long to find her. The cart was in the same spot as before, and he recognized her right away. She looked the same—green baseball cap and apron. It was early in the day for hot dogs, closer to breakfast than lunch, but it was summertime in Central Park, so she already had a customer, an older woman holding a leash with a tiny white poodle at the end of it. Dalton watched them chat until the woman walked away with the bottle of water she'd just purchased. He was starting to realize that even though Manhattan was surrounded by water, getting it in its purest form in clear plastic bottles was big business.

He approached the cart armed with his biggest smile. He'd done a pretty good job cleaning himself up that morning, washing from top to bottom when the restroom had been empty. His hair was clean, although still slightly damp, and he thought he'd taken care of the body odor problem. "Are you Trisha?" he asked, knowing the answer already.

"Yes?"

He could tell he'd started off on the wrong foot. His use of her name weirded her out and put her on guard. "I'm Dalton Bishop. I'm a friend of Matt Gower's?"

"I'm sorry. I don't follow." He was standing so near, he could see she was closer to forty than he'd thought. She was skinny with a ponytail sticking out of the back of her baseball cap. From a distance, she could have been mistaken for a teenager.

"The other evening, you gave him a hot dog when you were closing down for the night. Matt Gower? Brown hair, about this tall?" Dalton held his hand at eye level. "He's a veteran who served in Afghanistan."

"Oh, that Matt," she said, realization dawning. "I don't know him well. A guy was giving me problems one day and got super pushy and mean. He said I gave him the wrong change, but he hadn't actually bought anything, just walked up and started ranting. He got right in my face, swearing and waving his arms. I'm not embarrassed to say that I was afraid. Very afraid. Matt came to my rescue, told the guy to back off, and it worked. I don't know what I would have done if he hadn't shown up. He saved me."

"Sounds like Matt." Dalton didn't know Matt well, but everything he'd learned about him made him think he was a good guy, the kind who'd look out for someone in trouble. "I'm trying to track Matt down. His family and friends are worried about him. Do you see him on a regular basis?"

She shook her head. "Just here and there."

"If you see him again, can you tell him it's very important that he call Ellie?"

"Call Ellie."

"Yeah, she really misses him and wants him back. Can you remember that, or should I write it down?"

Trisha said, "No need to write it down. I've got it all up here." She pointed to the side of her head. "Tell Matt to call Ellie. She misses him and wants him back."

"Thanks—it's important."

"True love is always important." She picked up her metal tongs and snapped them together playfully. "Tell you what, I'll even let Matt use my phone if he doesn't have one."

"He might not want to call. I think he's a little embarrassed."

"Don't worry. I can be very persuasive."

They chatted then for a few minutes, and Dalton told her how he'd met Matt and been able to tell right away he was a good guy. She nodded sympathetically when he mentioned Matt's PTSD, said she knew a woman who'd gone for counseling for that. "So many people have such problems," Trisha said. "The older I get, the more I realize no one gets a free pass. Sooner or later, all of us have to take a turn carrying the load."

When a couple with a baby stopped at the cart, Dalton said goodbye and slipped away. Behind him, he heard Trisha making a fuss over the baby while getting their food ready. He felt good about their conversation, sure she'd remember to give Matt the message the next time she saw him. Would he call? Dalton hoped so. He'd neglected to tell Ellie about the hot dog vendor. Not on purpose—he'd just forgotten. Giving Trisha a message for Matt was his way of making up for it.

That done, he headed to Times Square to get something to eat. A breakfast sandwich at McDonald's would fill the gnawing spot in his stomach just fine. After that, he had the whole day free to entertain tourists with his two-song harmonica medley. If he could get enough money to put food in his belly, he'd consider the day a success.

CHAPTER NINETEEN

Back home, when Greta had pictured spending time with her very classy, high-society cousin, she'd never imagined they'd be walking through Times Square with Cece wearing Greta's sundress and pink baseball cap. They maneuvered around throngs of tourists, people who seemed to be from every corner of the world, judging from the languages she heard and the messages on their T-shirts. Cece was in her glory, taking it all in like someone seeing the world with fresh eyes. She was mesmerized by the ever-changing electronic billboards that loomed on all sides. Greta had to make an effort to keep up. The heat radiated off the pavement, and the crowd was thick, but none of it bothered Cece. Something had gotten into her—that much was sure. Greta couldn't believe the transformation from the girl she'd first met. Without Vance and Katrina there to rein her in, she'd become willful and crazy.

This expedition had started back at the apartment, after Nanny and Brenna left to go shopping. Greta and Cece had talked in the kitchen for two hours, Cece asking questions about Greta's life back home in Wisconsin, wanting to know every detail. She loved hearing stories about Greta and her brother when they were little kids. How their dad had built them a tree house in their backyard and how Greta's mom had started board game night on Sundays, blending virgin strawberry daiquiris for them to drink as they played. "For years, I thought that was what real strawberry daiquiris tasted like," Greta said. "When I ordered one in a bar, I almost spit it out."

None of the stories were exceptional, but Cece hung on to every word. "Maybe someday I can come and visit you?" she said, tilting her head to one side.

"Anytime. My mom would love it." They went up to Greta's room, where Cece looked with great interest at everything her cousin had brought from home. At Cece's request, Greta pulled out her clothing and laid it all out on the bed.

"Where did you get this?" she asked, holding up a cream-colored top. It was sleeveless with a shirred front.

"On the clearance rack at the Gap."

"The Gap?"

"You know the store—the Gap?"

She thought. "No, I don't know it, but then, I've never been to Wisconsin."

"It's not just in Wisconsin. They have them everywhere. It's a mall store."

Cece nodded and kept looking over each item. "Did you bring the red sweater?" she asked.

"What red sweater?"

"The red sweater with the bling around the neck?" She gestured to her throat. "It matched your Santa hat."

"Oh, sure." The Santa-hat reference cleared things up for Greta. Cece was talking about the red sweater she'd been wearing in the family's last Christmas card photo. "No, I left it at home. It would have been too warm for summer."

"Too bad. I liked that one." Cece rummaged through the closet, admiring the few sundresses Greta had brought, each of which she'd combined on the hanger with a little jacket or sweater. As an intern, she'd had this idea she'd be working in an office in New York, and so she had prepared to look nice. She knew what she'd brought probably wasn't the most professional, but she figured she'd add to her wardrobe once she knew what the other women wore to work. Now she saw that her clothes, most of them from the mall or Kohl's, looked cheap by comparison. But Cece didn't seem to look down on her clothing at all; if anything, she seemed intrigued. "What do you call this fabric?" she asked, running her fingers over the front of a ruffled top.

"Rayon, I guess? Some kind of synthetic."

"It feels cool."

"It's nice because it doesn't wrinkle."

As Cece riffled through her clothing, she chattered away. She told Greta how excited she was when her mother had Brenna. "I was an only child for so long. I was a teenager when she was born."

"I know. I remember your Christmas card that year. You were opening a gift, and the baby was inside."

Cece said, "Brenna was always my baby. Nanny used to let me feed her and take care of her and change her diaper, but my mother told me not to, that it was Nanny's job to do all that. So after that I just played with her. I could make her laugh so hard. She smiled when I walked into the room. It was amazing to have that kind of effect on someone so tiny." She held one of Greta's button-down shirts to her front for a moment, considering, and then set it down again. "One time a few years ago, Nanny took me and Brenna to her place in Brooklyn. We went undercover, and no one even knew who we were."

"For real?" The word *undercover* piqued Greta's interest. "How'd you do that?"

"We took the service elevator down and left out the basement door. We had to go past the maintenance man's apartment and take the stairs up to the street." She held up a sundress, a subtle paisley print with a halter neckline. "Can I borrow this?"

"Sure."

She dropped her robe, and it fell to her feet. Then she quickly slipped into the dress like a fish diving through water. "How do I look?"

she asked, once the dress was on and properly adjusted. She admired herself in the mirror, turning to check every angle.

"Beautiful."

"What shoes do you usually wear with this dress?"

Greta went over to the closet and took out a pair of strappy flats. "These sandals."

Cece sat down on the bed to put them on, then held her feet out, assessing the look. "We have the same size feet."

"Pretty close."

She went back to the mirror. "Now I look just like you, Greta."

"Not exactly. You wear it much better," Greta said admiringly. When she wore the dress, it fit snugly over her hips. On Cece, it swung freely.

She shook her head. "No. We look the same now." She slung her arm around Greta's shoulders and pulled her into view. "Almost exactly the same. Anyone might think we're sisters."

Greta stared at the reflection of the two of them and smiled. *Huh.* They did look similar. Maybe not sisters, but close enough to be related anyway. Without her signature dark-lined eyes, red lips, and flawless foundation, Cece could be anyone else. Especially wearing the sundress Greta had gotten from Kohl's three summers before at an end-of-season sale. "You look so different now," Greta said. "No one would even know it's you."

Cece must have agreed, because a second later, she put on Greta's pink baseball cap, grabbed her arm, and led her out of the apartment. "What are you doing?" Greta asked, laughing.

"You'll see." There was no stopping her. She was so insistent that Greta barely had time to grab her phone and sunglasses before they left. "No questions," she said. "Just come with me."

"Where are we going?" Greta asked after they'd left the apartment.

"Out on our own," she said. "To do whatever we want. No one to tell me what to do. Come on, Greta. It will be fun."

"Well, maybe just for a few minutes, and then we have to come right back." Greta had imagined they'd take a quick walk around the lobby or maybe a short trek around the block. Hopefully, a taste of freedom would tide her over.

They followed the exact route Cece had described when telling about the time she, Nanny, and Brenna had gone to Nanny's place incognito. The service elevator had padded walls and a scuffed vinyl floor. As they went down, Greta said, "I don't think this is a good idea, Cece. What if someone recognizes you and we get mobbed? You could get hurt. I would feel terrible if that happened." Cece's parents would be furious too. There was nothing about unauthorized excursions in the information Vance and Katrina had given her. Clearly, this just wasn't done.

"Oh, don't be like that!" Cece gently punched her arm. "This will be an adventure." The elevator door opened, and she led the way out. "I'm so glad you came. Katrina and Vance would never be on board for something like this."

Right before they exited the building by way of the service door, Cece leaned over and picked up a brown plastic doorstop and wedged it under the door, leaving it propped for their return. Outside, they climbed the concrete steps to street level. Greta had half expected a crowd of people to be waiting, but there was nothing there but a dumpster off to one side. Cece continued on, getting to the corner of the building and turning onto the sidewalk. The farther they got from her building, the more Greta worried. "Slow down." She could barely keep up with her. "I don't want to lose you."

Cece turned back, her expression exuberant. "Then hurry up, Greta!"

"Where are we going?" Greta asked, lengthening her stride to keep up. The sidewalks were getting crowded now, and they had to weave around people coming their way. No one noticed Cece. Her Wisconsin disguise was working, and she was just another face in the crowd.

"To Times Square!" She looped her arm through Greta's, like they were schoolgirls in an old movie. "To find me a date for the Forgotten Man Ball."

CHAPTER TWENTY

New York City has some of the finest restaurants in the world, but Dalton wanted something hot, fast, and cheap, so he headed to McDonald's for a breakfast sandwich. The place was packed, and the line moved slowly. Luckily, he had time. As he waited, he couldn't help but notice that the air-conditioning was not on full force. Maybe, he surmised, the management was trying to cut costs, or maybe it was a strategy employed to keep customers from lingering. In any event, when he returned outside, the heat was not a shock to his system.

He did a quick search for Matt, glancing down the side street where they'd first met and then walking the perimeter of Times Square. A pretty girl tried to hand him a flyer for a comedy club, and he took it just to be polite. "Thanks," he said, and she nodded with a smile. Down the block, he came to a trash receptacle and threw it out, first checking to make sure she wasn't looking his way.

Dalton still hoped he might run into Matt. Leaving the message at the hot dog stand was something, but he knew it would be more effective to talk to him in person. Matt needed to know that Ellie, the love of his life, hadn't moved on the way he'd thought. She loved him and was tormented by his absence. Matt had to call her, if only to assure her he was still alive. Dalton wanted more for those two than that, though. He'd never thought of himself as a romantic happy-endings kind of guy, but in this case, he wanted a happy outcome for Matt and Ellie. Those two belonged together. She was great. And Matt? Such a good guy but so sad. Despair radiated from him. Dalton wanted him to know that things could get better.

Dalton sat on the sidewalk of the side street where he'd first met Matt. Again, he put out his hat for donations and played the harmonica, alternating between the only two songs he knew. After two hours of playing on and off, and greeting people in between, he'd made a few dollars. He'd call that a success.

Time to stretch his legs.

Putting the money in his pocket and sticking the hat back on his head, he set out to walk around Times Square. Again, Dalton was struck by the energy of the place, the sounds of music mixed with conversation, the smell of delicious food. And the sights! So much to see. His dad was right. It was a big tourist trap, but what a magnificent trap. He walked over to the metal bleachers. When he'd first noticed them, it seemed a random place to put raised seating, but once he was a few rows up, he saw how perfect they were for getting an overview of the place. He sat and thought about his next meal and how hot it was getting now that the sun was climbing in the sky.

Without having someone to talk to, his thoughts just rattled around in his head, and a realization startled him. He wasn't just alone.

He was lonely.

Lonely. It wasn't just the loss of friends and family. He also felt as if he'd lost himself—the brother, friend, and son he'd once been. So very weird. He couldn't remember ever feeling quite that way before.

From his perch in the bleachers, Dalton watched the people milling around, some walking with bottled beverages in hand, more taking pictures—mostly selfies with the electronic billboards in the background. He started to narrow his focus to specific people, watching the way one couple walked together hand in hand, then noticing a mother pushing a stroller containing a sleeping toddler, a thumb in his mouth. A group of teenagers strode past wearing identical green T-shirts. There were ten or so. A school group, maybe?

And then he saw her. The young woman he'd seen getting out of Cece Vanderhaven's limo the other day. The one who'd given him a thumbs-up. She trailed a woman in a pink baseball cap who meandered like she was slightly drunk. The pink-capped woman wandered into one of the cheesy gift shops, the kind filled with "I heart New York" coffee mugs and T-shirts. The door to the shop was propped open, all the better to entice people to come in. Dalton couldn't see much, but he knew what was inside the store. He'd gone in there once to cool off, amazed that there were people in the world who still bought ashtrays and plastic snow globes. The second woman followed the pink-capped woman into the store. Thinking of how she'd looked outside the limo made him grin. He remembered the hesitant way she'd stood there, and how she'd caught him looking and smiled right back. Like they knew each other and shared a joke. In this enormous city, what were the chances they'd cross paths again?

But they really hadn't crossed paths. He'd spotted her from a distance.

After a few minutes, he stood up. They were still out of sight, but something inside of Dalton told him he needed to get closer or he might never see her again.

He climbed down the bleachers, zigzagging around other people on his way down. Once he was at ground level, he crossed the plaza and headed to the gift shop, veering around random tourists and performers dressed for photo ops. He also passed a food truck selling delicious-smelling empanadas. As he got to the gift shop door, an elderly couple was exiting, so he stood back to let them pass. Just as he was about to go inside, the pink-capped woman came flying out, bumping into him. She stopped, laughing at their collision. "Excuse me," Dalton said, although technically, it was her mistake.

On her heels, her friend came rushing out, and following *her* was an older man, yelling, "Come back here! You have to pay!"

Dalton noticed then that pink-cap wore a pair of sunglasses with the price tag still attached to the side piece. Her friend frantically said, "She didn't know. We'll put them back."

The man, who had to be the owner of the store, angrily said, "The hell you will. I'm calling the police." He raised a fist to the tourists passing by and shouted, "You shoplift from my store, you will be prosecuted!"

The pink-capped woman said, "I told them to put it on my account," her voice so soft and sweet, no one could have heard her but Dalton.

Her friend began arguing, saying the other woman didn't understand about paying at the register. The owner yelled back, repeating what he'd said about calling the police and the store's policy regarding shoplifting. Pretty soon, their voices began to overlap, neither one listening to the other.

"Please don't call the police. She didn't mean anything by it, honest." The young woman had stopped arguing and was pleading now. "We'll put the sunglasses back and go."

Talking right over her, the owner said, "No one steals from my store. Do you hear me? No one!" As his pointed finger got closer and closer to her face, she took a step back.

Through all of this, Dalton was right there in the thick of the group. Anyone glancing their way would think he was part of the altercation, but the only one who noticed him was the pink-capped woman, who repeated her line to him once again: "I told them to put it on my account."

Dalton put two fingers in his mouth and blew his loudest taxi-calling whistle. When both the owner and the friend stopped talking, he pulled cash out of his pocket. "Okay, let's settle this. How much do the sunglasses cost?"

"Five dollars," the owner said, folding his arms. "Plus tax."

"Here." Dalton shuffled through his cash and handed him a five and two singles. "That should cover it, right?"

The owner held the bills loosely in his hand, but only for a second, and then the money was in his pocket. He gave the girls a look of disgust.

"I'll let it go this time, but I never want to see you two in my store ever again. Now get out!" He turned and went back inside in a huff.

"How can we get out if we're already out?" the pink-capped girl asked, wide-eyed. She turned to her friend. "I don't want to go in his store again anyway, Greta. He was mean."

"He *was* mean," Dalton said, and then faced her friend, pleased that he had a name to match the face. "Greta, is it?" To his surprise, she started blushing. "Sorry, I couldn't help but overhear your name."

She glanced up through her lashes and said, "Thank you for helping us. I don't know what we would have done if you hadn't shown up." She pulled her friend away from the doorway and steered her down the sidewalk.

Dalton followed. When they stepped aside to let a guy using crutches pass, he pivoted in front of them. "No need to thank me. I was glad to help." He stuck out his hand. "My name's Dalton. Dalton Bradshaw." The fake last name came out without much thought. He didn't normally lie. He'd already given his correct name to Ellie and her sister, and to Trisha at the hot dog cart, so it wasn't exactly a secret. But now he wanted to keep his identity under wraps, at least for the time being. People who knew he came from the Bishop family viewed him differently, either looking down on him for coming from wealth or liking him for the same reason. He wanted this woman to judge him on his own merits.

"Nice to meet you, Dalton Bradshaw." She slipped her hand into his and that was it. Once their hands were pressed together, skin against skin, neither one made a move to separate. She blushed again, and then they locked eyes. He wasn't sure if she remembered him from the pizza parlor, but there was definitely something there, a connection. He would have remembered meeting someone named Greta, so he was certain they were strangers, but he got the strangest sense of familiarity. It was like they'd met before, maybe as kids at summer camp, or in a dream or another lifetime.

Her friend wearing the shoplifted sunglasses spoke, breaking the spell. "I told them to put the sunglasses on my account."

She seemed stuck on that one sentence. If her voice weren't so sweet, it might have been annoying. And then it hit Dalton that the girl behind the sunglasses was Cece Vanderhaven, the daughter of the very famous Harry Vanderhaven, the man he'd met at his dad's office. It was hard to tell with the hat, glasses, and baggy dress, but it was the voice that confirmed it. He'd never followed any of her accounts or watched her videos, but you'd have to live in a cave to avoid the commercials where she says, "Let me in." Same wispy little-girl voice. There was no mistaking it.

"I know," Greta responded to Cece. She let go of his hand and took Cece by the arm. "They don't do that here. You have to get in line and pay at the register."

"How inconvenient." The sunglasses slid down Cece's nose, and she pushed them up with one finger. She'd stolen a pair meant for someone with a bigger head.

"Yeah, but that's how a lot of places do it." Greta was leaning in and speaking softly and patiently. She looked up at him. "I don't want to be rude, but I have to get her home. We've been gone too long already."

"But we just got here!" Cece said, objecting. "I don't want to go home."

"Cece!" Greta said, then clapped her hand over her mouth and looked around to see if anyone had noticed. She lowered her hand. "We have to go. Now."

Cece didn't answer, but she didn't move either.

Dalton took this as his opening. "How about if I see you ladies safely home?" He extended the crook of his arm to Cece. "Please? It would be my pleasure."

Cece slid her hand over his elbow. "Only if we take the long way back."

"Works for me." He looked to Greta. "Are you fine with this?"

He saw gratitude in her eyes. She nodded. "Yes. Thank you, Dalton."

Hearing her say his name was the high point of this whole homeless-person experiment.

CHAPTER TWENTY-ONE

She wasn't one to swoon, but when Dalton said her name, Greta felt herself get lightheaded. Her reaction could only be from the sound of his voice. It wasn't the heat or the fear that someone would recognize Cece and this whole thing could go wrong in a big way. No, it happened the instant he'd said, "Greta." Like her name was a secret passcode known only to the two of them.

She didn't believe in love at first sight, but maybe attraction at first sight? He was very handsome, if a bit unkempt, and the way he'd taken charge with the Cece problem won him points as well.

But weren't there serial killers who charmed their victims and earned their trust before they went in for the kill? That was part of their plan all along. Dalton Bradshaw. Serial killer or sexy guy with a big heart?

Oh, she hoped it was the second one.

She walked on the other side of Cece, the side toward the street, listening as her cousin chattered on about trying on the glasses. The tall spindle rack that held the sunglasses fascinated her for some reason. "And this other woman kept stepping in front of me and spinning it around when I wasn't done looking in the mirror!" Even when she was irate, she sounded adorable.

"How rude," Dalton said. "She should have waited for you to be finished."

"I know, right?"

"People like that are so annoying."

Cece continued. "I hardly ever get to go places. We're always in a hurry. Did you know Greta is my cousin?"

"No, I didn't know that." Dalton smiled her way.

"She is."

"I do see a family resemblance."

Greta lagged behind to give oncoming pedestrians room to pass them. Now she was behind Cece and Dalton. She couldn't help but notice he looked great on both sides. That backpack, though? Totally hideous.

Cece said, "She's staying with me for the summer."

"Greta and Cece, roommates for the summer," Dalton said. Greta felt her heart drop when he said Cece's name. Had he recognized her, or did he notice when Greta had let her name slip? At the very least, he hadn't made a scene and given them away in public. He also hadn't taken any photos; in fact, she didn't even see a phone in his back pocket.

When they got a few blocks away from Times Square, Greta started to feel better. She'd been afraid that people would recognize Cece, and her worry diminished with every step. People were, she was starting to realize, very self-involved. Walking with their earbuds in, listening to music, or talking on the phone. Mothers with children concentrated on getting them safely to their destinations. Three people in their twenties barely gave them a glance.

I pulled it off, Greta thought with satisfaction. She'd given Cece the adventure she'd wanted, and soon enough, they'd be safely back at the Vanderhaven apartment. If Cece still didn't want to take Michael as her forgotten man, he could go as Greta's date, and they could ask someone else to accompany Cece, perhaps someone who worked in the building. The maintenance man, maybe? They hadn't seen him when they'd sneaked out through the basement, but Cece had pointed out the door to his place. Greta had pictured him as a gnarled Hunchback of Notre Dame type, but that was probably just her imagination at work. Most likely, he was a very nice guy who would jump at the chance to attend a black-tie event. Mentally, she shifted his appearance from hunchback to friendly, spry old-timer, the kind of man you'd see in commercials for the senior cell phones with the big numbers on the keypad. And if the maintenance man couldn't make it to the ball, they'd find someone else. Nanny might be able to help. If she lived in Brooklyn, she might have a family member or neighbor who could step in at the last minute.

And if Cece refused to go, Greta could go to the dreaded backup plan, which was to contact Leah Ann Miller and cancel. People canceled sometimes. They got the flu and bad headaches. Family emergencies cropped up. These kinds of things happened all the time. No one was exempt. It could plausibly happen to anyone, even Cece Vanderhaven. Really, who would know it was a lie? If her father was angry and it lost them the reality show deal, Greta would take the fall. It's not like they could sue her. Or could they?

No. She shook her head at the thought. What kind of person would sue a family member for not forcing his own daughter to attend a social function? That would be so messed up.

She'd been so caught up in her thoughts, she'd lost track of where they were going. Ahead of her, Cece and Dalton were still talking. At least, Cece was talking and Dalton was answering, mostly agreeing and nodding. Greta quickened her pace to catch up. "Cece, do you know where we are? I don't recognize anything."

In her hometown in Wisconsin, it was impossible to get lost. There were only two ways into town and out again, one on each end of the village. The small, charming downtown contained shops and restaurants and was surrounded by even more charming older homes along with the village hall, library, and post office. Circling around that area were the newer subdivisions, the houses with three-car attached garages and netted trampolines in the backyards. The village could be mapped out as concentric circles radiating outward. In theory, New York, being a grid, should have been even easier to navigate than her hometown, but she was the new girl and had no sense of where they were.

"I told you I was taking the long way, Greta," Cece said, laughing.

The long way? Oh no. She had a sinking feeling. What if Cece was deliberately getting them lost to extend the adventure? She considered getting out her phone and using GPS to find their location, but she'd have to stop to do that, and Cece had been unstoppable ever since they'd left the apartment.

Dalton talked around her. "Don't worry. We're heading in that general direction. Five minutes, and we'll be there."

So he knew her name and where she lived. Was the Vanderhaven address common knowledge among New Yorkers? It was likely. Still—and here her imagination ran wild—what if he was with the paparazzi, and he'd followed them from the apartment, and he'd been watching them the whole time? Then fake-rescued them and befriended Cece just to get a big story? It wasn't all that far fetched. Maybe all women fell madly in love with him at first handhold, and that was part of his routine. Dalton Bradshaw might not even be his real name. It sounded a little fake, like the name of a character in a daytime drama.

When she saw the apartment ahead, Greta began to feel better. At the next intersection, Cece rounded the corner, telling Dalton, "We need to go in the service door, or else all these people will rush up and bother us." She sounded exasperated. "It's so annoying."

"I bet," he said. "I would hate that."

His voice was so kind, Greta wanted to get lost in it. It was hard to believe someone could fake being that charming, that genuine. Or maybe she just didn't want to believe it was all an act. She thought of all the girls who had narrowly escaped getting into the car of a rapist or a serial killer. They'd say that some instinct told them something was off. Her instincts were on high alert, but she wasn't getting any warnings that he was dangerous. All her warnings were of the emotional variety, cautioning her against getting her hopes up. They were saying, *Even if he is the real deal, the genuine article, a super nice guy who also happens to be good looking, why would he be interested in you, Greta Hansen?* Out of all the young women in New York, most of them more sophisticated and all of them better dressed, why presume he'd felt the same connection she did?

The thing that she'd thought she'd felt, the jolt of lightning to her heart? It had to be one sided. She didn't come to New York to make herself an idiot over some guy she'd just met. Taking care of Cece had to be her priority.

When they got to the back of the building, Greta stopped. "Thank you for escorting us home, Dalton," she said, and could have smacked herself on the forehead. *Escorting us home?* What was she, a character in a Brontë novel? "I think we can take it from here." Off in the distance, a taxi horn blared.

Dalton nodded as if agreeing, but he didn't make a move to leave, and Cece still had her hand in the crook of his elbow. She and Dalton were each planted firmly on either side of Cece, like they were going to play tug-of-war.

She tried again. "Thank you. You were a lifesaver back in Times Square, and we appreciate it."

"My pleasure." He gave her a smile, flashing straight white teeth.

"We should probably say goodbye, Cece, so we can go inside and get ready for tonight." Greta had developed this cajoling tone during her teenage babysitting years. It wasn't any more effective now than it had been then.

"No." Cece shook her head. "I don't want him to go." She looked up at him. "Dalton, would you be my date tonight to the Forgotten Man Ball?"

Greta's mouth dropped open. How could she invite Dalton to be her date? He was a complete stranger! Sure, he was a hot stranger, but still, he was a stranger. "Oh, Cece, I don't know if that's a good idea." She turned to Dalton. "It's this ultra-formal black-tie dinner and dance, a fund-raiser." She waved a hand dismissively. "You're supposed to ask someone you know, which, as you're well aware, we just met you, so that doesn't work. The event is supposed to be like a thank-you—"

Before she could even finish, Dalton said, "I'd love to be your date tonight, Cece. Thank you for asking."

CHAPTER TWENTY-TWO

Going to a black-tie event wasn't in keeping with Dalton's plan for being homeless, but he'd vowed to be open to whatever came his way, and this definitely qualified. Besides, it was only for one evening.

It was pretty clear that Greta was trying to discourage Cece's invitation, but Dalton had steamrolled right over her objections. For one thing, he wasn't ready to walk away and never see Greta again. Second, she'd mentioned *dinner*. As in, a free meal, and probably something much better than a McDonald's breakfast sandwich. He had all the time in the world. With nothing else on his social calendar, he was in.

Even after he accepted the invitation, Greta kept going.

"That's so nice of you, Dalton, but I don't think it will work out. You'd have to wear a tuxedo. Plus, it's such short notice, I'm sure you must have other plans."

Cece leaned against Greta. "He doesn't have any other plans, Greta. He's a homeless person. Besides, you know the wardrobe people are going to bring tuxedos." She pushed her sunglasses to the top of her head and looked him over. "I'm willing to bet he'll fit in Vance's suit perfectly."

One of her words caught Greta's attention. "You're homeless?" She sounded shocked.

"Yes, ma'am, for the time being, anyway." Dalton smiled to reassure her it was all right, but he could see by the look on her face she found this troubling. "But I promise you, I'm harmless."

"Well, of course you are, Dalton!" Cece said, beckoning toward the door. "Hurry up, you two. I can't wait to tell Brenna and Nanny about all the fun we had today."

Greta wasn't budging. "Hold up a minute, Cece. Don't you think we should at least check his ID first before we go inside? He could be anyone."

Dalton winced. The jig was up. He had no ID, and worse yet, he'd given them a fake last name. The only way to fix this was to make up a story about losing his wallet or being robbed, or more honestly, he could simply explain why he was posing as a homeless person. His reasoning for the facade was honorable. That might win him points. He said, "This is going to sound hard to believe—"

Before he could finish, he was interrupted by the noise of three people, two guys and a woman rushing toward them.

"There she is!" the woman yelled, jogging their way. "I knew it was her."

One of the men, coming more slowly, held a phone in front of him, filming as he walked. "Cece? Can you answer a few questions?"

"Is it true you were caught shoplifting in Times Square?" the other guy shouted.

Initially startled, all three of them froze, but as they got closer, Greta sprang into action, guiding Cece down the concrete steps, yanking the door open and kicking the rubber stopper aside. Dalton grabbed the edge of the door right before it shut and followed. He closed the door firmly behind them, then made sure it was locked.

It was a narrow escape.

CHAPTER TWENTY-THREE

"How much fun was that?" Cece nudged her with her elbow. "And you were so worried, Greta. Everything turned out fine."

It wasn't that Greta had worried for herself. It was Cece she was protecting. She'd been put in charge of keeping her cousin's reputation intact and took the responsibility seriously. Firstborn Daughter, Inc. and Cece's parents were counting on her. She imagined Cece's company losing sales because of something that had happened on her watch. Lost sales could mean decreased revenue, which could lead to jobs being eliminated. Employees without salaries could lose their houses. Couples might wind up divorced from the stress. Their children might not get what they wanted for Christmas.

The trickle-down ramifications as a result of her failure would be vast and serious. She was starting to understand she was not made for the stress of corporate life.

As they reached the top of the stairs, Greta realized that Dalton was still right behind them. She glanced down to see his face tipped up toward her, and man, he was even cuter from this angle.

"You okay?" he asked with a smile.

"Fine," she said, resigned to him being there. It's not like she had much to say about it. Cece was the one who had invited him. Plus, he had helped them when the store owner was going to prosecute Cece for shoplifting. Both good reasons to use as a defense when Cece's parents took her to task for letting the whole day go off course. They couldn't blame her for something that wasn't her fault, could they?

According to Vance and Katrina, they definitely could.

She followed Cece, very much aware of Dalton right behind them. When they got to the apartment, Cece ushered them in, chattering away about the Forgotten Man Ball. "Greta can go with Michael, since that's already set up." She cupped a hand to one side of her mouth and said, "Sorry, Greta!" She laughed. "And Dalton can wear Vance's tuxedo, and Greta can wear Katrina's dress." Once again, she looked him over. "I think you're almost exactly the same size as him. I can't believe how perfectly this is working out." She clasped her hands together.

Katrina's dress. Greta hoped it would fit and not make her look like a stuffed sausage. And if she couldn't wear it, she hoped the wardrobe woman could find something else suitable. She hadn't brought anything even remotely appropriate.

"You're sure you want Dalton to go?" she asked Cece. "I mean, he seems like a great guy, but no offense, Dalton, we don't know anything about you."

"None taken."

"He could be a serial killer or a violent psychopath."

"Or a violent psychopathic serial killer," he chimed in, clearly amused.

"For all you know, he could be a reporter or photographer gathering dirt for one of the tabloids."

"One of the tabloids?" Dalton's mouth quirked. "I always saw myself as more of a *People* magazine kind of guy. Or maybe TMZ?"

Greta said, "See, he's joking about it, but that doesn't mean it's not true. The thing is, we don't know either way."

Cece waved away her concerns. "It's going to be fine, Greta. You always worry too much. It's time to live a little."

She slung her arm around Greta's shoulders, and some of her anxiety melted away. Greta did have a tendency to worry too much; Cece was right about that. And it was true that Greta was due to live a little, so maybe it was okay just to go with it. They weren't changing the plan too much. And Katrina and Vance had just left them stranded. Greta was making do as best she could.

Plus, as her mom often said, life is short. If you don't live now, when will you?

Cece turned her attention back to Dalton. "Do you want to get a tour of the apartment?"

"Sure."

Really? Cece was offering to show a stranger the apartment, when Greta hadn't even gotten a full tour yet? Oh well, she'd be seeing it now.

Cece led them through the apartment, throwing open doors and showing them rooms Greta didn't know existed. The Vanderhavens, it turned out, had a media room with theater seats, surround sound, and a freestanding popcorn machine. It was clean and empty but still gave off the faint smell of butter.

"Do you have a media room like this at your house?" Dalton asked Greta.

"Not exactly." Did anyone else in the world have a media room like this? Probably, but not in her social circle.

From there, they kept going, with Cece noting focal points in each room. One room had floor-to-ceiling glass cases that held her mother's collection of figurines. Then there was the library with a display of her father's first-edition copies of all the American classics. The two kitchens were next, each with its own style: one more industrial, the other as pretty as a magazine feature. Once done with the main floor, they climbed an expansive open staircase up to the third floor. When Cece flung open the door to Greta's room, Greta was glad she'd straightened up earlier. "Nice," Dalton said, peering inside. "Very tidy."

"Greta just got here," Cece said. "She hasn't had enough time to make a mess."

After seeing all the unused rooms on the third floor, they ventured down the stairs, ending up at Cece's room on the second floor. Greta had seen it in bits but only on the small screen in video clips, usually when she was opening the door to let Vance and Katrina in, or when they'd come in to surprise her and wake her up. She'd always wondered what was on the edges of the screen, hoping they'd pan around her room, but they never did. Greta went inside to get a closer look. The room was big, but then again, all the rooms were big. It was a little untidy, with random clothing on the floor and the bed unmade. Dalton and Cece followed behind her.

"I like it," Dalton said, nodding approvingly. "It's the first room that's made me feel at home."

Cece smiled. "I don't let them come in and clean unless I'm here to watch. They always want to move things around." She wrinkled her nose. "And I have things I like to keep private."

Greta wanted to ask, *Like what?* But that seemed intrusive, and Dalton was nodding again, like he understood completely. She wandered over to Cece's desk, which was cluttered with odds and ends of jewelry, a random pile of paper, and a sketch pad. She flipped the cover to find fashion drawings, all of them featuring Cece as the sketched model. The drawings were bold and crazy: One set had wild colors and a 1960s vibe. Another was flapper-inspired, complete with fringed dress and headpiece. Yet another few pages hinted at the wide skirts of the 1950s.

"This is so cool," Greta said, flipping through the pages. "Is Firstborn Daughter, Inc. going to come out with these?"

"I wish." Cece rolled her eyes. "They never let me use my designs for the company. They say they're not mainstream enough. They don't have widespread appeal. They'd cost too much to mass-produce. So other people design different fashions, and I get my name put on them. I don't even like most of them." She sighed. "I have so many good ideas, but no one ever listens."

"What kind of ideas?"

"Like, for instance, I think every evening gown should have hidden pockets. Deep ones that can be secured—so that you don't have to take a purse along."

"That is a good idea." Greta always hated getting up to dance and having to ask someone else to watch her things. Sometimes there was a coat check, but that wasn't always secure, and when she wanted something—lipstick, a tampon, whatever—retrieving it was always an ordeal. "Why don't they put pockets in automatically?"

"It brings up the cost," she said with a sigh. "So they would never do it for me. But"—she brightened—"I begged and begged, and finally they made two of my own designs for my own personal use, and they did them just the way I wanted." She came over and stood next to Greta and flipped through the book. "This one." She jabbed her finger at a dress that had an old Hollywood look to it, white with a halter neckline and feathered skirt. "I found a place that makes artificial feathers, so it doesn't use any animal products. The other dress was one I had them make for Katrina." She flipped to the next page to reveal a sleek black evening gown with crisscrossed panels across the midsection. "Isn't it cool?"

"It is cool." Lucky Katrina having an elegant dress custom-made just for her. "You have a talent for design."

"No one else thinks so."

"Well, they're wrong. Your designs are stunning." Greta had seen the Firstborn Daughter, Inc. designs, and while they were pretty enough, nothing stood out for her. She didn't see any dress in that clothing line that made her want to buy it, but the dress Cece had designed for Katrina was something else. Any woman who put it on would be transformed. It was glamorous and elegant, like old Hollywood with a modern twist. And Cece's dress, the white one with a feathered skirt, was even better. It was an evening gown that would make an entrance. Once someone saw that dress, they'd never forget it.

Greta laid a finger on the page. "When are you going to wear it?"

"I don't know. I ask every time, and they always put it off."

"Why?"

"They say it's not appropriate for the event, or that I have to wear a certain designer because we owe them a favor or something. It's never the right time."

Cece closed the book and turned to face Dalton. "I guess that's about it. Now you've seen my whole house."

"Except for the roof," Greta said, not thinking.

"What's on the roof?" Dalton asked.

A flash of emotion came across Cece's face, like a shadow passing. Then she smiled. "There's a pool up there. We don't use it anymore. Not since the accident. They keep the door locked so no one can get in. Even if I wanted to, I couldn't get up there to show it to you."

"There was an accident? What happened?" Dalton asked the million-dollar question, the one Greta had wanted to ask.

Cece said, "A few years ago, I was swimming with my little sister. She dropped her bracelet in the pool, so I ducked down to get it, and then something happened and I lost consciousness." She pursed her lips and shook her head. "Brenna got out of the pool and ran for help, and one of the maids came running up and pulled me out and revived me."

"So the maid saved your life," Dalton said.

"Yes, she did."

"Wow, that's quite a story. Your sister must have been pretty little when that happened."

"She was only four years old."

Dalton whistled. "Four years old, and she knew to go and get help like that. Your parents must be very proud of her."

"I wouldn't know. We never talk about it," Cece said. "Please don't repeat it to anyone. My parents don't want people to know."

"I won't." He crossed his heart with his index finger. "I won't say a thing. I promise."

He sounded sincere. Greta hoped he was a man of his word.

CHAPTER TWENTY-FOUR

After Cece was done giving them the tour of her apartment, things happened pretty quickly. They were joined in the kitchen by two more people: Brenna and her nanny. Nanny seemed only a little surprised to hear that Cece had a new friend named Dalton who was going to be her date to the Forgotten Man Ball. If she objected at all, it didn't show.

If anyone was concerned about Dalton's presence, it was little Brenna, who gave him a suspicious stare. "Do you like my sister?" she finally asked.

"I just met her, but she seems very nice."

"She is very nice. She's the sweetest and the best." Brenna narrowed her eyes and frowned, giving him the once-over. He got the unspoken message that she was putting him on notice. Brenna obviously treasured her sister.

"Then I guess I should be on my best behavior," Dalton said.

"Don't let anything bad happen to her."

"I won't," he promised.

For such a big apartment, there didn't seem to be anyone else there. Cece explained to Dalton that he wouldn't be meeting her parents because they were in Europe, so that saved him from having to get patriarchal approval. He could generally pull off meeting someone's father, but in his current hygienically challenged state, it would be more difficult to convince someone he was an upstanding young man. He wasn't sure that a firm handshake and extreme politeness would override his uncombed hair and rumpled clothing.

They made small talk in the kitchen, something Dalton recognized as being the epicenter of most people's homes. One of his friends from prep school had an entire mansion at his disposal, but every time Dalton slept over, they had breakfast on barstools at the counter while his parents fluttered around nearby, going over the day's events and filling their mugs with coffee. Meanwhile, in an adjacent room, there was a dining room table that could have seated their whole soccer team.

Greta never took her gaze off him, especially when he was talking to Cece. Dalton wasn't sure if it was because they'd had a moment and she was a little jealous that he was going to be her cousin's date, or if she still wasn't sure whom she was dealing with. He got his answer when there was a pause in the conversation. "What did you say your last name was again, Dalton?" she asked.

Dalton knew the last name he'd said. He had it locked in his brain because he'd settled on that particular alias before he'd even started this project, but the suddenness of the question threw him off. He hesitated for just a second and then tried so hard to force it out quickly that he stammered. "Buh-Bradshaw."

"Buh-Bradshaw?" she said, one hand on her hip.

Dalton sighed. "Just Bradshaw. I used to stutter when I was a kid, and sometimes it still comes out." Only a little true. He did have a speech impediment as a kid, but it wasn't a stutter. As a toddler, he did the classic Elmer Fudd switcheroo, substituting a *w* for the *r* sound. *Wabbit. Wainbow.* That sort of thing. The way his mom told it, his speech was very cute for a little kid, but she was relieved when he outgrew it.

His phony explanation did the trick because now, he could tell, Greta felt terrible about pointing out his speech flaw.

"Oh." Her hand flew to her mouth, and her eyes widened in embarrassment. "I'm so sorry. I don't know where that came from. I'm not usually rude like that."

"I like the name Dalton Bradshaw," Cece said, smoothing things over.

"Yes, it's a great name." Greta smiled weakly. "Sorry."

"Don't worry about it."

The wardrobe team arrived, along with two makeup artists and a camera crew carrying all kinds of gear. The wardrobe people had multiple black-zippered garment bags, which they wheeled in on a rolling rack. One guy flipped open a large silver reflector while directing his assistant to set up the tripod. Dalton's family was financially well off, but he'd never seen anything like this circus.

Cece watched the cameraman with her arms folded across her chest. The chatter in the apartment echoed off the ceilings. Cece opened her mouth to speak. "Just a minute," she said, but her voice didn't make a dent in the wall of sound. "I'd like to say something." She held up a hand as if she were a third grader with the correct answer.

Greta nudged Dalton's arm. "I think Cece needs your whistle."

He stuck two fingers in his mouth, and a second later the sound that came out was deafening—part whistle, part shrieking teakettle. The crew stopped and looked at him. "I think the lady has something to say," Dalton said, indicating Cece.

Cece clapped her hands. "We won't need the camera crew tonight. You may leave."

The crew exchanged a look, not knowing what to do. It was almost as if they weren't used to her being in charge. Dalton glanced back and saw that Nanny and Brenna had already slipped out of the room. "Are you sure?" asked one man, consulting his phone. "We're scheduled to film the preparation, including you getting ready and putting on your jewelry, and then we'll follow along when you leave, filming you going into the limo and documenting the ride to the hotel where the ball is being held. We're booked for two and a half to three hours. The directions I got said we can extend it up to four if it takes longer. Regardless, you're paying us for a two-hour minimum."

"I don't care about the money," Cece said. "I just don't want you here."

"Are you sure?" This guy was either afraid of getting in trouble or thinking about his lost income.

"I'm sure I don't want to be filmed tonight," Cece said.

"Sweet," said the assistant, folding the reflector up and slipping it into its case.

"But . . ." The first guy didn't want to let this go. "Was this cleared with Vance? Because when I talked to him, he was pretty clear on what he wanted."

"Vance isn't here right now," Cece said. "I'm here."

"Has this been approved?"

Greta stepped forward, and her voice rang out loud and clear. "It's been approved. You can go." She stood over the guys as they packed up, then told Cece she'd see them out. Dalton heard her thanking them for coming as they left the room, as if they were party guests.

"That's my cousin," Cece said happily. "She looks out for me."

"I can see that," he said.

"I heard that when Greta was a little girl, she was painfully shy. Painfully," Cece said, emphasizing her point. "And she was scared of her own shadow. But over the years, she's come into her own."

"Has she ever." So little Greta was the mouse that roared. Dalton thought of her pulling Cece down the concrete steps away from the paparazzi. And now, walking the camera crew out to make sure they would actually go. She could be bold when necessary, yet she'd immediately felt terrible for mocking him when he'd stuttered. What an intriguing woman.

When Greta returned, she had a tall, thin man with her. "Look who I found," she said, gesturing toward him. This was the kind of thing people usually said when they were excited to run into someone, but her tone lacked that kind of enthusiasm.

"I'm here," the man said with a sigh. "Right on time."

"Hi, Michael." Cece turned to Dalton. "Michael is our driver. He's going to be Greta's date tonight to the ball." She whispered out of the side of her mouth, "He would have been my date if I hadn't found you."

"Lucky thing you found me then."

"You're right about that." Cece threw her arms around Dalton's neck and raised herself on tiptoe to speak in his ear. "I don't really care much for Michael."

Dalton took her point. Michael resembled the bad guy in every cheesy late-night movie. His slicked-back hair had comb marks as distinct as furrows in a farm field. His forced smile was a grim line, and he twitched even at rest. The way he sighed while looking at his watch gave the impression he wished the night were over already.

Cece addressed the woman who seemed to be in charge of wardrobe. "Libby, Dalton will be wearing Vance's tuxedo tonight."

Libby frowned, then whipped out a tape measure and measured his waist, inseam, arm length, and shoulder span. Finally, she stood and compared the numbers to the size on the suit. "His measurements are close enough. It should work." She instructed one of the young men to take Dalton to a guest room where he could shower before getting ready for the evening.

"Honest," Dalton said, "you can just give me directions, and I can figure out where to go."

She shook her head and continued explaining to the young guy, whose name was Duffy, how to get to the right room. "I want everything done correctly," she said.

"Okay, Libby."

Duffy accompanied Dalton up the stairs, enthusiastically telling him about his experiences as a film student. "Working on the prep crew for Cece Vanderhaven is going to look good on my résumé. I mostly just carry stuff, but I had to go through all kinds of screening to get cleared. They tested me for drugs and had me fingerprinted and interviewed my professors."

"Sounds intense."

"Libby is a piece of work, but I just keep my mouth shut and do the job."

A lot of talking for someone who prided himself on keeping his mouth shut.

Duffy kept going, even though he hadn't been encouraged. "This would all be worth it if I could get some kind of endorsement from the Vanderhavens. I'd love to ask Cece for a letter of recommendation, but we're not supposed to talk to her. Most of the time they keep her secluded, and I never even hear her speak, except for the lines they have her say for the filming." He snapped his fingers. "Hey, maybe you could put in a good word for me? Even if it's not a letter, a note saying I was an asset to the team would help. Are you a good friend of hers?"

Dalton shook his head. "I wouldn't say very."

He was glad to end the conversation and head into the bathroom. The shower in the guest room had a rainfall showerhead and jets that shot out water from all sides. Dalton's family had one like this at their house, and it got mixed reviews. His mom loved it, while his dad said he hated getting pelted with water. Dalton appreciated any shower at this point, and being able to use shampoo seemed the ultimate in luxury.

After he toweled off, he found a terry cloth bathrobe hanging on a hook next to the sink. He wore it while shaving with the travel-size disposable razor and shaving cream he found along with other assorted toiletries in a basket next to the sink. Here he'd been sleeping in the park when a room like this stood empty, proving once again that life was so much easier when you had friends in high places.

He left the bathroom to go into the adjacent bedroom and almost fell over at the sight of Duffy sitting on the bed, next to a garment bag. On the floor next to his feet sat a pair of shiny black shoes. Despite the reflexive clench of his jaw, Dalton was able to say, "Can I help you?"

"I went down, and they made me come back to help you get dressed," he said, like this was a reasonable thing. As if a grown guy helping another adult man get dressed was something that was commonly done. Dalton had been getting himself dressed for almost two decades. He'd never needed a Duffy before, and he sure didn't need one now.

"That's nice of you," he said. "But I think I've got it."

"Are you sure?" Duffy didn't move a muscle. "'Cause Libby is making me responsible for your attire."

"Absolutely." Dalton gestured toward the bag. "Is everything there—shirt, socks, the whole nine yards?"

His head bobbed up and down. "The entire ensemble. You've got yourself head-to-toe coverage right here."

"Then I'm good, Duffy. Thanks."

As it turned out, Dalton managed on his own, even doing the cummerbund and bow tie correctly. Once dressed, he rooted through his backpack, taking out the ReadyHelp device and his money. After tucking them into separate jacket pockets, he was finished. His shiny shoes clicked on the stairs on the way down, but no one seemed to be around on the first floor, so he sat on the bottom step and waited.

CHAPTER TWENTY-FIVE

Libby was, Greta noticed, really, really bossy and unbelievably overbearing. She led them up the stairs to Cece's room, walking at a fast clip. They were followed by Libby's beleaguered assistant, a young woman who toted bags slung over her back and stacked boxes carried in front. Greta thought of offering to help but was afraid she'd throw off the woman's balance and send her tumbling down the stairs.

Libby had her assistant unzip the bags and lay the dresses out across Cece's bed, along with the appropriate undergarments, footwear, and jewelry. She'd prepared sketches of how each ensemble would look and brought out glossy color wheels showing the color palate for the evening's chosen cosmetics. "I emailed the colors to the makeup artist ahead of time," she said. "Make sure they adhere to my choices."

Greta couldn't imagine anyone contradicting her, but Cece did. From the way Libby reacted, this was not something that had happened before.

It started when Libby asked about Katrina's whereabouts. "What time is Katrina arriving?" she asked, frowning. "She's usually on time."

"Not today," Cece said. "Katrina isn't going to be here tonight. Or ever, probably." It struck Greta how easily she'd accepted her best friends' abandonment. Greta knew they were friends for pay, but Cece didn't know that. Their absence had to sting, but Cece was putting up a brave front.

"But she has to be here." Libby's brow furrowed. "I have a dress that's been fitted especially for her."

Like a model on a game show gesturing to a new convertible, her assistant waved her arm toward one of the dresses. The gown she pointed to was a one-shoulder design, beige with a big fake flower on one side.

"Katrina won't be coming," Cece said. "Greta is taking her place tonight."

"Greta?" Libby turned and gave Greta a haughty stare, as if she'd just noticed her presence and didn't like what she saw. "Greta can't go. I discussed this with Vance. Her storyline is one of gradual transformation. She's the duckling who will become a swan. We have several weeks before she can appear at a black-tie event for the big reveal. Right now she's supposed to look dumpy and Midwestern. Besides," she said with a sniff, "her coloring is all wrong for the dress. The bisque would be lovely against Katrina's skin, but it would be all washed out on this girl."

"We don't want to wear the dresses you brought," Cece said. "We'll be wearing the dresses I actually designed. I can wear the white one with the feathers, and Greta will wear Katrina's black gown."

"No, no, no!" Was it Greta's imagination, or did Libby grow taller with every word? "That's not acceptable. The gowns I brought are the ones in your new line. We're debuting them tonight. The whole marketing campaign revolves around your wearing them this evening. By the time Firstborn Daughter, Inc. is done hyping them, every high school girl in the nation will dream of buying these dresses for the prom."

Really? Greta tried to imagine a sixteen-year-old wearing the beige dress with the fake flower on one side. Maybe with the flower taken off and the right jewelry, it wouldn't look too terrible. No, who was she kidding? There was no saving that dress.

"You can put that dress away," Cece said. "I don't want to wear it."

Libby got out her phone. "I need to talk to Vance."

While she dialed, Cece went to her closet and pulled out two dresses covered with plastic bags. She handed one to Greta, who followed her lead, taking it out of the plastic and laying it across the bed. Cece shoved the other two dresses aside. She said, "I hope Vance doesn't tell her to make us wear those ugly dresses."

"You don't have to worry about that."

"I don't?"

"No, you don't," Greta said firmly. Why did Cece think she didn't have a choice? When did the lunatics start running the asylum? "Vance isn't here anymore, but even if he was, you can be in charge of your own life. Firstborn Daughter, Inc. is your company, right?"

"Right." Even as she agreed, she still looked skeptical.

"And it's your body and your life."

"That's true," Cece said, mulling over her words.

"Besides, all these people work for you. Why does she think she can boss you around?" Greta glanced over at Libby, who was in the middle of leaving a scathing voice mail for Vance. Something about Cece having a temper tantrum like a spoiled child. "She's *your* employee."

The assistant, who'd overheard them talking, came over and nervously said, "No one says no to Libby." The poor girl looked like she was about to get sick.

"Well, you're going to see someone say no to Libby today," Greta said. "Right, Cece?"

"Right." She smoothed the front of her shirt and cleared her throat.

"Remember how you told the camera crew to go? This is the same thing. Just say the word, and send her away." Libby was a whole lot meaner than the camera crew, but she didn't mention that. "You should be able to wear any dress you want to wear." It occurred to Greta that by encouraging Cece to mutiny, she was going against her assigned job as transferred to her by Katrina and Vance, but she was starting to think, *The hell with that.* The whole thing was ludicrous. Deborah

Vanderhaven had brought her here under false pretenses, promising her an internship in one of their companies. She hadn't come to New York to become Cece's handler. She was her cousin and, hopefully, now her friend. Greta was beginning to see that Cece needed a friend, a real one, not one on the payroll.

If the Vanderhavens were going to sue her, let them. It's not like she had much to lose financially. If there were ever a good time in her life to be sued, it was right now when her student loans outweighed the numbers in her bank account. Good luck getting something from a negative. She wasn't a math major, but even she could do those calculations.

When Libby was done leaving the message, she turned to Cece and said, "I am quite sure Vance will be calling back directly. In the meantime, I suggest we get started if you're going to get to the ball on time."

"Cece?" Greta prompted.

Cece straightened up and addressed Libby. "You may go."

"Pardon me?" Libby narrowed her eyes in a way that said, *How dare you?*

"You may leave. I won't need your help tonight."

"No." She shook her head. "I'm not going. I was hired to be the wardrobe supervisor, and that's exactly what I'm going to do. If you leave here not properly attired, who's going to be blamed? Me, that's who. I'm responsible for your entire look. I came to do my job, and I'm seeing it through." Her impossibly high eyebrows got even higher.

Greta sucked in a breath, wondering what Cece would say. She would have banked on her capitulating, given that independent thinking was new to her. But she would have been wrong. In a show of solidarity, Cece slipped her hand in Greta's. "No, you're leaving," she said calmly. "You work for Firstborn Daughter, Inc., which is my company, which means I'm in charge."

"Not technically," Libby said.

She never got a chance to finish that thought because Cece kept talking, her voice getting louder with each word. "I don't want someone working for me who doesn't listen to me, so you're fired."

"You're firing me?" Libby said in disbelief. "You can't fire me. You weren't the one who hired me."

Cece looked to Greta, who nodded encouragingly. She said, "You don't work for Firstborn Daughter, Inc. anymore. You may go."

There was an audible gasp in the room. It came from Libby's assistant.

"Cece Vanderhaven, you're making a big mistake." Libby gathered up her purse and headed for the door. On her way out, she couldn't resist adding, "Wait until your father and Vance hear about this. Come along, Gabriella." She stormed out of the room.

As her assistant, Gabriella, went to follow her, Cece stopped her. "Just a minute."

The girl paused in the doorway. "Yes?"

"Do you like working for Libby?"

She hesitated. "I've learned a lot under her tutelage and am making some great connections in the industry."

From down the stairs, they heard Libby's voice call out, "Gabriella, now!"

Cece ignored her and asked, "But honestly, do you enjoy your job?"

"I wouldn't say I *enjoy* it."

"Why not?" Cece asked.

"Well, because . . ." Here, the girl held up both hands and looked anxiously behind her. "I don't get much say in anything. Let's just say I'm putting in my time, trying to build some experience."

"Hold that thought," Greta said, one finger raised. She took Cece aside. "You should hire her. With Vance and Katrina gone, you're coming up short on personnel."

"I have you."

"Yes, but I'm only here for the summer."

Cece tapped her lips thoughtfully. "Would you like to come work for me, Gabriella?"

The girl's shoulders relaxed. "Are you offering me a job? For real?"

"Yes."

"Wow." She smiled. "Yes, absolutely yes! I mean, as long as it's full-time. I can't afford to do it otherwise."

"It'll be full-time," Greta said. "Right?"

"I guess it could be," Cece said.

"I'd love to! I mean, as long as the pay is comparable to what I'm already getting."

Cece said, "I didn't know there were so many things to think about when you get a job offer."

Gabriella said, "I definitely want the job. It's a matter of paying my bills. I'm cutting it kind of close as it is. I can't take less pay than I'm already getting."

"I will give you more than Libby is paying you," Cece decided.

"And full benefits," Greta suggested.

Cece turned to her. "What's that?"

"Health insurance and vacation days, things like that."

"Doesn't that come automatically?"

"No. You'd be surprised. It's not as common as you'd think."

"You shall have full benefits, Gabriella," Cece said, as if bestowing a royal title.

From the bottom of the stairs, they heard Libby yell, "Gabriella! Now!"

Gabriella broke into a grin. "Can I run down and tell her I quit?"

Getting approval, she took off out the door, looking so much happier than what they'd seen on the climb up the stairs, when she'd resembled a burdened pack mule. Greta felt happier too, a weight lifted since she'd first arrived in New York. She'd had a lot to process, and then Katrina and Vance had left, leaving her in the lurch. She'd never wanted to be in charge. Without realizing it, she'd handed over some of the burden to Cece, who was more than willing to share the load. She was also proving to be capable of deciding what she wanted.

Gabriella came back and helped them into their dresses, the ones Cece had designed, and then Brenna came in and sat on the bed to watch them get ready. Greta breathed a sigh of relief upon discovering Katrina's dress fit her. There was some give to the crisscross bodice, spandex or something that stretched to conform to her body. As a design element, it was one most women would appreciate. When they were dressed in finery from head to toe, the hair and makeup people set up chairs, put paper capes around their shoulders, and did their magic. Cece was used to this routine and knew when to purse her lips and when to close her eyes and all the rest of it, while Greta needed instruction.

Once done, they stood side by side, looking into Cece's full-length mirror. "Twins," her cousin exclaimed.

Greta almost didn't recognize herself. She had never looked this good in her entire life. She didn't know she *could* look this good and was pretty certain she never would again. Her skin no longer had pores. Her eyes had gotten bigger, and her lips looked luscious without looking garish. The dress was incredible, giving her curves in all the right places. The shoes were pretty awesome too, with crystals across the ankles and toe straps. The whole ensemble made her feel like a different person. Glamorous. Saucy. Bold. She felt a small hand brush against her arm and looked down to see Brenna, her eyes wide. "So how do we look?" Greta asked.

"Beautiful. Like princesses."

"Thank you, sweetie."

While the crew was packing up their supplies and Cece was talking to Gabriella, Brenna motioned for Greta to come closer. "Yes?" She crouched down to her level.

"Will you watch my sister tonight?" she asked, her voice quavering. "To make sure nothing bad happens to her?"

"I'll be with her the whole evening." Greta shot a look at Cece, who didn't appear to be in any danger. "Nothing bad will happen to her. She'll be fine."

Brenna tugged at her dress and whispered right in her ear. "You have to watch her every minute." Her worry was endearing. "My dad said sometimes she has poor impulse control. From being in the pool." Her eyes were tearing up, as if she were about to cry. Poor little thing. She'd obviously overheard the adults talking about her sister and taken the worry on to herself. Greta knew the feeling well. She'd spent a lot of her own childhood worrying about things that never happened.

"You don't need to worry, Brenna. Believe me, I will watch her."

She still looked dubious. "You have to promise."

Greta tapped her heart. "I swear on my life that I will watch Cece every minute and will keep anything bad from happening to her."

"And she'll come home safe."

"Yes." She reached out and gave her cousin a reassuring hug. "Cece will come home safe and sound. You can be sure of that."

CHAPTER TWENTY-SIX

Dalton sat on the bottom step for what felt like a long time. He was alone until he wasn't anymore. When a herd of people came thundering down the steps, most of them carrying cases of cosmetics and hair supplies, he got up and stepped out of their way, leaving his spot to lean against a pillar. They nodded as they went past and headed toward the exit. Once they were out of view, he heard their voices, the chattering of women who were done working and were now making plans for the rest of the evening. One of them jovially called out, "First round of drinks is on Carrie."

Another woman's voice called back, "Like hell."

Hearing this friendly exchange gave him a pang. He'd become so entrenched in living the life of the homeless that he'd almost forgotten the casual fun of going out with friends. Now it was all coming back: the pleasure of grabbing a bite or getting a drink in the company of people he enjoyed. The comradery of joking among friends. It was such an ordinary thing to do, but his current lifestyle wouldn't allow him to spend money so frivolously. He missed being able to socialize on a moment's notice. Part of him wanted to run after them and say, "Wait up! I'm coming too."

He felt that way for only a second, because the next thing he heard was Greta coming down the stairs. He looked up to see she wasn't so much stepping as gliding, one hand lightly skimming the banister, the skirt of her black dress moving with the twitch of her hips. She gave him a shy smile that erupted into a grin mirroring his own. Man, she looked great.

"You look gorgeous," Dalton said when she reached the bottom. "Great dress."

"Thanks," she said. "We need to talk." She grabbed the lapel of his tux and steered him to the other side of the pillar. "Quick, before Cece comes down. What's your story?" She still looked gorgeous, but she wasn't smiling anymore.

"My story?"

"I googled *Dalton Bradshaw* and couldn't find you anywhere."

"No?" He raised one eyebrow. His former girlfriend had thought this looked sexy, but of course, this was the same girlfriend who'd broken off the relationship because she'd found her someone, and it wasn't him. Judging from Greta's expression, the eyebrow lift wasn't getting him anywhere.

"There were some Dalton Bradshaws out there, but none of them looked like you. So what gives?"

She had him there. If she had searched for his real name, Dalton Bishop, she would have found his social media accounts, LinkedIn page, and articles about the service projects and scholarship funds he'd helped establish at the university. But as Dalton Bradshaw, he'd done nothing. "I know there's not much out there," he said. "I'm not big into social media. I kind of like to keep a low profile."

"Try again." She crossed her arms in front of her, trying to look menacing, but it was like being threatened by a rabbit. "Are you homeless, like Cece said? And how is it that you keep showing up wherever we are? Are you a stalker?"

"Okay." Dalton lowered his voice. "Just between us, I am currently homeless, but it's a temporary situation. I didn't plan to run into you, and I'm not stalking you or Cece. That part is a coincidence." He glanced up to see Cece at the top of the stairs. "I don't want to get into it right now, but I promise you, I'm a good guy."

"Is your name even Dalton Bradshaw?"

"Not Bradshaw, but I promise you that Dalton is my first name. Is, has been, and always will be." He hoped that would be good enough for her.

As they heard Cece coming down the stairs, Greta quickly said, "Whoever you are, you better not mess with my cousin. If I find out you're secretly filming her or selling information to the media, you will live to regret it."

Bunny threats. So adorable. "Understood."

"Greta?" Cece called out. They stepped around the pillar to see her descending the staircase with the grace of royalty. All she needed was a crown and a velvet cape, and anyone would kneel before her.

"I'm right here," Greta said. "I was just threatening Dalton and telling him he'd better behave tonight."

"Behave?" Cece said. "Well, I certainly hope he doesn't behave. That would be no fun at all."

CHAPTER TWENTY-SEVEN

Greta reflected on what she'd just learned, which wasn't much. He'd said his first name was Dalton, but now the plot thickened. She couldn't think of one good reason why he would be temporarily homeless and give them a phony last name.

Was she supposed to just trust that he was a good guy? Isn't that what all bad guys said? *Trust me. I promise. Believe me.* Words guys used to lure girls in and win them over. Maybe he thought that because she was from Wisconsin, she was from farm country and could easily be duped. Funny that Cece, the one from Manhattan, was so trusting while she was cautious. But then again, Cece had always been surrounded by people who took care of these kinds of things, so she didn't have much experience dealing with lowlifes and con artists. Greta didn't, either, but she'd seen every single episode of *Law & Order SVU.* She knew plenty.

When Cece came down the stairs, she looked so beautiful, she took Greta's breath away. When Cece had pulled her over to the full-length mirror earlier, she'd said they looked like twins, but that wasn't entirely true. Anyone could see they were related, but Cece had the more refined features. Another difference? Cece moved with grace and certainty while Greta always felt like she wasn't quite sure of herself. At times, her elbows seemed to operate on their own. Talk about awkward. She didn't contradict Cece's view of them together. If Cece wanted to pull Greta onto her carousel, she was happy to be along for the ride. Cece's world was one of beauty and privilege. Greta was lucky to be able to stand in her shadow.

While they waited for Michael, Cece flirted shamelessly with Dalton, telling him he looked extremely hot in a tux and goading her into agreeing. "Greta, doesn't Dalton look handsome in his tux?"

"I might think so, except it's not technically *his* tux," she said.

In response, Dalton mimed a dagger to the heart, while Cece gave him a playful slap on the arm. "Just ignore Greta. She's having some fun with you."

Cece rested her hand on her shoulder and said that from now on, she was doing things her way. "I'm tired of playing by the rules," she said. "Tonight I say we all live large and do whatever we want."

"Works for me," Dalton said.

Brenna and Nanny came out of the kitchen to say goodbye, and a few minutes later, the pocket in Cece's evening gown pinged. Pulling her phone out, she read the text and said, "It's Michael. The car is out front."

Brenna tugged on Greta's dress and pulled her down to her height. "Don't forget," she whispered into her ear.

"I won't."

Nanny gave Cece a hug. "Have fun at the ball. Be good."

Cece laughed. "No promises!" She looked even happier than in the perfume commercial, when she'd been frolicking in a fountain somewhere in Europe. Tonight, she was jubilant.

She slipped her hand over Dalton's arm, and together they looked like a couple heading out to the Academy Awards. Greta did think he looked exceptionally handsome in that tux, not that she wanted to give him the satisfaction of hearing her say it.

As they headed to the elevator, Greta walked behind them, Cinderella's somewhat pretty but gawky cousin who was visiting from the Midwest and had to be invited along out of sheer politeness. Not that she was complaining.

She was just glad to be included.

CHAPTER TWENTY-EIGHT

When the trio left the apartment building, a few tourists recognized Cece and came up to say hello. It was nowhere near the throng Dalton had seen the other day, just half a dozen people who happened to be walking by at the time. Cece beamed when they asked for photos and posed for all of them, giving one little girl a hug and high-fiving a bike delivery guy who'd paused from his route, leaning his bike against a sign post upon spotting her. Greta stood silently nearby, while inside the car, Michael waited behind the wheel. When Dalton noticed Greta's distraught expression, he asked, "What's wrong?"

She said, "Oh, man, Dalton, I completely messed up. I forgot to call the security detail this morning and set up the schedule for them to accompany us. It was in the packet Katrina gave me, marked *very important*. She highlighted it, even. Cece's not supposed to go anywhere without security."

He knew the sound of guilt when he heard it. He'd felt it himself, every time he'd let his father down. Greta thought she'd screwed up big-time. Poor girl. He hated that she was beating herself up over this. "So who says Cece's not supposed to go anywhere without security?"

"Katrina and Vance. It was in the packet. They were very adamant about her safety protocols."

"And where are Katrina and Vance now?"

"I don't know," she admitted, shrugging. "They took off and left me in charge. Even Cece didn't know they were leaving until after they were gone."

"Then I say, screw 'em and their instructions. If it was so important, they shouldn't have left. They should be here taking care of things. It was unfair of them to dump it on you and expect you to cover their duties."

"Well, I said I would . . . "

"I'm sure you did, but it sounds like coordinating all of this is a massive job, probably too much for one person, much less someone who's new to it. Besides, look at Cece. Does she seem upset that her Secret Service hasn't shown up?"

Cece was happily showing a woman how the skirt of her dress moved when she swayed. Greta smiled. Shy, uncertain, but a real genuine smile of relief. "I guess it will be okay for one night," she said.

"I'll help you keep her safe."

Greta looked relieved. "Thank you."

Michael tapped on the horn, then opened the window and said, "Sorry," as if he'd hit it by accident. Dalton opened the car door, and Cece reluctantly left her fans and slid inside. He gestured for Greta to go next and then got in after them.

It struck Dalton as odd that Michael was attending the event and driving as well, but when he asked him about it, the guy only grunted and said, "I'm the driver." What could Dalton say to that? Michael had phrased it as if there were no other options, as if New York was devoid of people who were capable of driving that limo.

When they arrived at the venue, a crowd had formed on either side of the velvet ropes. In between, a red carpet ran from the curb up some steps and into the building. The event had its own security team on-site, men who opened the car doors as guests arrived and kept the peasants from breaching the perimeter. "See," Dalton said to Greta, "you didn't need your guys, after all."

As Cece exited, the crowd called out in excitement. "Cece Vanderhaven!"

"Cece, over here!"

Cece stepped aside so that Greta and Dalton could join her on the sidewalk, then went over to the rope to talk to her fans.

"Gorgeous dress, Cece. Who's the designer?"

Upon hearing the question, she posed, one hand on her hip. "I designed this myself," she said and began describing the fabric and other details about the styling and construction. "It was created using synthetic feathers that are as soft as goose down. It creates movement." One woman reached over the rope to touch the skirt, then nodded approvingly to her friend. "My favorite feature?" Cece tucked her hands into her pockets. "Built-in pockets, so there's no need to bring a handbag to an elegant event."

The crowd chimed in.

"What a great idea!"

"Why don't all dresses come like that?"

"Beautiful *and* practical."

Cece gestured to her cousin. "Greta, come over here." When Greta complied, Cece slipped an arm around her waist and pulled her closer. "This is my cousin Greta. Isn't she beautiful?"

The crowd agreed. One woman said, "You look like sisters!"

Greta blushed and looked around, as if unsure what the correct response should be. A woman reached out to touch her dress, and Greta flinched for only for a second, then stood stock-still, as if determined to endure the attention. As much as Cece was in her glory interacting with crowds of adoring fans, her cousin wasn't loving it. Dalton picked up on her discomfort and provided her with an exit strategy, stepping forward and touching each of them lightly on the back. "Ladies? I believe they're waiting for us inside."

Greta turned and gave Dalton a relieved smile. "Of course." She nudged Cece. "We need to go to the ball."

Not wanting to leave either of them out, Dalton crooked both arms and wound up with a beautiful woman on either side of him. A pretty good place to be. Michael had driven off after letting them out. At the time, Dalton had wondered if they'd ever see him again, but now he realized it didn't matter. Regardless, the three of them would be fine.

"Cece?" A yell came out from the crowd, accompanied by the flash of a camera. "Who's your date?"

She stopped to answer. "This is my new friend, Dalton. Isn't he handsome?"

"Cece! Cece! Look over here!"

Cece spoke to Greta and Dalton. "Let's turn right before the door and give them a good picture." They went about five feet before she had them pivot to face the crowd. Cece's smile stretched wide, and even Greta started to relax a little, knowing they'd soon be inside.

"Gorgeous, Cece! This way!"

"Love you, Cece!"

One man's voice rose over the crowd. "Cece, what about the reports that Vance and Katrina got married in Vegas? Reportedly, Katrina is pregnant. Did you know?"

Katrina and Vance got married? Dalton tried to remember what he'd heard about Cece's former sidekicks. Wasn't Vance supposedly her gay boyfriend? Greta had just said they'd taken off on short notice, which really didn't tell him much. If any of this was news to Cece, she didn't show it. "Of course I knew," she said. "I adore both of them and wish them every happiness."

CHAPTER TWENTY-NINE

Greta had never seen so many stunning women in one place before. With their perfect hair, fabulous gowns, sparkling jewelry, and flawless faces, all of them looked like they were supermodels ready to walk down a runway. And Cece was the most gorgeous of them all. Greta wasn't sure if it was the dress or her newfound freedom, but her cousin positively glowed.

Greta, on the other hand, felt as if she stood out, as if everyone there could see that a plain girl had somehow wandered in among the beauties. She was only dispelled of this notion when she went to visit the ladies' room and a man at the bar caught her eye and said, "Hello, lovely." She'd glanced around to see if he could be speaking to someone else, but there was no mistake. He meant it for her. A little creepy, but still it was a compliment. She found it oddly unsettling being put in the same class as all these strikingly attractive women, but it was also somewhat thrilling. As new experiences went, it was one of the better ones. She could definitely get used to it.

The evening started off with drinks in a large hall flanked by two bars. Servers came around with trays of champagne, and the bars kept busy mixing cocktails and pouring wine. Waiters carried trays of appetizers on tiny skewers. None of the other women in the room opted for the food, but many of the forgotten men chowed down, taking multiples and balancing them on cocktail napkins. One side of the room was lined with small tables, bar height. After they found an empty table, each of them accepted a glass of champagne.

An older woman, slightly plump with upswept hair and glittering drop earrings, sat at a grand piano in one corner, playing soft background music. Her fingers fluttered over the keys while she kept her head high and her posture perfect.

"What's the song she's playing?" Greta nodded toward the piano.

Dalton said, "I don't know the specific song. I think it falls under easy listening."

"Cocktail party music," Cece added. "It all sounds the same."

The other female guests mingled, throwing their arms around each other, giving air kisses, and admiring each other's gowns and jewelry. From what Greta overheard, there were a lot of connections from summer camp, sororities, and mutual friends. Summer camp sounded like it was a big deal, much different from the time she spent a week as a Girl Scout at Camp Alice Chester, the highlight of which was making a dream catcher at the craft table. From what she could tell, their camp experiences lasted for weeks and took place in lavish rural retreats in other states. On visiting day, their parents brought wrapped gifts and gourmet treats. "Remember when your mother brought those trays of fresh sushi?" one woman said.

So many of the young women talked about trips they'd recently taken, citing the names of places Greta wouldn't be able to find on a globe for any amount of money. The act of introducing their dates to the other women seemed to be an afterthought.

When she saw Michael enter the hall, Greta raised a hand to get his attention, and he strode straight to their table, tapping Cece on the shoulder. When she turned, he said, "I will be at the bar if you need anything." She nodded in acknowledgment, and off he went.

"He's really supposed to be part of this, isn't he?" Greta asked, watching as he deftly wove his way around clusters of chatting guests.

Cece shrugged. "It's fine. He didn't choose to come here, so if he'd rather not join us, I understand." She smiled. "Besides, I don't need his bad mood tonight."

Leah Ann Miller, their hostess for the evening, had been making the rounds. When she got to their end of the ballroom, she shrieked at the sight of Cece and threw her arms around her. "Cece Vanderhaven!" she said. "I'm so happy you're here." Noticing Dalton, her eyes widened. "And who might you be? It's hard to believe you could be a forgotten man."

"This is Dalton," Cece said. "He only qualifies because when we met, he was homeless."

"My, my," Leah Ann said, suddenly lapsing into a Southern accent. "That's a hard one to believe. A man as good-looking as you without a home? You can leave your shoes under my bed anytime you want, Dalton."

Cece stepped between them, pulling Greta to her side. "This is my cousin Greta. She's here for the summer."

"It's nice to meet you, Greta," Leah Ann said, her eyes still on Dalton. Next to her, a man in a tweed jacket with dark-framed glasses fidgeted nervously. He was lanky with pale skin; a lock of hair fell over his forehead.

"It's nice to meet you too," Greta said. "I don't believe we've met your date."

"This is Roger," she said dismissively. "My little sister's tutor. My first choice for a forgotten man got sick, so Roger filled in at the last minute."

Cece extended her hand. "Lovely to meet you, Roger."

Roger twitched, startled, but recovered quickly, taking her hand with a smile, then leaning down and pressing his lips briefly to her fingers. "It is an honor to make your acquaintance," he said, his eyes flicking up to meet hers.

If Cece found this old-fashioned phrasing odd, she didn't show it. "How charming," she said, looking pleased. "Leah Ann, I hope you don't mind, but I've decided to steal Roger for the evening. My little party of three seems to be short a forgotten man." It sounded like she wasn't counting on Michael coming back at all.

Leah Ann let out an unattractive laugh. "You're welcome to him." She clapped a hand on Roger's back. "I'm in so much demand this evening, he wouldn't have seen much of me, anyway."

Roger looked pleased. "That's so nice of you," he told Cece.

Leah Ann wasn't done. "Speaking of coming up short, where are your partners in crime tonight? I haven't seen you without Katrina and Vance in ages. Usually, they keep you in such close quarters, we barely get to speak."

"Katrina and Vance?" Cece waved a hand. "They couldn't be here. Recently, we decided we were all due for a change, so off they went. The last I heard, they got married in Las Vegas."

"Vance and Katrina? Married?" Leah Ann said. "How scandalous!"

"Not at all. It's what they wanted all along," Cece said, turning to Roger and changing the subject. "Roger, would you go with me to the bar? I would love an apple martini."

"Anything you want, Miss Vanderhaven."

"Call me Cece." She rested her hand on Dalton's arm. "You don't mind, do you? Greta can keep you company."

"Whatever you want," he said, giving her a smile.

Leah Ann had treated Roger with such disdain, Greta was glad that Cece had added him to their group. She had a big heart, her cousin. Of course, that left Greta with Dalton, which wasn't all that bad except for the way his eyes followed Cece to the bar. She wondered if he was disappointed being left behind with her. What had Katrina called her? Frumpy. Yes, that was it. Such an odd word. You almost never heard anyone use the word *frumpy* anymore, and yet Katrina had somehow decided that it fit Greta.

"Did you want to go to the bar for a drink?" Dalton asked, breaking into her thoughts.

"I have a drink." Greta lifted her barely touched glass of champagne.

"I mean, to keep an eye on Cece? You were worried I was a scam artist, and here she's with Roger, who's also a complete stranger . . . "

"Ha! There's no comparison. Roger is Leah Ann Miller's younger sister's tutor, so he comes with a recommendation. You're a guy we picked up on the street. If anything, I'd say Roger is more likely to be trustworthy." Roger was not as easy on the eyes as Dalton, but at least someone was vouching for him. "I don't even know who you are."

"I told you, my name is Dalton," he said, looking amused.

"Okay, that's a start. Now how about a last name?"

"Mine or yours?"

She crossed her arms. "Yours, of course. I know my last name. Hansen. Greta Hansen."

Dalton gave a little laugh. Despite her intention not to let him off the hook, she couldn't help but smile. Oh, he was charming. "Greta Hansen," he said approvingly. "I don't think I've ever met a Hansen before."

"Move to Wisconsin, and you'll find it hard to avoid them."

"So you're from Wisconsin?"

"Yes. You?"

"Connecticut. What part of Wisconsin are you from?"

"Nice try," Greta said. "But you can't steer the conversation that way. We're talking about you. Do you have some proof of your identity?"

CHAPTER THIRTY

"What constitutes proof?" Dalton was stalling. From the look in her eyes, she knew it.

"A picture ID would work. Driver's license, passport, whatever you have."

He shook his head, trying to look sad. "Believe me, I'd love to have something to show you." Dalton patted his pockets, feeling the ReadyHelp device in one pocket and the folded bills in another, neither of which would prove his identity. "I got nothing."

"Every adult I know carries something with their name on it. Credit cards, a library card, insurance cards. No one leaves the house without *something*."

"I know. That's how it usually works."

"But you have nothing with you. Why?"

She wanted an answer, and he wanted to give her one. There was no need for her to think he was a serial killer or one of the paparazzi. "Okay, I'll tell you." Behind them a group of girls laughed uproariously, drowning out his words. After they went by, he moved closer to Greta and spoke into her ear. "My family is well off. I have an apartment in Connecticut, but I'm living the life of a homeless person as an experiment."

She pulled away and regarded him warily. “So you live in Connecticut, but came to New York to pretend to be homeless. As an experiment.”

“That’s right.”

“I don’t get it. Why pretend to be homeless? Why the ruse?”

“It’s a long, not very interesting story. Basically, I have something to prove to my father.”

They were interrupted by Cece, who’d pushed her way through a throng of people, towing Roger behind her. They both held oversize martini glasses filled with a green liquid. “Greta, you won’t believe it! Roger knew the bartender from middle school, and they did their secret handshake for me.” She laughed and set the drink on the table. “It was hilarious. You should have seen it.”

Roger modestly said, “It wasn’t that big of a deal. I’m surprised he remembered it.”

“You have to teach it to me,” she said, giving him a grin. “Seriously, Greta, you would have died. It was so funny.”

“You know what’s *really* funny?” Greta said. “Turns out Dalton is only pretending to be homeless. His family is rich.”

“I’m not rich. My parents are.” He could not stress that enough. The amount in his actual bank account lacked the multitude of zeroes found one generation up.

“That’s what all rich guys say,” Roger said, making Cece laugh again. She thought he was an absolute riot. He made finger quotes. “I’m not rich. My parents are.”

Dalton didn’t know why Cece thought that was so funny. If anything, her family was the wealthier of the two. Everything she had could be traced back to her family connections. Without them, she’d be sending out her résumé and going to interviews like everyone else. Dalton didn’t think it was a crime to get help from his family. Despite his background, he was trying to be his own man and follow his own social conscience. That should count for something.

"You shouldn't have lied to us," Greta said.

"I know. That was wrong of me," he said. "I was trying to keep a low profile and keep my family name out of it. If I had to do it over again, I would have been truthful right from the start. I made a mistake. I'm sorry."

"Apology accepted." Cece lifted her glass and took a sip. "Ooh, this is good. I could drink these all night." She made a face. "Vance used to make me stop after two. He said I became unpredictable."

Dalton turned to Greta. "Do you accept my apology?"

"Do I have a choice?" The words were snarky, but the amused quirk of her lips said otherwise. She tucked a wave of hair behind her ear, uncovering a dangling gemstone earring.

"Well, of course you do. I have to warn you, though, if you don't accept my apology, I'll spend the rest of my life currying your favor in an attempt to get you to reconsider."

"In that case, I'm holding off for a bit. I'd like to see what that looks like."

CHAPTER THIRTY-ONE

Greta didn't entirely trust him. For one thing, his story sounded unlikely. He decided to go homeless to prove something to his wealthy father? *Please.* She'd have to know a lot more to make sense of that scenario. Offhand, she couldn't think of anything that would fit.

He had a certain something, though, an ease in the way he moved and spoke, an innate charm that was hard to resist. When he smiled her way, it was intense. And any guy who used a phrase like *currying favor* won points with her. She liked a man who knew his way around the dictionary.

The conversation in the room quieted with the ringing of a bell. Servers walked through, stopping at each cluster of assembled guests to invite them to proceed across the hall to the dining room. It was a slow process with most people ignoring the announcements at first, but slowly, after the second and third announcements, there was a drift in that direction. In the other room, staff escorted guests to their tables. Most of them were set for eight people, but their table had only four place settings.

"We seem to be short a few places," Roger said. "Our invisible friends don't have any silverware."

Cece laughed. "Vance bought out eight spots. He didn't want anyone else sitting with us. He was always afraid I'd say something stupid and ruin my image. I was encouraged to pretend to be someone else."

Roger opened his mouth, aghast. "That's horrible. You're so much fun. Why would anyone want you to act like someone else?"

"They told me it was a game," Cece explained. "I had to be mysterious and vague, and I don't know what else." She took another sip of her apple martini. "I got dragged around everywhere. They were always talking to each other off to the side, whispering about me. Whenever I asked them to let me in, they brushed me off and said they were talking about things that didn't concern me, but I knew better." She tapped her fingernails against the linen tablecloth. "They never let me in. I hated it."

Roger sympathized, telling her he knew just how she felt. He launched into a childhood story about how his two older brothers told him he couldn't be part of the Cool Kids' Club unless he did exactly what they told him to do. He had a funny way of telling the story, doing voices and acting out the motions, all of which cheered Cece up immensely. Dalton found him funny too, leaning in his direction to hang on every word. Both of them were amused by his storytelling, but Greta had trouble concentrating, because something her cousin had said caught her attention.

They never let me in.

Greta could imagine Cece in the commercial for her signature fragrance, the camera zooming in on her beautiful face, her perfect lips whispering, *Let me in.* In the context of the ad, her words sounded romantic, seductive even, but now, knowing what she knew, Greta realized what had happened. Somehow a camera had caught her saying the phrase more than once, and the machine that was Firstborn Daughter, Inc. felt compelled to explain it—so an entire product and ad campaign were built around it.

Roger finished his story by saying, "Turned out there was no Cool Kids' Club. They just told me that so I'd do their chores."

When everyone else at the table finished laughing, Greta asked, "Cece, you didn't seem surprised that Katrina and Vance left and got married. Did you know they were a couple?"

She nodded. "They didn't think I knew, but I did. They wanted to leave so badly. I would hear them whispering about the contract and how stuck they were. It was tiresome. I said, 'Just leave if you want to,' but then they pretended I misunderstood, and they hugged me and said they loved me and that they didn't want to go. They thought I was clueless."

Greta felt for her. "Oh, I'm sure they didn't think that."

"But they did. I heard Katrina say it once." She picked up her plate and looked at her reflection, then tilted it back and forth.

Roger followed her lead, picking up his plate as well. "Cool," he said. "Look at the way the light reflects." The light from the chandelier above bounced off the china. Roger directed it at his water glass, taking it to the next level. Rays of light shimmied across the table. Cece grinned and aimed her plate the same way, creating her own beams of light.

At the next table, there were hushed whispers from the other guests. Greta had a feeling they were commenting on Cece's behavior.

Dalton gave her a look, shrugged, and picked up his plate and followed suit. Not to be left out, Greta did it too. Cece let out a peal of laughter, and Roger gave her an admiring look. He said, "This evening is turning out to be a lot more fun than I thought it would be."

Cece said, "And the evening is only just starting."

CHAPTER THIRTY-TWO

Dalton had to agree with Vance: Cece was unpredictable after two drinks. All of them put their plates down when the servers came with the salads, then listened politely when Leah Ann Miller stepped up to the podium on the dais to thank everyone for attending her dinner and dance to benefit the Museum of Modern Art. Apparently, each seat in the room raised $3,000 for the museum, even the four empty ones at their table. Each occupied table cost $24,000. Dalton tried to do some quick math, counting the tables and doing some mental multiplication, but he got bogged down midway through and never did come up with a total. Regardless, Leah Ann Miller's event had raised a cartload of money for the museum.

Leah Ann spoke into the microphone, saying, "Please hold your applause," even though there was no sign of anyone starting to clap, "and remain silent during a five-minute video about the museum."

It was during the video that Cece got the giggles. It started with a slight smirk and built from there. Her efforts to rein in her laughter only made it worse, and Roger seemingly encouraged her by whispering in her ear. At one point, she held her breath and turned red and slapped Roger away, as if one word from him would make her go ballistic.

Finally, just as the video finished, she got up and left the room. Greta followed. Dalton could hear Cece's explosion of laughter just outside the banquet hall.

"What's up?" Dalton whispered to Roger, who shook his head like he had no idea.

While Cece and Greta were gone, they heard a distinguished-looking man from the museum board talk about the history of the museum. His talk went on and on, punctuating the fact that the girls had been gone a really long time. When they finally returned and slid back into their seats, Cece had composed herself and Greta looked relieved. "Everything okay?" Dalton asked.

Greta nodded. "All good."

Leah Ann went back up to the front and spoke into the microphone once again. "Just one more important announcement before dinner is served." She held her hands together as if praying. "The Vanderhaven Corporation has generously offered to match any additional donations from tonight's attendees contributed in the next thirty days." She motioned to their table. "Thank you to Cece Vanderhaven and her family. Cece, would you stand, please?"

Cece got up from her seat and gave a little wave while the room applauded. As she sat down, she murmured, "This is the first I've heard of this."

A formal event was not normally something Dalton enjoyed, but he was looking forward to the dancing portion of the evening. Sometime in middle school, he'd figured out that slow dancing was the safest and easiest way to get a girl to embrace him. One added bonus? He would look like a perfect gentleman just for asking. It was, he thought with a smile, one of the most self-serving things a guy could do in the name of being polite. Now that Cece and Roger had hit it off, he was free to ask Greta without looking like he was a total jerk to his date. When Cece had first invited him to attend this event, he'd had no idea it would work out this perfectly. It was like he'd wished for something and it had magically happened. If only all of life worked that way.

The servers came around periodically with champagne. Even though Cece and Roger weren't done with their martinis, they each took a glass. They toasted each other and clinked glasses, and when Greta said, her face scrunched in worry, "Don't you think you've had enough?" Cece brushed her off.

"Enough? I'm not even halfway to enough." Cece patted Greta's arm. "I feel fabulous. I wish everyone in the world felt this good." She lifted her glass overhead, and champagne sloshed over the rim, splattering the tablecloth. "Everyone!" Her laughter was so delightful, it was impossible not to smile.

Cece was out of control and loving it. Greta, meanwhile, looked like a parent chaperone who'd lost a first-grader during a field trip to the zoo.

By the time the tables were cleared and the band started up, Greta wasn't even trying to look like she was enjoying herself. Her eyes were focused on Cece, and her hand fluttered nervously on the tabletop like she was ready to take action but wasn't quite sure what would help. Dalton was just gearing up to ask her to dance when Cece leaned across the table and called out, "Dalton, when are you going to ask my beautiful cousin to dance?"

Inwardly, Dalton sighed. Cece had gotten ahead of him, and now he wouldn't get credit for the idea. Nothing to it but to do it. "Greta," he said, very seriously, "would you dance with me?"

Greta hesitated, shaking her head. "I don't really—"

"Please?" Dalton put his hand over hers. "I don't want to beg, but I will if I have to." He gave her fingers a gentle squeeze.

"Make him beg!" Cece cried out.

Even Roger looked amused. "Do it, man. Beg the woman."

Dalton got off his chair and dropped to one knee. "Greta Hansen, I'm begging you to please dance with me. If you would, my life will be complete."

Her face flushed adorably red as she realized they were attracting the attention of everyone in the room. "Get up," she said, her eyes darting back and forth. "People are looking."

"Let them look," he said. "I will not get up until you agree to dance with me."

"Make him wait," Roger suggested. "Keep him kneeling."

"No! That's mean." Cece slapped Roger's arm. "Don't torture him, Greta. Just dance with him."

"Fine," she said. "I accept."

Dalton scrambled to his feet and extended a hand, which she took with a reluctant glance back at Cece. He led the way, holding Greta's hand behind his back, and when they got to an opening on the dance floor, he turned around and pulled her toward him in one smooth move.

"You seem like you've done this before," she said.

"On the count of three, I'm going to flip you." Dalton grinned.

"No!" she cried out, then laughed when she realized he'd been teasing.

As they continued to dance, Greta's attention began to stray, her gaze darting back to the table, watching her cousin. "You're not responsible for her," Dalton said. "She's an adult."

"She's acting out because she's had too much to drink," Greta said, shaking her head sadly.

"Because you forced her to?" They were swaying now to some orchestral tune he'd never heard before. Old-people music, but perfect for his purposes.

"Of course not." She glanced up and met his eyes. "But I'm in charge of Cece now that Katrina and Vance left. They've been carefully cultivating her image for years now. I don't want to be the one to blow all their hard work in one night."

Dalton shot a look at Cece, who had one hand resting on Roger's cheek. "She looks pretty happy to me. I don't think you need to worry."

"It's not about her being happy. I mean, I want her to be happy, but out in public, she's supposed to be conducting herself a certain way. They have this big-deal thing coming up that I'm not supposed to talk about, but it's time-sensitive and might mean millions of dollars. And all of that is riding on my shoulders, so please don't tell me not to worry."

He nodded. "Okay, I'm sorry. I have no right to tell you how to feel." She relaxed in his arms. "How about you give some of that worry to me? Hand it right over. I will gladly take it."

She laughed. "It doesn't work like that."

"Why not? People share happiness. Why not worry?"

"Okay, fair enough. I'm giving you half."

"I'll take more than half. I want to lighten your load."

The music was so nondescript that nothing stood out for him except the swell of violins. Still, he hoped the song would last forever. When she rested her chin against his shoulder, her body relaxing against his, he had a quick pulse of gratitude, taking it as a sign of trust. He noticed now that her hair had a wonderful scent—coconut, he thought. When the song finished, Greta pulled apart and politely clapped, but Dalton was intently looking at her face, noticing the half smile and the sparkle in her eyes. The hold she had on his attention was unnerving. Everything else just faded into the background.

"What?" she asked, noticing his stare.

He wasn't going to say anything stupid and ruin the moment. He'd planned on letting this thing, this attraction or whatever it was, just evolve naturally. But the evening was going so quickly, and he felt compelled to get his thoughts out while he still had the chance. Too soon the night would be over, and if he didn't say it now, he might never say it. "Has this ever happened to you before?"

"What?"

People were drifting off the dance floor, but they didn't move. He gestured back and forth between them. "This thing between us. I'm not sure what it is. Chemistry, maybe? It happened the moment I saw you across the street at the pizza parlor right before you went into Bellemont. We had a connection." More than a connection. It was a recognition. He'd felt an attraction to her at first sight, something that confounded him. Even though they hadn't known each other very long, he had a good sense of who she was. He knew her. Everything she said and did struck him as being just right. Even her worrying was adorable.

Out of nowhere, he was hit with a sudden realization: Greta Hansen was his someone.

She blushed and said, "I'm not sure what you mean."

Her blush contradicted her words. Dalton was fairly certain she knew exactly what he meant, but he resisted the urge to press the issue. A moment later when the music started up, she stepped forward and put her arm on his shoulder, and once again they were dancing.

CHAPTER THIRTY-THREE

When Dalton asked if this had ever happened to her before, she couldn't believe it. For an instant, she couldn't think straight and just blurted out, "What?" Then when he clarified what he meant, she was even more stunned, because he was describing exactly what she'd felt. It was like having a dream about someone and finding out they'd dreamed the exact same thing.

Unlikely.

Uncanny.

Unbelievable.

Things like this didn't happen to Greta. She was the quiet girl, the one who didn't like to be the center of attention. She never put herself out there, not if she could help it. Jacey once had asked why she always looked so weighted down. One winter night as they crossed campus, she'd made Greta practice walking with swagger. "Wear the coat! Don't let the coat wear you," she yelled as Greta did her best to strut with confidence. Both of them had laughed so hard, they had to stop to catch their breath. Greta could do it in practice, when just Jacey was looking, but in everyday life, she fell back into her old ways.

Did she give off an unapproachable vibe? She thought that might be the case. When she went to bars with friends, sometimes she was the only one not approached by a guy. Or else she was the leftover girl in the group, the one stuck talking to the leftover guy. At times like that, she really thought she would die old and alone. Not that being single was so terrible, but the not knowing was killer. She could live fifty more years, and it would be nice to know what to expect.

She was never one to believe in love at first sight, even for other people. Jacey loved telling the story of how she'd spotted her boyfriend on the other side of a crowded bar. They'd locked eyes, and that was it. She said he was the one. When Greta had asked how she'd known, she'd said she just did. At the time, Greta had thought it was drunken wish fulfillment, but now she was willing to concede it might be true.

Oh, why had she been such an idiot? He'd taken a risk asking if she'd felt a connection too, and in return, she'd told him she didn't know what he meant. She did know what he meant. She was just caught off guard because it seemed too good to be true.

She clung to him as the music played, wishing and hoping that she hadn't messed things up between them. On the strains of the violins, questions floated through her mind. How could she feel such a pull for a man she knew nothing about? What if he were really only interested in Cece and using her to gain access? It wasn't that far-fetched an idea. Cece was a woman in demand, while Greta was her not-so-in-demand cousin. Maybe he'd noticed her noticing him and decided to play off her interest in order to get closer to Cece.

These were the doubts running through her brain. She knew what she hoped to be true. She just didn't know if she could allow herself to believe it.

When the music stopped, they paused, waiting for the next song, and then when it started up, they continued dancing. With Dalton holding on to more than half of her worry, she let her concerns melt away. What the hell. Life was too short to overthink everything.

After the fourth or fifth song, or maybe even longer, she glanced back at their table. "Where's Cece?" She looked up at Dalton, who surveyed the room.

"I don't know," he said.

She let go of his hand and broke away from his hold. A second earlier, she'd memorized the feel of his hand resting on her waist and wished the song would last forever, but now she could kick herself for not being more vigilant. The dancing had been so wonderful, she'd let her guard down. She went to the table, looking for some clue as to where Cece might have gone, but there was nothing. She turned to a group of people nearby. "Do you know where Cece and Roger went?"

A tall woman with silvery white hair cascading over her shoulders shook her head. "I didn't see."

Dalton caught up to her. "Don't panic. She probably went to the restroom."

Greta whirled around. "Both of them? What are the chances?"

"You saw how Roger was with her. I wouldn't put it past him to follow her into the ladies' room."

She got out her phone and texted: Where are you? Before Cece could respond, Greta punched in her number to call, but she didn't pick up. Greta listened to her cousin's voice mail and scanned the room for signs of either of them, but they'd simply vanished. "She's just gone," she said to Dalton. She had one responsibility that night. All she needed to do was keep Cece safe, and she'd failed.

"Let's not panic," Dalton said. "We'll find them. They couldn't have gone far."

They couldn't have gone far. Famous last words.

He suggested they each take half of the ballroom and walk through, searching and asking if anyone had seen Cece along the way. "They all know who she is," he said. "And even if they didn't, it would be hard to miss that dress." After they got through the ballroom, he said they'd check out the bathrooms.

"And then what?" Greta asked.

"Then we can panic."

Greta covered every square foot of her half of the ballroom, asking about Cece as she went. Several people had witnessed Cece and Roger leaving the room, but no one knew where they had gone. When she reached the doors on the far side, Dalton was waiting for her. She could tell from his expression and the slow shake of his head that he didn't have any luck either. They went silently to the bathrooms, each of them heading into their respective rooms. "Cece," Greta called out, leaning over to check out the shoes in the stall.

"She's not here." The voice came from behind stall number three. The door swung open, and out stepped a petite redhead with a tattoo of a phoenix across one shoulder. "She and that guy with the glasses left."

"Left the building?"

"Yeah. I heard her say she was bored." She snapped open her purse and pulled out a lipstick, then sashayed to the mirror.

"Did she say where they were going?"

"Not a clue." She deftly applied her lipstick, then blotted her lips with a tissue. "I heard her say something about going wild, and then they ran out laughing. Believe me when I say Leah Ann will not be happy that her star guest ducked out so early."

Greta dashed out the swinging bathroom door, almost running into Dalton. "A guy overheard them talk about hitting some bars," he said, all in a rush. "Fifteen minutes ago."

"A girl in there said Cece said something about going wild." She checked her phone again. Still no response. "We need to find them."

"Let's go down to street level and see if anyone saw them walking or getting into a cab." He touched the small of her back as they walked quickly down the hall. They heard piano music coming from the bar area. Someone was loudly playing a blues song. The double doors were wide open. Looking in, they saw the room was empty except for a bartender at each station, and Michael, who sat at the grand piano, fingers flying over the keys, his entire body getting into the music.

He was, Greta realized with a start, an incredibly good piano player. She rushed to his side and tapped his arm. "Michael!"

He shook his head and continued to play, giving the keys a workout. The expression on his face was pure bliss.

"Michael!" Now she raised her voice, yelling over the music. "I'm looking for Cece. She left with a guy named Roger. Do you know where they went?"

His brow furrowed, and he shook his head, but he didn't stop playing.

"Do you know where she'd go if she said she wanted to go bar hopping?"

It was as if he hadn't even heard her. He leaned in even more, merging with the music.

Dalton stepped forward and slammed a hand on the far end of the keys, making a discordant sound and breaking the spell. Michael stopped and looked up in annoyance. "Why did you have to do that? I was almost done."

"Dude, could you stop for a minute and answer Greta's questions?"

Michael said, "What would you like to know?"

She tried again. "Did you know that Cece left with some guy named Roger?"

He nodded. "They came to me. I gave them the keys to the limo. They didn't want me to drive. She said I should stay and enjoy myself." He lifted a cocktail glass off the top of the piano and took a sip. "I don't know where they went."

"Where did you park the limo?"

"On the street. Down a block or two." Michael squinted and pointed. "That way. Or maybe that way." He put a fist to his chin. "No, wait, I'm pretty sure it was that way."

"Thanks," Greta said, motioning to Dalton.

They took the elevator down to the first floor. "Does the limo have a GPS that can be tracked?" Dalton asked as the doors opened.

"Probably," she said. "But how would we track it? I don't think you can randomly track other people's vehicles. And I think the vehicle would have to be reported as stolen or something, and we can't do that. It doesn't even belong to us."

"Maybe we can see them outside and catch up with them."

The doorman pointed down the street to the right when they asked if he'd noticed which way Cece Vanderhaven had gone, and the uniformed valet standing by the curb confirmed it. Dalton and Greta stood on the sidewalk, staring in that direction. The velvet ropes and red carpet from earlier in the evening were gone, and so were the admiring crowds.

They walked in that direction, scanning the streets for the limo. When they'd gotten half a mile away, it seemed time to admit defeat. "This is where the trail runs cold," Dalton said. "Unless we happen to see the limo drive by, I can't think of any way we can find them."

Above Greta's head, an imaginary light bulb flicked on and she said, "I know a way."

CHAPTER THIRTY-FOUR

Greta whipped out her phone. "For years, I've been following Cece on social media. I know every account, every hashtag, every nickname." She peered down at the screen, tapping away.

"You think she's posting?" It seemed to Dalton that Cece was more into laughing it up with Roger than updating her status.

"Not her." Greta tucked her hair back behind one ear. "Other people. Usually, you can literally follow her movements just by doing a search. It's up to the minute, in real time. And then other people share or retweet or whatever."

Dalton stood so close, he could have rested his chin on her head. "What are you planning to do when you find her?"

"Hopefully bring her home before she does anything to seriously mess up the Firstborn Daughter image." She scrolled with her thumb, dismissing images taken earlier in the evening.

Edging in closer, Dalton looked over her shoulder. "That's a good one of you. You look gorgeous." He pointed to a photo of her with Cece. It had been taken in front of the building, right after Cece had introduced her as her cousin and said, "Isn't she beautiful?"

"Hmmm."

"You disagree?"

Greta wasn't sure if she agreed or not; she was too busy focusing on her current mission. "I found her," Greta said, showing him the screen. "Someone who goes by Parky4U spotted Cece with a 'cute nerd type' at a place called Marcie's."

Dalton hadn't heard of Marcie's, but from the photo, it looked like a dive bar. Roger and Cece were at a table in the corner, Cece sitting on his lap. There were shots of a cherry-colored liquor lined up in front of them, and Cece had one glass in her hand. Other people clustered around the edges of the photo. It looked like they were cheering her on.

Two images later, Cece was dancing on top of the bar next to Roger, who appeared to be clapping. They'd packed a lot of fun into a short period of time. "I guess we're heading to Marcie's," Dalton said.

One cab ride later, Greta and Dalton were heading into Marcie's, which turned out to be as classy as it looked in the photos. Going inside was like walking into a cave. They had to give their eyes time to adjust, and once they did, they could see the whole place at a glance. No sign of Cece and Roger, although the table in the corner matched the photos they'd seen online, complete with abandoned shot glasses. "Let me ask," Dalton said to Greta, who looked distraught.

"Okay."

Dalton went up to the edge of the bar. "Excuse me?" He waved to get the bartender's attention.

"Yeah." He pulled down a handle to fill a beer mug.

"Cece Vanderhaven and the dark-haired guy who was with her. Any idea where they went?"

He shook his head, tipping the mug to crown it with the proper amount of foam. "A cop came in and said they couldn't park the limo out front, so they took off. Too bad, because that's the most excitement we've had in a long time."

He set the beer in front of a dark-haired woman. She took a sudden interest in Dalton. "Are you someone famous too?"

"No."

"Huh." She took a pull of beer. "Too bad. You look like a sexy penguin in that suit."

"Thanks."

He got back to Greta and said, "They left. You'll have to do your search magic and see if you can find out where they went." He hated that she looked so sad and guilty, but in all honesty, he didn't care where Cece had gone. He just liked hanging out with Greta. He'd chase Cece all over the city if it meant he could spend more time with her cousin.

CHAPTER THIRTY-FIVE

Eventually, Greta got a new lead on Cece's whereabouts. According to soccermom685 on Instagram, Cece and an "unidentified geeky guy" had just arrived at the Crazy Night Karaoke Bar. Judging by the photo, Greta and Dalton agreed that the place looked like it was frequented by married couples out for date night. Greta had to give it to Cece; she was trying new things, the kinds of things Greta had never seen her do before. Slumming it at a karaoke lounge.

With no cabs in sight, they decided to request an Uber. They stood outside on the sidewalk waiting for their ride, watching as cars whizzed past. Occasionally, someone would walk by, or go in or out of the bar, and they'd step aside to get out of the way. Even in her worried state, Greta relished being here. There was something about New York, an energy and diversity she'd never experienced anywhere else before. New York wasn't her home, but it was an excellent place to be.

She found herself looking at Dalton and admiring the firm line of his jaw, the wavy hair that fell past his collar. She committed his mannerisms to memory—the casual way he ran his hand through his hair, lips pressed together in thought, the tap of one foot. None of it was extraordinary, but combined in total, it made up who he was.

Dalton caught her staring and told her, "You're a good cousin and a great friend."

She felt her cheeks flush at the not-entirely-deserved compliment. As concerned as she'd been about Cece, she hadn't been thinking about her for the last few minutes. "Thank you."

"You two must be really close. Did you grow up together?"

"Actually, we just met the other day."

"No!" He seemed genuinely surprised.

"It's true. We're second cousins, and we'd never met until recently. I only knew of her from her family's Christmas card photos, and then when she became a celebrity, I heard about her like everyone else did." Like everyone else if they were slightly obsessed with Cece Vanderhaven.

He whistled in disbelief. "I never would have guessed. You seem like such close friends. She so clearly adores you."

"Oh, I don't know about that." Sheepishly, her gaze dropped to her shoes, the expensive shoes that were on loan for the evening. They'd gotten more street wear than intended; they'd be wrecked before the night was through.

"I do," he said adamantly. "I can tell she thinks the world of you. Believe me, most of the time, gorgeous women are catty to each other, but you two aren't like that. It's obvious you care about her, and she's definitely got your back."

Nice of him to say, except it was clear Cece didn't have her back, or she wouldn't have ditched her at the Forgotten Man Ball and made them follow her all around the city. If she were looking out for Greta, she'd have behaved herself tonight and saved her a lot of stress and worry.

Her mind shifted from their conversation about Cece and went back to the compliment, the one he'd slid in oh-so-casually, the one that made her flush with pleasure even as she tried not to show it. She had to ask. "Do you really think I'm gorgeous? Because I know Cece is, but I'm more on the average side. You're being nice, right? Be honest."

Some emotion Greta couldn't place flashed across his face. Confusion? Pity? She wasn't entirely sure.

"I wouldn't say it if I didn't think it," he said. "But it's not a matter of opinion. I've got eyes. It's a fact. You're clearly gorgeous." Two guys, biker dudes, approached, and when they were within earshot, he called out, "Would you say this woman is gorgeous?" His pointer finger curved down above her head.

"Hell yeah."

They were closer now, and she could see they each had a chain that ran from their belts to their back pockets. The larger of the two had a full beard. His smaller friend had a bandanna wrapped around his head.

"No doubt," the second one said approvingly. "Gorgeous!"

They kept going, and at the end of the block, the bigger one glanced back and grinned.

"Did you really have to do that?" Greta asked. Dalton had a way of throwing her off balance in the best possible way.

"Just making a point." He gestured in their direction. "If you can't trust those guys to tell the truth, who can you trust?"

"Okay, I'll admit I look pretty good tonight, but I had a whole team of people working on me." She tugged at the waist of the dress so it hugged her middle just above her hip bones. "You give the average girl a fabulous dress and professional hair and makeup, and she'll look completely different."

"You forget that I saw you before. You were gorgeous without all that extra stuff, and you're even gorgeouser now."

"*Gorgeouser* isn't a word." Greta gave his shoulder a gentle push, making him chuckle.

"Oh, but it is. It's the perfect word to describe you."

She knew from experience that guys would say anything to get on a woman's good side, but it didn't seem like he was trying to seduce her. At the ball, his hands hadn't strayed down to her backside, and he hadn't pressed against her in a way that made her feel uncomfortable.

He seemed interested in her but in a gentlemanly way. Were there still guys like that? She honestly didn't think he was using her to get to Cece; Dalton seemed so sincere. Greta leaned back against the building, her hands in her pockets, as happy as she'd ever been. Her cousin was still out of reach, out in the city somewhere. Most likely, this fiasco would cause her to lose her internship or get fired or whatever, but this night wasn't over, and already she would have said it was worth it. Even if nothing happened with Dalton, she'd come away with a great memory and an interesting story to tell.

Talking about professional hair and makeup reminded Greta of something ridiculous she used to do, and the buzz from the drinks she'd had earlier made her want to share. "Do you want to know a secret?" she asked.

"I always want to know a secret." He leaned in to listen.

"I probably shouldn't tell you this. You'll think less of me."

"Go on." His lips stretched into a wide smile.

"Our conversation reminded me of something I used to do in high school. It's just the worst thing I've ever done. You're going to think I'm terrible."

"Now I'm even more interested."

"Sometimes," she said, "when I was at work or school and I couldn't stand to be there anymore, I'd excuse myself to go to the bathroom, wash off all my makeup, and go back and say I was sick and I had to go. Every single time, some guy would tell me that I looked awful, that I really needed to go home and get some rest." He was laughing now. "Seriously. They'd say I looked terrible. That's how much of a difference it makes. Without makeup, guys would think I had the bubonic plague."

"Please, stop." Still laughing, he leaned over, his hands on his knees.

"You don't believe me?"

He straightened up and composed himself before answering. "I'm not doubting your experience; I just think it's absolutely adorable that you consider this the worst thing you've ever done. What's the second worst thing? Sometimes you don't recycle? Occasionally you drive five miles over the speed limit?"

"I know it doesn't sound like a big deal," Greta said. "But for me, it was. I always felt terrible about lying. I made a decision a few years ago that I wanted to be the kind of person who is honest and has integrity. I try to be kind and caring. At the end of my life, I want to know that I made a difference, you know? In a good way."

He nodded thoughtfully and said, "I understand." As their driver pulled up to take them to the karaoke bar, he reached for her hand and said, "Greta, I have to tell you that in my whole life, I've never met anyone like you."

His smile told her it was a compliment.

CHAPTER THIRTY-SIX

When the car pulled up in front of the Crazy Night Karaoke Bar, Dalton dug in his pocket for some cash and tipped the driver. "I've got this," he said before Greta could add a tip using the app. True, he was posing as a homeless person and couldn't afford to part with much money, but he was also a guy hanging out with a beautiful woman. It felt like they were on a date, even if that wasn't technically the case, and he hated being a freeloader. It wasn't who he was. He was a good guy, one who didn't like to impose or take advantage of other people. Greta nodded, and Dalton got out first, giving her a hand to help her over the curb.

Halfway down the block, they saw the limo. Whoever had driven it had tried parallel parking into a space along the curb, decided there wasn't enough room, then just given up and left it on the street sticking out at an angle. Ingenious, but so wrong.

The lounge was old-school, plush booths along the back with café tables filling the space between the booths and the stage. A stage by definition only, more of a small platform with a monitor to display the lyrics, and a microphone in a traditional stand. Cece stood in the spotlight, her hand wrapped around the base of the microphone, singing in a breathy Marilyn Monroe voice. The song was "Unforgettable," and she was a sight, there in her white dress, the stage light reflecting off her necklace and earrings. She was old Hollywood glamour and New York contemporary fashion, all rolled into one. She saw them walk in, and her expression changed from utmost concentration to one of sheer delight. She stopped singing, waved, and said, "Everybody, meet my cousin Greta and Dalton, a friend of ours. He's a good man."

Cece went back to singing, and the crowd turned to look, some of them shouting their names.

"Hey, cousin Greta!"

"Good man Dalton!"

"Welcome, you two!"

"Hello, beautiful cousin!"

"Hi, Dalton!"

Their initial assessment of the crowd as middle-aged people out on date night appeared to be spot-on, but what the audience lacked in cool, they made up for in enthusiasm. Dalton waved in response to their cheers while Greta, who also waved, managed to look embarrassed and pleased all at the same time.

They joined Roger at his table, and he stood up and enthusiastically shook Dalton's hand. "So glad you guys caught up to us," he said.

"Why did you leave without saying anything?" Greta asked as they sat down.

Roger shrugged. "Don't ask me; ask Cece. She said she wanted to forget the Forgotten Man Ball; the place was suffocating her. I asked about you guys, and she said you'd be fine, that you needed some alone time."

When Cece was done with the song, the room filled with the sound of clapping. Some of the crowd even whooped, and one guy pounded his feet. Cece bowed and smiled. "And now," she said, her mouth close to the microphone, "my darling cousin Greta and her date tonight, Dalton, will be singing a duet. Let's give it up for Greta and Dalton!"

The crowd went wild. At least as wild as that particular crowd could get. The guy who'd pounded his feet kept doing it, and everyone clapped, some of them yelling their names. Dalton looked at Greta as if to say, *What do you think?* and she shook her head, looking terrified, like she wanted the world to end right that minute.

Cece said, "I think Greta needs a show of support. Please, Greta? This is a friendly crowd. Let's give it up for Greta!"

Dalton stood up and reached out to take her hand. All around them people clapped and shouted.

"C'mon, Greta!"

"Please, Greta!"

"Greta, sing!"

The sound built to the point that it was just her name being chanted over and over again. "Greta! Greta! Greta! Greta!" She stood finally, not sure what else to do, and took Dalton's hand. They walked up to the stage, him leading, her lagging behind as if she were debating making a run for it.

The steps to the platform were off to the side, and they climbed them together. Cece came to that side of the stage and grabbed Greta's other hand, towing them over to the mike stand. "I picked the best song for these two," Cece exclaimed. "'Perfect' by Ed Sheeran."

The crowd reacted as if this were their favorite song in the entire world and they couldn't believe their good luck in hearing Greta and Dalton sing it. Clapping, foot pounding, cheering, a tidal wave of sound came their way. Cece left the stage to join Roger, and Dalton squeezed Greta's hand to show her it was going to be fine. As the music began and the audience settled down, he leaned over and whispered, "They are *so* drunk," which made her smile.

Dalton took the lead in singing the song, knowing Greta wasn't quite ready yet. After the first few words, he relaxed, knowing he didn't sound too bad. He was able to hold a tune, nothing fancy, but he'd been good enough in eighth grade to get a solo during one all-school assembly. Luckily for them, Cece had picked a song that required more emotion than vocal ability. People in the audience were singing along, which took the pressure off as well. He got through the first verse, and when it came time to sing the chorus, Greta still looked shell-shocked, so he kept going.

Singing the lyrics, it was easy to feel like this song was written specifically for him and Greta. The lines about finding a beautiful and sweet girl, dancing in each other's arms, and seeing the future in each other's eyes perfectly encapsulated their experience that evening. That Cece was a crafty one. How had she known?

Greta relaxed, and her eyes glittered with tears as she squeezed his hand. Just when it looked like he might be singing the whole song by himself, she jumped in and took the next line. Her voice was soft and wobbled a bit, but she sounded pretty good. Her eyes were locked on his, like she wanted to ignore the fact that fifty people were watching them.

"Louder!" came a yell from in back.

"We can't hear you!"

Greta sang more loudly, and when it came to the chorus, they did it together. Nothing complicated, no harmonizing, just Dalton and Greta holding hands and singing perfectly in sync. At the end, she brought it home, doing the final line solo and wrapping up the song, then grinning at Dalton.

When they finished, Dalton felt the kind of endorphin rush people get when they reach the top of Mount Everest. He was overjoyed, not for him but for Greta, who'd started off afraid but then rose to the occasion and totally nailed it. Over the course of the evening, he'd shared her anxiety and her joy. Funny how easy it was for him to read her frame of mind. He'd dated women for months and hadn't felt as in sync with them as he did with her.

When the room erupted into applause, they bowed, and then unexpectedly, Greta threw her arms around him and kissed him on the cheek. It took him by surprise, but looking out into the audience, he glimpsed Cece, who was smiling broadly. From her satisfied expression, the kiss didn't surprise her at all.

CHAPTER THIRTY-SEVEN

Nothing Greta had done that day was in character. Never in her life could she have dreamed of a scenario that would require her to get glammed up and attend a charity event with debutantes. In the short time she'd been in New York, she'd tried new things, met new people, and taken chances she never would have taken at home. Throwing her arms around a man she barely knew and kissing him on the cheek was a pretty innocent thing to do, something most women wouldn't think twice about, but it wasn't a Greta Hansen thing to do. She usually had to think about things for a long time, consider all the details, weigh all the possibilities. Greta, impulsive? Never. Follow her heart? She wanted to, but she wasn't that bold.

She wasn't the kind of person who'd jump in the pool of love without at least dipping a toe in first.

So why did she wrap her arms around Dalton and kiss him? She didn't honestly know. Maybe it was the alcohol kicking in, or maybe she just got caught up in the moment. Or perhaps—and this is the one reason that rang true to her—it was because he'd opened his heart to her first. What had he called it? *This thing between us.* An irresistible magnetic pull felt by both of them.

As they stepped down off the stage, Dalton still holding her hand, she saw that Cece was now surrounded by people taking selfies and asking her questions. An older man took the stage, reading off the next singer's name. "Amy Cooper from South Orange, New Jersey, is going to entertain us by singing Neil Diamond's 'Sweet Caroline'!" he announced. As Amy got up from her chair, it occurred to Greta that she and Dalton had jumped the line. If anyone minded, she didn't notice.

While Amy bounded up to the stage, Greta went straight to their table to retrieve her cousin. Cece had succeeded in having an unconventional night of fun without doing anything too outrageous, and if they went home now, it might still be okay. She pushed through the row of admirers and interrupted. "Cece, do you mind if we go?"

Her sweet face looked up, puzzled. "Go where?"

"Back to your apartment. I think I've had enough for the night." She put her fingertips to her forehead as if she had a headache. Not a lie, exactly.

"Oh no." She looked so sad that Greta felt a little guilty, but an instant later, Cece smiled when a woman came over for a selfie. After the flash went off, Cece got back to Greta. "Of course we can go," she said, standing. To those around her, she said, "I'm sorry, but I have to leave. My cousin is feeling sick."

Roger and Dalton got the cue and helped shepherd Cece out of the lounge. Navigating through the crowd, the three of them formed a protective circle, surrounding her while she smiled and waved. As they headed out the door onto the sidewalk, they heard Amy belt out, "So good, so good!" during the instrumental part of her song.

A few minutes later, they were inside the limo, Roger at the wheel and Cece next to him, giving him directions back to her place. "Can you believe I've never driven anything this large before?" he said, pulling out of the space.

A few stray people had followed them out of the club and were leaning on the car, so he edged forward slowly. As he drove through the city, Cece opened her window and stuck her arm out, waving like she was in a parade. "Hello, beautiful people!" she yelled to pedestrians as they drove past. "Hello, night sky! Hello, New York City, best city in the whole world! Hello, people on the sidewalk! I love you all."

Dalton leaned in, his lips almost to Greta's ear. "See, it all worked out. And you were so worried."

It would have been impossible for her not to smile. The only negative was that once the night was over and they were back at the apartment, Dalton would be changing into his regular clothes and leaving. She wasn't too worried about it, though. It was late, and they'd been drinking. Maybe she could suggest that he crash at Cece's for the night? There was no shortage of guest rooms, and with Mr. and Mrs. Vanderhaven in Europe, there was no one there to object. They would have time together, plenty of time, and soon he could explain why he was voluntarily, temporarily homeless. There had to be a good reason.

Cece turned around. "How do you feel, Greta?"

"I think I'm going to be fine," she said. "I don't know what was wrong. It might have just been the noise in the lounge that got to me."

"I'm so glad you feel better." She turned back to Roger, and they chatted about something Greta couldn't quite hear.

Dalton's hand rested over hers, his thumb caressing her knuckles while he alternated between smiling at her and glancing out the window. "Roger!" he called out suddenly. "We went past it."

"It's okay!" Cece called back. "Now that Greta feels better, I thought we could drive through Central Park before we go home." She turned back to Roger. "Katrina and Vance would never let me go anywhere that wasn't approved ahead of time. And it will be fun for Greta too. She's never been to the park."

Greta felt a knot of anxiety. "I don't know about this," she said to Dalton.

"It's going to be okay, Greta," he whispered. "I'm pretty sure Central Park is closed to traffic at night. We'll get to a barricade and have to turn back."

But they never reached the barricade, because after Roger turned on Fifty-Ninth Street, Cece pointed. "Just park here, and we can walk." She called back to them, "Central Park at night! I can hear Vance now." Her voice deepened. "Maybe another day, Cece. We don't have time on the schedule for that." She laughed, delighted with herself. "Ha! Now I have my own schedule."

At the sound of her cousin's jubilation, Greta relaxed. Cece was like a caged bird finally set loose. Only someone who was pretty coldhearted would deny her this taste of freedom.

At that moment, she decided to give up trying to protect her cousin's carefully crafted image. Cece was an adult and knew what she wanted. If her parents and the Vanderhaven Corporation didn't like her choices, that was their issue. Greta was ready to stop being her babysitter and start being her friend.

Dalton leaned in. "We'll keep a close eye on her. It'll be okay." He spoke with quiet and sincere concern.

"I know." She patted his hand. "Whatever happens, it'll be fine."

Ahead of them, a horse and carriage pulled away from the curb. The driver, wearing a top hat, sat tall in his seat. A young couple sat in the back, their heads close together. As the horses clopped off, Roger pulled into the newly available space.

Dalton said, "I don't think you can park here," but by the time he got to the end of his sentence, Cece had already opened the door and was out of the vehicle.

"I think we should just go with it," Greta said, lifting the handle and scrambling out. When Dalton joined her, Cece and Roger were already running ahead, carefree as kids. Without saying a word, she and Dalton followed. He took her hand, and a lightness washed over her, a burden lifted. She was young and carefree, enjoying the best city in the world. A good-looking guy was at her side, giving her admiring glances, something that never happened. The weather was perfect too. Now that the sun had set, it was cooler. If none of this was real, if she woke up tomorrow and was in trouble for going off script with Cece, or if it turned out that Dalton was a scam artist or even a not-so-nice guy, so be it. That was tomorrow's problem. Tonight, she was living in the moment, and that moment was the absolute best.

They hurried to keep up with Cece and Roger, who'd briskly run ahead, down some steps, and then turned onto a path paralleling a large body of water. She marveled at how quickly Cece could move while wearing stilettos, because the heels of her own shoes weren't nearly as high and her feet were torturing her. As if reading her mind, Dalton said, "I have no idea how you're moving so fast in those shoes."

"It's not easy," Greta said. Her tone was lighthearted, even as her feet protested.

When Cece and Roger slowed and veered off the path, stepping onto some rocks that jutted over the water, Greta took the opportunity to stop thirty feet behind them. "Let's give them a moment to look at the lake," she said.

"It's actually a pond."

"A pond." It was larger than any pond she'd ever seen. "Really, it's a pond? You're not joking?" The water shimmered from the light of the moon, the surface calm. "That's one big pond."

"The Central Park Lake is even bigger. The most beautiful night sky I ever saw was when I was standing on the Bow Bridge. You can get a great view of the city after dark there. I'll show it to you the next time there's a full moon."

To Greta, it sounded like a date. "I'd like that." She still didn't know anything about Dalton, really. Didn't know if he had siblings or what type of music he liked or what sports teams he followed. All she knew was what was right in front of her. It was entirely possible he was misrepresenting himself, but somehow, she didn't think so. In her heart, she thought she knew him. Wishful thinking? Maybe. But she was ready for wishful thinking, ready to take the leap. She heard Cece laugh, the kind of deep-bellied laughter that can't be kept back, and the sound punctuated her own elation.

Greta crooked her finger and beckoned for Dalton to come closer. When he did, she pulled on his lapels until their faces aligned. They lingered that way for a second, or maybe a fraction of a second, or maybe an eternity, his eyes searching hers, both of them wanting the same thing, and then she broke the spell. She kissed him, and he kissed her back. When he pulled back for a moment, cupping her face in his hands, he gave her an appreciative look of surprise, which might have made her laugh, except he came right back for more, and she was too busy kissing him to do anything else. She closed her eyes, and the universe spiraled toward them, narrowing and narrowing until they were at the epicenter of everything, all of time leading up to that moment, every star in the sky existing to shine upon the two of them. Glorious.

And then, a miracle. She didn't envy Cece anymore, a habit of a lifetime gone in a moment. Ever since she was a little girl, she'd thought her cousin had the perfect life, but she'd found that appearances could be deceiving, and now she wouldn't trade places with Cece for anything.

Turned out, being Greta Hansen suited her just fine.

Roger laughed, and the sound echoed across the water. She was glad for them but happier for herself.

Dalton pulled her closer. As if on cue, the wind gusted, lifting the hem of her dress and blowing her hair, like she was the lead in a romantic movie. It was all so perfect.

A possible future appeared before her. A life she never even could have imagined presented itself, unfolding before her eyes. She could see them together, now and forever, traveling, getting married, having kids, laughing and loving. Getting old with Dalton by her side. She saw memories of the future, a montage of shared experiences, glimpses of everything that could be.

Her thoughts were interrupted by a rush of people heading their way. She would have kept going with the kissing, honestly. She stopped to look only because Dalton did.

Turning, they saw a thundering herd, eight or nine people running, cell phones in hand. All of them were young—teenagers or slightly older. When the crowd spotted them, one of the girls yelled, "I told you that was Cece's limo! That girl was with her at the ball."

Another voice rang out, asking, "Where's Cece?"

Dalton pulled her aside, and the whole group, having spotted Cece and Roger ahead, suddenly forgot about them and ran past. Greta's worry knot came back with a vengeance.

Reflexively, she took off after them, knowing a group of people running crazily and yelling Cece's name meant something was about to happen to her. And it couldn't be good.

CHAPTER THIRTY-EIGHT

Greta and Dalton saw the crowd of teenagers enthusiastically ambush Cece. The suddenness of their appearance seemed to take the couple by surprise. Not thinking, Roger stepped out of their way, deferring to the group. They were a boisterous bunch, crowding in to take video and selfies with the pond in the background, admiring Cece's dress, and asking her questions.

"I love you, Cece!" one of the girls shouted.

"Why weren't you at Vance and Katrina's wedding? Did you guys have a fight or something?"

"I have so many dresses from your clothing line, and I wear your perfume too!"

"This way, Cece! Smile!"

"Would you mind leaving a message on my friend Carver's phone?"

Dalton would have thought this kind of thing was commonplace to Cece, that she would have encountered curious, adoring fans everywhere she went, but the stunned look on her face said otherwise. She didn't answer any of their questions, and she flinched with every flash, looking around, as if searching for an out. As they crowded nearer, she stepped back. In response, they got even closer, and she backed up again.

Anticipating what was about to happen, Greta yelled, "Cece, no, stop!" so loudly that her voice echoed off the water. Hearing her cousin's warning, Cece turned to look at Greta just before she stumbled backward, her arms flailing as she went. She fell in with a loud splash, and the teenagers cried out as they rushed to the edge to look down.

Greta charged ahead, taking off her shoes as she went and randomly tossing them, then stepping in and sloshing through the water. Dalton hesitated for only a second before following her, wading in with his shoes still on. Cece was underwater, just under the surface, her arms splayed out, hair floating like a halo around her head. The water was shallow, no more than three or four feet, but she didn't struggle to get up, just lay there until Greta crouched down and lifted her from underneath. Cece gasped and coughed, then turned her head to one side and spit out some brackish water. All the while, Greta murmured, "You're okay, you're okay. I'm here. You're fine."

From the shore, Roger yelled, "Should I call 911?"

No one answered. Slowly, Greta helped Cece to a standing position, then brushed her hair away from her face. She whispered something, and Cece nodded yes. Dalton came and helped Greta walk Cece to shore.

When they got out of the water and onto dry land, Greta addressed the teenagers standing in their way, still taking pictures. "What is wrong with you people? Back off!"

The crowd retreated far enough to let them move past. Roger came and put his jacket around Cece's shoulders. Dalton did the same for Greta, who nodded and said, "Thank you."

Roger said, "Are you okay? Do you want to go to the hospital?"

Cece wiped off her wet brow and shook her head. "No, I'm fine."

"Let's get you home," Greta said, still guiding her. Dalton gathered up Greta's shoes, noticing the strap had broken on one. Maybe she wouldn't ever wear them again, but he didn't want the teenagers to grab them as souvenirs.

When they got to the limo, they ignored the looks of the tourists coming and going from their carriage rides and climbed in without a word. Roger got behind the wheel, and Cece sat up front next to him. Greta shook her head, guilt and worry written across her face. "It could have happened even if you had been standing right next to her," Dalton said.

She shook her head. "No, that's not true. I wouldn't have let it happen. I should have been with her."

They were about two blocks away from the park, stopped at a traffic light, when Dalton looked out the window and saw him on the sidewalk. Matt, sitting with his back to a building, his cardboard sign propped up alongside him. His eyes were half-shut, like he was dozing off. "Give me a second," Dalton said, opening the car door. "I have to talk to that guy."

He trotted over to Matt and crouched down to his level. His baseball cap with only a few coins inside sat next to the sign. Sweat beaded on his forehead, and his skin was pasty white. "Matt, buddy, are you okay?"

His eyes flicked open and then shut. He mumbled something unintelligible. Pedestrians walked by, barely glancing their way. Clearly he was out of it, so something was wrong. Dalton didn't smell alcohol, but that didn't mean he wasn't drunk or on drugs. "Did you get my message from Trisha at the park? Did she tell you to call Ellie?"

"What?"

Behind them, the sound of car horns blared. He turned to see the light had turned green and the limo was blocking traffic.

Cece lowered the window. "Dalton, we have to go."

"Go without me," he yelled, gesturing for the limo to go forward. "I'll catch up later."

From the sidewalk, a woman shouted, "That's Cece Vanderhaven!" Heads turned, and a few people darted toward the vehicle. Before they were able to reach it, Cece had raised the window. A few seconds later, the limo took off.

CHAPTER THIRTY-NINE

The mystery of Dalton deepened when he suddenly bolted out of the limo to talk to some guy sitting on the sidewalk. Greta hadn't even noticed the homeless man because she was too caught up in her own problems: Cece's distress, her own sopping-wet clothing, and their urgent need to go back to the Vanderhavens' apartment to get cleaned up.

Dalton had told her he wasn't actually homeless, so how was it he was friends with this guy who clearly was? He'd dashed out of the limo like this guy was his best friend. Greta's mind churned with possibilities: They'd served in the military together, or maybe they were actors doing research for a role. Or maybe he really was homeless due to mental illness or an addiction. She didn't want to think that last possibility could be true, but she didn't know what else to think.

Greta turned to look back at Dalton, who, still in his wet tuxedo pants, dress shirt, and bow tie, was now crouched on the sidewalk. She saw him put his hand on the man's forehead, the way a parent would to a sick child. It was the kind of gesture you'd bestow on a family member or good friend. Someone you truly cared about.

Under different circumstances, she would have been tempted to get out of the limo to join Dalton, but she was soaked to the skin and didn't want to abandon her cousin. Dalton knew where she lived, and his well-worn backpack was still there. If he wanted to, he could find her.

The limo barreled forward, leaving Dalton behind.

CHAPTER FORTY

When Cece called out from the limo, Dalton made a split-second decision. He couldn't be in two places at once, so he decided to stay with Matt. He'd spent hours looking for him all over New York City, and having located him at last, he wasn't going to lose him again. Also, from up close, it was evident something was seriously wrong with Matt. Dalton couldn't leave him.

Parting from Greta killed him. He felt like they'd had a major emotional connection, and here he'd abandoned her when she needed help dealing with Cece. He didn't really have a choice, though.

He turned back to Matt. "Hey, Matt, remember me? Dalton? We talked just a few days ago?"

With great effort, Matt murmured something hard to decipher. Dalton thought he caught his own name, but it was hard to tell for sure.

"Matt, are you okay? You don't look so good, buddy." Matt's head lolled to one side like he was having trouble controlling his muscles. It was a summer evening and the air was warm, but even so, the amount of perspiration on his face was excessive. Dalton put a hand on his forehead and was shocked at how hot he was. Matt was burning up with fever.

He called out to those walking past. "This man is sick. Can I get some help here?" No one paid any attention.

"Please? Can anyone help me?"

A couple with a baby in a stroller came by, and as they went past, the guy said, "Sorry, dude."

He stood up when a young woman approached and said, "Can I use your phone to call 911? My friend is seriously sick. He needs an ambulance."

She stopped in her tracks. "Oh no! What happened?"

"I'm not sure. He's not responsive, and he has a high fever. I'd call myself, but I had a run-in with the Central Park pond." Dalton gestured to his wet pants. "Turns out cell phones don't do well when they're wet."

"I hear you." She nodded sympathetically while unzipping her purse and taking out her phone. "I dropped a cell phone in a puddle once, and that rice thing didn't work for me at all." Pressing her thumb to the bottom, she unlocked it, then handed it to him.

"Thank you. I can't tell you how much I appreciate this." Dalton dialed 911 and filled the operator in when she asked, "What's your emergency?"

The owner of the cell phone, whom he learned was named Rachel, waited with him until the ambulance arrived. Once they got Matt on a gurney and started assessing him, Dalton looked to thank her again, but she had simply vanished. Nowhere in sight. An angel impersonating a regular human being? Or maybe a human being acting as an angel. Either way, he was glad she'd arrived at the right moment.

When they got to the hospital emergency room, he became Matt's voice and advocate, telling them his name, age, and marital status. He also knew that he was a US veteran who'd served in Afghanistan, had PTSD, and had been homeless for several months. When Dalton explained that he didn't know him well, that they'd just met recently, they asked for contact information for his family. "I can't help you with that," he said, shaking his head. "But I know who can. His girlfriend's name is Ellie Fronk. I know her phone number." The day that Ellie had handed him her number written on a scrap of paper, he'd committed it to memory. He rattled it off now, and the nurse marked it down, saying they'd give her a call.

CHAPTER FORTY-ONE

After Roger left and Cece and Greta had each taken a shower, the cousins stayed up for hours talking, Cece on one side of her enormous bed, Greta on the other. In the dark, fueled by just the right amount of alcohol and exhaustion, Greta found that confidences could be easily shared.

They talked about Roger and Dalton, and how the whole evening had played out. Already the memory of her time with Dalton had a dreamlike feeling. Saying his name helped make him real.

"I can't believe I fell into the water," Cece said. "I just lost my footing. So stupid of me."

"You seemed calm," Greta said. "When I got there, you were floating under the surface."

"It was so odd. I wasn't afraid at all. I was waiting."

"Waiting for what?"

"For you. I saw you coming my way. I knew you'd save me."

Cece knew she'd come and save her? How could she be so sure? Before she could ask, Cece started talking about something she did know all about—her childhood. "I used to love seeing your family's Christmas cards." Her voice floated in the dark. "I couldn't wait to see how much you and Travis had changed from the year before. I have all of them, still, in my dresser drawer."

"I loved looking at yours too, and my mom let me keep them all," Greta confessed. "We were boring compared to your family. You always had cool costumes or elegant clothing, and each year you had a different theme. Your family was so glamorous. I loved that."

Cece groaned. "I hated dressing up for those pictures. And it took hours for them to get just the right shot. We had to keep posing until my dad was happy."

"But look how great they turned out. That circus one was killer."

"That one was the *worst*. I was terrified of the clowns, and the fire-eater was this creepy guy. The circus ring smelled like dung."

"From the elephants?"

"No." Cece sighed. "The elephants were added later on. Photo manipulation. I guess the smell was left over from before." It was quiet for a minute, and then she said, "I always loved that your Christmas cards were the same. You always held that sign that said—"

Before she could say it, Greta cut in, saying, "We're still the Hansens!" They both burst out laughing. When they finally settled down, she said, "That was so lame."

"No!" Cece said, sounding indignant. "I thought it was cool. And your brother's sign always said, 'Merry Christmas and Happy New Year.' The same signs every year. I could count on it. You were always standing in front of the same tree, so I could see how much you grew since the last Christmas. I used to think about what it would be like to trade places with you."

"With me? Why would you want to do that?" Why would anyone want to do that? Her life was boring, mundane.

"You grew up with a brother, and I was the only one here, until Brenna was born. So that was one thing. And then I loved all the notes your mom sent with the cards. She was so proud of you and Travis. My mom and dad were gone all the time, and when they were around, all they talked about was how I could do better in school, or that I should be spending more hours practicing the piano. When my family came back from parties, we had meetings to discuss what I'd said and how I could improve. My dad has very high expectations. He wanted a daughter who was brilliant and beautiful and clever, but all he got was me."

"I think you're all those things. Everyone wants to be you or be near you or be your friend. I think you're perfect." There was silence on Cece's side of the bed, so Greta asked, "What did my mom's notes say about me?"

"Oh, they were *so* nice! She used to talk about how shy you were when you were little and how you worked to get past it. That she could see the fear in your eyes whenever you tried something new, but you did it anyway. Your mom really understands who you are."

Greta smiled. "Yeah, she does."

"Some of the notes mentioned clever things you said or did, like when you and your brother invented that game with the hose and the basketball hoop in your driveway."

"We called it Water Ball," she said, remembering. It wasn't much of a game, but they loved it. They'd set the nozzle on the spray setting and string it over the hoop. On hot days, there was nothing like a pickup game of Water Ball.

"We never had a driveway," Cece said, a little sadly. "That must be nice."

"It is until you have to shovel the snow off it."

"Your mom would write about how kind you were to kids who were being picked on at school. I thought that was heroic. She talked about when your high school swim team won at regionals, and you set a record for the front crawl."

That particular swim meet had been Greta's personal best. When she climbed out of the pool, she saw her parents in the bleachers, her mom totally losing it, jumping up and down, screaming her head off. "That record still stands, by the way."

"Oh, I remember another good one!" Cece said. "The year when you figured out that the anagram of Greta was the word *great*. Your mom said you were so pleased. Oh, I wished I had a cooler name then, one that could be twisted around into a word. That was the year this boy in my class used to follow me around whispering, 'Cece is a ree-ree.' It was awful."

"What a jerk," Greta said. "I always thought the name Cece Vanderhaven sounded so elegant."

They talked far into the night, telling each other stories about their lives. Despite Cece's lavish upbringing and Greta's own modest middle-class childhood, they weren't that far apart when it came to the important things.

"I always wanted to do something with my life that makes a difference," Greta said. "Otherwise, what's the point? Why even live and breathe and spend time on this planet?"

"If it makes you feel any better, you've already made a difference to me," Cece said.

"I'm glad." The pauses between each side of their conversation were getting longer. "Do you think I'll ever see Dalton again?" Only a few hours had passed, but the evening spent with him already felt distant.

"Absolutely."

"You seem pretty sure."

"I am *very* sure," Cece said confidently, her voice drowsy. Right before they drifted off to sleep, Cece said, "Didn't we have the best night ever?"

"Yes, we did," Greta said.

"Wasn't it smart of me to set you up with Dalton? I could tell the two of you had a thing for each other." There was a wink in her voice. "So I made him fall in love with you."

Falling asleep, Greta thought that between the two of them, Cece was definitely the more clever one. Would she ever see Dalton again? Oh, she hoped so.

CHAPTER FORTY-TWO

By the time Ellie and Mia arrived, the hospital staff had taken a sample of Matt's blood and run a few other tests, put him on oxygen, and gotten some intravenous fluids into him. They'd already decided to admit him, but he was still in the ER, waiting for both a room assignment and a diagnosis.

Dalton had told the hospital staff he was a friend, but one of the nurses corrected him. "It says here you're his cousin." She stared at him over the top of her glasses.

"No, I—" And then he got it. "Thank you for taking such good care of my cousin."

"It's what I do," she said gruffly, before checking Matt's vitals and moving on to the next patient.

When Ellie arrived, she rushed to the bed and crouched down to get close to Matt's face. "Matt? I'm here, baby. It's Ellie."

Matt had been completely out of it up until then, but at the sound of her voice, his eyes opened, and a smile tugged at the corners of his mouth. His voice croaked out something that sounded like her name. It obviously took great effort on his part.

"You don't have to say anything. I'm here." She pulled a chair alongside the bed, sat down, and reached over to stroke his hair. "Everything's going to be okay." Dalton got up and offered his chair to Mia.

They wanted to know where he'd found Matt and what the doctors had said, and he clued them in as best he could, but the dynamic had changed. He was an outsider now. Ellie and Mia had the love and personal connection covered, and the hospital staff was providing the medical care. Matt was in the best possible hands. Dalton still stuck around for a while, but once the doctor came up with a diagnosis of strep accompanied by dehydration and then started to get Matt ready to be transferred to a regular room, his work was done. "Can I call you to check and see how he's doing?" he asked Ellie.

"Sure." She got out her phone.

Dalton held up a hand. "I already have your number, but I don't have my phone on me right now. Can I borrow yours for a minute to make a quick call?"

She handed it over without a moment's hesitation. "Anything for the guy who helped me find Matt."

"Thanks. It'll just be a minute." He gestured to the doorway. "I'll step out into the hall to talk."

CHAPTER FORTY-THREE

Cece and Greta slept in the next day, or at least they tried to. They were awakened by Brenna, who'd crawled onto the bed, whispering her sister's name. From the doorway, Nanny quietly said, "I held her off as long as I could, but it's noon, and she's been worried about you." Nanny crept away, leaving Brenna behind.

"Cece?" Brenna's whisper was loud enough to wake the dead, or the hungover, in Greta's case. Her stomach wasn't a problem; it was her head doing the protesting. She couldn't speak for Cece.

"Yes?" Cece asked.

"Are you okay?" The blinds were partway down so the room was dimly lit, but she heard the concern in Brenna's voice. "I saw you fall in the water."

"You did?" Cece's voice had a sleepy quality. "Where did you see it?"

"It's all over the place. Nanny said I had to stop watching it online because it was making me upset. It looked like you drowned."

"No, honey, I'm fine. Better than fine. You know how I was afraid to go into water? I'm not so afraid anymore."

Brenna lay down next to her sister, and Greta heard them talk in the way only sisters could. She wasn't part of it, and it wasn't her business, but she listened anyway. They talked about the incident in the pool the day Cece had been pulled out unconscious and rushed to the hospital.

"I didn't mean to hit you in the head," Brenna said, sounding anguished. "I was just practicing my kicking. I'm sorry, Cece."

"Oh, baby, I know that. You don't have to keep apologizing. It was a long time ago, and it was just an accident. Accidents happen all the time. It was nobody's fault." Cece made soothing noises while she stroked her sister's hair. They kept talking almost as if they had forgotten Greta was there. She listened, piecing together the whole story from what they said. Brenna, who'd had water wings on her arms, had dropped her bracelet, and Cece had ducked down to get it. In the split second her head was below the surface, Brenna had practiced her kicking, knocking Cece against the side of the pool. Cece said, "You were only four years old, and you were smart enough to run for help. You saved my life, baby girl. You're my sister, and I love you. You need to stop worrying. Believe me, I'm okay now."

"So you're not afraid of the water anymore?" Brenna said, sounding dubious.

"No, I decided I am not. I'm done with that."

Slowly, Greta drifted from grogginess to being fully awake. Eventually, flinging the covers aside, she got up and went to her room to take an ibuprofen and get dressed. It was a slow process. Her limbs were so uncooperative, it was like walking through maple syrup.

When she went down to breakfast, the Vanderhaven girls and Nanny were already in the kitchen, Brenna eating lunch at the counter next to Cece, whose hands were wrapped around a mug of coffee. Their attention was on a tablet propped up in front of them.

Greta walked around to their side of the counter just in time to see a clip of Katrina and Vance speaking to an interviewer. The camera was focused on them with the skyline of Las Vegas in the background.

Offscreen the male interviewer asked, "Vance, you came to fame as Cece Vanderhaven's gay boyfriend, so I think we're all a little surprised that you and Katrina are now married. Can you explain this to us?"

Vance smiled, his arm around Katrina's shoulders. "I had no idea that people took Cece's little nickname for me so literally. I was happy to be Cece's gay boyfriend, and I'm even more excited to be Katrina's husband and for the two of us to start this new chapter of our lives together."

The interviewer moved the microphone closer. "What about the reports you're pregnant, Katrina? Any truth to that?"

She grinned at Vance. "None whatsoever. We hope to start a family someday, but we're not there yet."

The interviewer nodded and said, "What about the rumor you had a falling-out with Cece?"

Katrina said, "Not true at all. We both think the world of Cece. She will always be important to us, especially because without her, we never would have met."

Vance nodded. "If you see this, Cece, we love you!" Katrina gave a little finger wave and made one of the goofy faces she'd made famous as Cece's sidekick.

"So you aren't upset that she's now said her cousin Greta is her best friend?"

"Are you kidding?" Katrina said. "Greta is fabulous, and did you see the footage from last night? Crazy times. I think all of America is going to want to see more of Greta and Cece."

The interviewer said, "So what's next for the two of you?"

Katrina smiled. "We both want to pursue acting careers, so that will be our focus going forward."

"I wish you both the best of luck."

"Thanks!" Katrina and Vance spoke in unison, and then he leaned over and kissed her on the cheek. They made a cute couple.

After the interview was over, Cece shut the device down. Greta asked, "What did they mean about last night's footage and crazy times?"

"It's all over the place," Brenna piped up. "I saw you guys singing, and I saw when Cece fell in the water and you got her out. And when she was at the place with all the teeny tiny glasses." She took a sip of her orange juice and then held the glass up, assessing the size.

"Basically, the whole evening is now online," Cece said. "And everyone is speculating as to what this new side of me means. Am I going to have a new reality series, or have I gone crazy?" She laughed.

"What *does* it mean?" Brenna asked.

"It means your sister just wanted to be herself," Greta answered. Cece nodded in confirmation.

"I was tired of not being able to make my own decisions." Cece sighed. "After the pool accident, everyone thought my personality changed because I had some sort of brain damage. But that wasn't it. I tried to tell them that I was different because I came so close to dying, but no one paid any attention. They thought I was impulsive and unpredictable. Maybe I was, but it wasn't because of an injury. I just wanted to make every moment count."

CHAPTER FORTY-FOUR

Dalton called, and Will came to pick him up. Even though it was the middle of the night, Will said it was no problem. That was the kind of friend he was.

When he walked into the building and spotted Dalton in the lobby, he said, "You know, when you said to pick you up at the hospital, I had a little breakdown, thinking something happened to you."

"Sorry about that. I should have explained first thing."

"What's with the monkey suit?" He pointed at Dalton's white shirt, bow tie, now-dried dress pants, and shiny shoes. "You go to a prom for the homeless?"

"Something like that. I'll explain in the car."

Will had brought a paper bag containing his wallet, apartment keys, and cell phone. Dalton rooted through the bag, eager to reclaim the things that made up his life. Driving away from the hospital, Will commented, "You didn't last two weeks."

"True that." He turned on his phone.

"And you lost the gross backpack and are wearing someone else's clothes."

"I know. Things didn't quite happen the way I planned, but I got the information I needed and then some." When his phone came to life and the screen lit up, he let out a sigh of relief.

Will glanced his way, eyebrows raised, then turned his attention back to the road. He drove a fast car made even faster by his heavy foot. City driving held him back, but Dalton knew that once they reached the open roads, they'd be flying. They'd arrive in Connecticut in no time at all.

Will asked, "And then some?"

"Yeah." Dalton couldn't help but smile. "I met a girl. A woman, I mean. She's really something."

"Every good story involves a girl. Spill."

He gave him the details of what had happened, right from the start, and when he was done, Will let out a long whistle. "You're probably, like, the only guy I know who can do an undercover homeless gig and wind up in a tuxedo hanging out with celebrities and meeting a cool girl. Surreal."

"That's the right word for it."

"And her name is Greta Hansen? Greta Hansen from Wisconsin." He did his best to say it with a *Fargo*-esque accent, which wasn't how Greta talked, but whatever. "Are you going to see her again?"

"Yes, I'm going to see her again. And again and again and again." While he spoke, his eyes were on his phone, already seeing her. He'd found her Instagram account and could now see the faces of her friends and her parents and her brother, Travis, all of which he found interesting, but most of his attention was drawn to the photos of Greta. *There you are,* he thought. *It's you.* One day, hopefully soon, he'd be in her photos.

When the car pulled up in front of his apartment complex, he thanked Will for the ride and got out. Will sped off as soon as the door closed, presumably to go home and get some sleep.

Dalton made a mental list of things to do, then set out to do them. He showered, shaved, and changed clothes. His fridge was pretty empty, but he found some frozen organic black bean enchiladas. Four minutes in the microwave, and he had a meal. Once done eating, he spent a few more minutes looking at photos of Greta online before sitting down to create the document that would define his future.

Three hours later, he'd created a business plan, one that would please his father. Dalton knew what he expected: a clear and concise description of what the project entailed, along with the services offered, an estimate of needed funds, and the number of necessary employees to get started. He'd found studies online with statistics and graphs and included them in his report. His father would love that. "Give me a visual," he always said. Dalton also outlined the estimated impact on society if his plan were successfully implemented.

He'd been angry with his father when they'd first discussed Dalton's role in the family corporation. His brother, Grant, excelled at the business end of it and was destined to take over when his father stepped down. Grant was a competitor through and through. Dalton was always what their mother called "the gentle one," something that made him cringe, even though she wasn't too far off. He had a penchant for helping those who seemed lost or in pain. Offering a helping hand came naturally. If that was a weakness, he had to claim it as his own.

When he'd finished his master's degree, Dalton had suggested that he could contribute to the family business in his own way. His idea involved revamping the family charitable foundation, a small division of the corporation that had been set up primarily for tax advantages. One woman in his father's office distributed checks to charities at the end of the year. It seemed like money shuffling to Dalton. He had big ideas for expanding it.

He'd asked his dad to meet with him to discuss his place in the organization. At the onset, the meeting had gone well. His father had been enthused about his sudden interest, shaken his hand when he arrived, and listened to his prepared speech. Dalton had gone over it in his head dozens of times and thought it was impassioned and convincing. He could tell his dad was losing interest halfway through, but he still wasn't prepared for his reaction at the end.

His dad had scoffed. Seriously, he made that noise people make when they're being completely dismissive. Then he said, "What a bunch of idealistic blather." His voice changed to mock Dalton. "I want to make the world a better place. I want to really help people and make a difference."

Dalton found this last bit totally obnoxious.

And for the record, he was misquoting Dalton. What he'd actually said was that the Bishop Foundation had an opportunity to make the world a better place and make a real difference in people's lives. He was ready to walk out right that minute, but he knew his father. If he just waited for it, sometimes there was an addendum. He said, "So you don't like my idea?"

His father sat back, his arms crossed. "No, I think it's a good idea. We've discussed expanding the foundation and getting more directly involved with the recipients but never found the time to follow through. My guess is that you're just the man for the job. The problem, as I see it, is that you didn't give me a plan. You gave me an idea. Ideas are a dime a dozen. Ideas are just thoughts until they're put into play. You have to decide what your focus will be. You say homeless people, but that's a pretty large population."

"It's a pretty large problem," Dalton said.

His father continued as if he hadn't spoken. "Who specifically will benefit, and how? And will there be long-term benefits, or are we going to just provide short-term food and shelter? I'm opposed to the latter, by the way. I'm against enabling people. You have to think about how to go about solving the problem."

"Solving the problem." Dalton nodded, even as his mind reeled with the enormity of it all.

"I'm always thinking about the endgame. I also think opening a shelter comes with additional costs that the Bishop Foundation is not prepared to incur. Once you buy a building, you have maintenance, insurance, property tax, utilities . . ." His father ticked them off on his fingers. "You'll have to come up with some other idea, some program that doesn't require buying or renting real estate. I would hope that with all your education, you were at some point instructed in the art of creating an effective business plan. Submit one for approval, and we'll take it from there."

Dalton had left that meeting heartened. His father had liked his idea and thought he might be just the man for the job. His dad didn't hand out gold stars for nothing. After that, Dalton had racked his brain thinking of programs and ideas that might make a long-term difference to the homeless, but he was always looking at the problem from the outside. How could he possibly know what would be most helpful to someone on the streets?

His two weeks on the streets were intended as a fact-finding mission. He didn't tell anyone what he was doing except for Will, in case it backfired somehow.

Crazy as it sounded, it had worked. Now he had a plan. He wanted to focus on homeless vets, providing them with one-on-one caseworkers, someone who could shepherd them through the process, letting them know what benefits they were entitled to, and actually drive them to appointments, if need be. Each client would say what they wanted and needed, whether it was help in getting medical treatment, finding a place to live, providing transportation, or just having someone to listen to their concerns. One person to follow them through the whole process of becoming whole again. And the clients would provide them with a quick way to connect with their caseworker so that, in the event of an emergency, they could get access to help quickly. It was a simple plan, but not an easy one. He knew of at least one vet he wanted to help as soon as possible.

He thought of the young couple, Lauren and Diego, the ones who'd been selling water in the park. Maybe they'd want jobs helping him find applicants for his program. If his father approved his plan, there was no end to the people he could help.

Dalton printed up his business plan, wrote a cover letter, and then clipped the pages in a plastic report cover. After getting a few hours of sleep, he drove to his parents' house, planning to drop off his paperwork, say hello, and then leave, but the visit took a different turn when his dad ushered him into his home office. Dalton took a seat and handed him the plan. Fifteen long excruciating minutes later, his father looked up from reading and addressed him from across the desk. "I like the graphs."

"I knew you would."

"And this ReadyHelp device you're proposing to give each client? They can get help with the push of a button?"

"Yes, sir. It's easier than making a phone call. Nothing to turn on, just one button to push. When someone is having a panic attack or needs help, they can get an immediate response. It has built-in GPS and fall detection, so we can find them if need be. The expense is minimal compared to the peace of mind."

"Good idea."

"The newest version has a battery that lasts a week before it has to be recharged, so as long as the client meets with their mentor at least once a week, they'll always be connected."

"I see."

After what seemed to be a long pause, Dalton asked, "What do you think about my business plan overall?"

He nodded in approval. "It's lacking a few details, but nothing that can't be filled in as we go along. Come in to the office first thing on Monday morning, and we'll hammer it all out."

Dalton exhaled in relief. "Sounds good. I'll be there. Thank you, sir."

His father came around to his side of the desk and shook his hand. "This is a good thing you're doing, Dalton. I'm especially impressed that you've chosen to help veterans. I like the idea of honoring those who've served our country."

"Yes, sir."

"Are you staying for Sunday dinner? Your mother would like that."

"Can I take a rain check? I have to go see someone."

CHAPTER FORTY-FIVE

Things were different now. Greta's narrow worldview had been broken wide open. She'd arrived in New York City insecure and unsure, and in a few short days, she'd found strength she hadn't known she had. And in acquiring strength, she'd found love too.

Or at least, it felt like love.

Cece seemed certain that she would see Dalton again. "Don't even worry about it. He'll be back." One night of freedom, and she'd become a more assertive woman. Her father had called after the news of her wild antics had reached him in Paris, and she'd handled the call like a boss, telling him that she'd known Katrina and Vance had been a couple all along and she'd given them her blessing. Greta only had access to her side of the conversation, but from what she heard, Cece was a woman in charge. "Dad," she said at one point, "what I did last night was typical for someone my age. Isn't that right, Greta?" She turned to Greta for confirmation, then got back to the conversation. "Greta's nodding. I didn't do anything wrong, and no one coerced me. No, you don't need to hire anyone. I don't need babysitters anymore. I'm twenty-three. I can make my own decisions."

She listened for a moment. "Yes, I'm going to see Roger again. We're going out tonight. You can meet him when you get home." A long pause. "No, I'm not interested in having my own reality show. I'm going to be doing my own clothing designs." Another very long pause. Her father's voice on the other end sounded agitated. "No, I've canceled all my scheduled activities for the next few weeks. I need time to clear my head and sort things out." He must have asked what she was sorting out because she answered, "I'm not sure yet. I'll let you know. Love you, Dad. Goodbye."

After she hung up, she said, "I feel much better now."

"I bet." It was unclear what role Greta would play in Cece's new life, but she was up for anything.

Later Cece and Roger invited her to go along with them for a night on the town, but she turned them down. "You guys don't need to have an extra person on your date, and I could do with some downtime. Besides, I'm in for the night." She indicated her yoga pants and T-shirt, just a step up from pajamas. "Aren't you guys worried about getting rushed by fans?"

Cece shrugged. "I've snuck out before without getting noticed. If I dress the right way, I'll be able to blend in."

After she and Roger left, Greta had dinner with Nanny and Brenna, then retired to her room to send texts to a few friends, who couldn't help but notice there were photos and video footage of her all over social media. She'd even garnered a few mentions on the cable entertainment news shows. She sat back on her bed and watched the clip of her and Dalton singing together over and over again. That night, she had been so worried about making a fool of herself, she'd forgotten to fully embrace the experience. Turned out she relished it more in retrospect than she did at the time. When the video zoomed in on Dalton, it was evident that he was singing only to her.

She scanned the comments below the video clips, looking to see if anyone mentioned knowing him in real life, but there was nothing.

What was his story? Greta wondered. What terrible tragedy would explain his sudden spate of homelessness? She wanted to help. She hadn't gotten her first paycheck from Firstborn Daughter, Inc. and didn't know if she ever would, now that she and Cece had gone rogue. She didn't have much money to spare, but if he needed a job, perhaps Cece or her family could help.

If she ever heard from him again. He knew her name and where she was currently living, while all she knew about Dalton was that he was from Connecticut. She could hardly drive around the state, yelling his name. All she could do was wait. What if they never connected? She could go her whole life wondering and anticipating something that never came to be.

As her mind ran through worst-case scenarios, she spotted his tuxedo jacket still draped over the desk chair where she'd left it the night before. On a hunch, she got up and searched through all the pockets. Besides some random money, all of them were empty except for one interior pocket, which had a slight bulge to it. She reached in and pulled out what looked like an amulet. It was an oval piece of plastic with the word *ReadyHelp* on the back. The front had a red button in the middle. She pressed it, and a woman's voice came through, startling her. "Mr. Bishop, did you need assistance?"

"What?"

"Am I speaking to Dalton Bishop?" Creepy how clear her voice was, like she was in the room with Greta.

"No, this is Greta Hansen. I found this ReadyHelp thing in Dalton's coat pocket. Can you tell me how to reach him?"

"Is Mr. Bishop there?"

If he were there, would she be asking how to reach him? "No, he's not here. Can you tell me how to reach him, so I can return this thing to him?"

"Are you experiencing an emergency?"

"No."

They went back and forth a few more times. Since Greta wasn't in danger and wasn't the account holder of the device, the company was limited in what it could do for her. The woman apologized and said she'd make a note on Dalton's account saying that Greta had the device, so if he called and requested a replacement, they could let him know where it was. She requested Greta's cell phone number, and that was it.

But Greta did get something out of their exchange: Dalton's last name, Bishop. Greta went back to her tablet and googled his full name, then pushed "Images." There he was, Dalton Bishop, the man who'd won her over with his caring manner and gorgeous, inviting smile.

She sat down on the bed, taking in all the new information, then searched for and found his Facebook and Instagram accounts. Most of the pictures he'd posted were of other people or the places he'd visited. He'd gone on mission trips in previous summers to install wells in villages in third-world countries, and closer to home, he'd helped build houses for Habitat for Humanity. He didn't seem to update very often. His Facebook account seemed to be primarily for his grandmother, who had the first comment after every single post. She was very proud of him.

Greta did a search for the family name, and what she found was an eye-opener. The Bishops were rich. Maybe not Vanderhaven rich, but then again, few people were. He was Dalton Bishop of the Bishop Corporation.

So why would a guy that wealthy pretend to be homeless? It didn't make any sense. She did some more digging and discovered his family had been affluent going back four generations. Decade after decade, while the Bishops were winning at life, the Hansens were working to pay their bills, put dinner on the table, keep a roof over their heads, and save for a few fun extras. A good life, but nothing lavish.

They had, she realized with a pang of sadness, nothing in common except for one shared awesome evening. At least, it had been awesome for her.

She went back to the video clip of them singing at the karaoke place and searched his face, looking for signs of sincerity. When he sang the line about meeting an angel in person, his gaze was right on her.

She took a deep breath, wondering if she was assigning meaning where there was none.

Greta watched the video clips over and over again, focusing on Dalton. It would be nice to know it was real and that he felt the same way she did.

If only she had a way to reach him right this minute.

Finally, she set the tablet down and went to the window. He was out there somewhere. She lifted the blinds and saw the moon hanging over Manhattan, a bit of mist creating a halo around the periphery.

The moon. A perfect yellow orb. From where she stood, it looked like a full moon.

A full moon.

Greta did a mental rewind, going back to what Dalton had said the previous evening when she'd pulled Cece out of the pond. She'd thought the pond was a lake, and he'd let her know otherwise, informing her that Central Park did have a lake, and then he'd said, "The most beautiful night sky I ever saw was when I was standing on the Bow Bridge." And something about a great view of the city. The next sentence she remembered verbatim: *I'll show it to you the next time there's a full moon.*

Greta went to her tablet to check. Yes, it was indeed a full moon. She made an impulsive, split-second, out-of-character decision. She threw a hoodie over her yoga pants and T-shirt; left a note on the kitchen table for Nanny, Brenna, and Cece; and headed out.

CHAPTER FORTY-SIX

Dalton drove into the city and left his car in a parking garage, finding it easier to navigate Manhattan by foot or taxi. His first stop was the hospital to check on Matt. He found him sitting up in bed, talking to Ellie, and looking remarkably better.

"Hello," Dalton said, coming into the room. It was the tail end of visiting hours, but he wasn't planning on staying very long.

They took one look at his newly shaved face and each did a double take. Ellie pointed to his chin. "Hey, Dalton, you lost your scruff."

"Yep, it looks like I have a job now, working for my dad."

Matt said, "See, I knew you'd work it out with your family."

Dalton explained that he was going to be helping to set up a non-profit that would serve veterans. "Once it gets going, I'll get in touch to see if we can do anything to help you."

"Cool," he said with a nod. "That's good of you."

"Not good of me," Dalton said with a shake of his head. "You served our country. The least we can do is help you get back on your feet."

They talked about Matt's health, and then Dalton said he had to get going. Ellie followed him out the door, thanking him profusely for his part in connecting her with Matt.

"It was nothing," he said, feeling sheepish about getting credit for doing the right thing.

"Well, it was everything to me." Her eyes filled with tears, and she gave him a quick hug before going back to Matt.

He felt lighter as he left the hospital and caught a cab to Cece Vanderhaven's apartment. He longed to see Greta again, to have her smile at him. Most importantly, he wanted her to know the truth, to have her understand and approve of his ruse. To forgive his lie and know that he was really a good guy. And then maybe they could go from there.

Getting out of the cab, he handed the driver the money, slammed the door closed, and almost sprinted to the front door. He was stopped by a burly doorman, who wanted to know if he was expected. "Not expected, but I know Cece Vanderhaven, and I need to speak with her cousin Greta Hansen." He took out his phone and showed him the footage of Cece introducing him and Greta right before they started singing. Proof positive, but the man barely glanced at it.

"Anyone can doctor footage," he said. "This is a private building. If you're not on our list, you don't get in."

"I didn't doctor it," Dalton said, exasperated. "This happened last night. It's been a big deal on the internet."

"This isn't the internet. This is the real world, and you're not on our list. Move along."

"If you see Greta, can you tell her Dalton stopped by?"

"Yeah, I'll do that," he said, sounding bored and clearly humoring him.

A young guy carrying a cellophane-wrapped bouquet of red roses edged him out of the way and told the doorman he had a delivery for Cece Vanderhaven. The doorman shook his head. "Sorry, not happening. Have the florist call the front desk, and then you'll be on the list." The guy dropped the bouquet of flowers onto the sidewalk and wandered away.

"Hey!" Dalton yelled after him. "Don't you want these?" He stooped over to pick them up.

The doorman said, "Don't bother. He's a scam artist. Tries this kind of thing every other week."

Dalton shrugged and kept the flowers, then wandered around the building to see if the door used by the maintenance man was unlocked. Nope. Sealed shut. He knocked for a few minutes, and when no one answered, he went back to the front.

Standing on the sidewalk and looking up, he thought about Greta being up there while he was down below, with no way of connecting except through social media. He didn't want to leave a comment on her Instagram or send her a friend request on Facebook. It just seemed wrong. Impersonal. Juvenile.

As he stood there, two women passed by, walking a dog. He heard the jangle of tags against a collar and the dog's whine. When he turned to see, one of the women said to the other, "A full moon tonight. Look, how beautiful!" They paused for just a second until the dog, a big curly-haired thing, tugged at the leash, and they continued on.

A full moon. Dalton looked up at the night sky and thought about what he'd said to Greta the night before. That he'd take her to the Bow Bridge the next time there was a full moon. Clearly, that wasn't going to happen, but he could go there himself, take a selfie, and include it in his message, saying he'd thought of her and wished she'd been there.

A little lame, but a lot smoother than saying, *Hey! Remember me from the other night?* Now that he had a plan, he set off in the direction of the park. The weather was beautiful for a June evening in the city, and the sidewalks were busy.

He was, after all, in the city that never sleeps.

The perimeter of Central Park was buzzing with activity, but as he got farther into the park, he encountered fewer people, just a few couples holding hands and some runners grinding out the miles in a scenic place.

The Bow Bridge was known as a romantic spot, but it was a long bridge, and he knew that even if there were couples there, he wouldn't be crowding anyone out. The opposite side of the bridge led to the Ramble, a wilderness area that wasn't the best place to visit after dark, so he wouldn't be crossing over.

When he saw the Bow Bridge, he remembered that it wasn't brightly lit at night, part of its allure for lovers. The full moon was covered by a gauzy mist, but the city lights ahead were gorgeous and the reflection on the water a masterpiece. It would have been a perfect night to bring Greta. He was about a third of the way onto the bridge when an older lady approached. Her silver hair fell to her shoulders, and she had a pretty peppy walk for someone who used a cane. "Oh," she said, spotting the flowers in his hand. "Roses! How nice. Young love! There's nothing like it. Someone is going to be very happy to get that bouquet."

"Actually," Dalton said, "I brought them to give to the first beautiful woman I saw tonight. These are for you." He held them out, touched to see her free hand cover her heart.

She had a twinkle in her eye. "Are you teasing an old lady?"

"I would never do that. I would sincerely like you to have them."

"Thank you." She took them from his hand and clutched them to her front. "I can't remember the last time a man gave me flowers. You can tell your mother she raised you well."

"I certainly will."

CHAPTER FORTY-SEVEN

More people were in the park late on a Sunday night than Greta would have thought. Still, it was peaceful. Tranquility right in the heart of the city. She walked the path as it took twists and turns, passing a fountain along the way. It seemed to take forever, but she kept the faith, following the instructions on her phone and fighting the urge to turn back. Eventually, just when she'd wondered if she was hopelessly lost, she came to the bridge. She walked onto it and, when she reached the center, stopped to take it all in. On top of the railings on either side were planters filled with flowers. The sides of the bridge were made up of decorative circles. The water below rippled gently.

Dalton was right. It was a beautiful spot.

She got out her phone and took a few photos, posting them to Instagram for the benefit of her Wisconsin friends. She entered the location and wrote, I made it to Central Park! #fullmoon #Sundaynightfun #CentralPark #NYC #WisconsingirlinManhattan. And for her friend Jacey: #yolo. Within about five seconds, Jacey had left a comment: Lucky!

Greta stood on the bridge, aware of people around her, all of them careful not to crowd anyone else. Besides the couples in love, there was one old woman with a cane who walked past to the end of the bridge, then did an about-face and came back. Greta smiled at her, and she said, "Good evening." People in New York were friendlier than she'd been led to believe.

Greta was still watching the old woman when she spotted Dalton striding onto the bridge. She felt a pulse of surprise, followed by the feeling of no surprise at all. Of course he was there. Somehow, even as she'd told herself she might never see him again, she'd been sure he would show up. Or maybe not sure but hoping, or perhaps she'd tried to wish it into happening, but regardless, here he was, striding onto the bridge, carrying a bunch of flowers. The whole world shifted on its axis, and everything was right again.

She walked his way, just in time to overhear the old woman admire the bouquet and Dalton say, "Actually, I brought them to give to the first beautiful woman I saw tonight. These are for you."

She stopped in her tracks. She couldn't see the old woman's face, but she heard the wonder in her voice when she realized he wasn't playing a cruel trick but really wanted her to have them. Such a kind thing to do. She said something about his mother raising him well, but Greta knew better. His mother probably did raise him well, but that wellspring of compassion came right from his soul. Dalton was a good man.

His back was to her now as he turned to watch the old woman leave the bridge, the flowers clutched to her front.

Greta knew this man. She'd danced with him, held his hand, sung a duet with him before an audience, and kissed his cheek. She'd yearned to get the chance to see him again, but now that she had the opportunity and he was only an arm's length away, she was suddenly unsure. Should she tap him on the shoulder? Give him a hug? What if his presence here was merely a coincidence, and he was meeting someone else?

And then he went to rest his elbows on the railing, and he happened to see her out of the corner of his eye. He stood up and smiled in recognition. "Oh, thank God. It *is* you. For a minute, I thought I was imagining things."

She didn't say a word, just crossed the few feet between them and pulled his face down to hers and kissed him. The two of them together felt right. His hands slipped down to her waist, steadying her, and she rested a hand on his cheek.

He pulled back and gazed at her face. "Greta, I have so much to tell you. I know I've got a lot to explain."

"Luckily," she said, "we have plenty of time. You want to get a bite?"

He tipped his head to one side, considering. "I could eat."

They walked off the bridge, hand in hand. She was officially happier than she ever remembered being, and that was saying a lot, because she'd had more than her share of happy moments. They walked along the path, their fingers intertwined. When they approached the fountain, they came upon the silver-haired lady, still holding on to the flowers. When she saw them, a grin came over her face. She pointed the bouquet in their direction and said, "Young love. There's really nothing like it."

And Greta had to agree.

AFTERWORD

This novel wouldn't exist if not for a touch of insomnia and some late-night television. On the night in question, I was randomly channel flipping when I came across a film from 1936 called *My Man Godfrey* starring Carole Lombard and William Powell. In the movie, a socialite offers a bum named Godfrey five dollars to be her "forgotten man" for a scavenger hunt. Eventually, he is invited to be her wealthy family's butler. Of course, there's more to Godfrey than is initially thought, hilarity ensues, and the two fall in love. This type of movie was once known as a screwball comedy, so the humor was greatly exaggerated, but the dialogue was witty, and since I'm a fan of happy endings, I found it entertaining. There were some parts, though, that hadn't aged all that well. As I watched it, I couldn't help but wonder what a modern-day version would look like.

I went to bed and didn't think any more of it, but my brain must have been working on it—a few months later, *Good Man, Dalton* came to me almost fully formed. Truthfully, it shares little with the movie that inspired it except for the idea of inviting a forgotten man to a high-society event.

And, of course, the happy ending.

I hope you enjoyed my story.

ACKNOWLEDGMENTS

I'd like to start by thanking everyone at Lake Union Publishing, my home at Amazon Publishing. The team there is beyond compare. I regret that I don't know all of your names (or I would certainly be acknowledging you here), but please know you are appreciated.

To Danielle Marshall, you are a rock star among editors, and so much fun to speak to on the phone that I often forget we're talking *serious business*. Thank you for everything.

Jeff Belle, you should know that sometimes I take out my old contracts and marvel at your signature, happy to have a few from before the days of DocuSign. Having them in my possession makes me feel cool.

Gabriella Dumpit, I'm thankful that you're always there for my questions and concerns. Your attention to detail and speedy follow-up do not go unnoticed.

A special shout-out to Nicole Pomeroy, who oversees the transformation of my pages from manuscript to book. Thanks for doing your magic!

A debt of gratitude to my copy editors and proofreaders: Valerie Kalfrin, Kellie Osborne, and Karin Silver. They are the unsung heroes of the publishing world and have saved me from myself more than once. I will claim any remaining errors as being wholly mine, as they were mine to begin with.

To Kay Bratt and Kate Danley, I'm glad to be included in the weekly check-in. You help keep me on track and provide wise counsel, which is no small thing, as you well know.

I hereby credit Charlie McQuestion as the inventor of Water Ball, which was mentioned in this story, and recognize Kevin Becker, Josh Carter, Aaron Fiscal, Dan Lynch, and (always a favorite) Zach Trecker, all of whom participated in said game on our driveway back in the day. Good times.

A thank-you to Dr. Nick and Meredith Chill, at whose wedding I heard the story of the Cool Kids' Club. I appropriated the concept for the dinnertime conversation at the Forgotten Man Ball in this novel. I hope you don't mind.

To the beta readers of this book—Kay Bratt, Kay Ehlers, Michelle San Juan, and Alice L. Kent—like Liam Neeson, you each have a particular set of skills, and for that, I am grateful. I owe you!

I'm lucky to have a family who offers me endless love and support. Many thanks to my beloved husband, Greg, who keeps me level; Charlie, who provides the humor; Rachel, the best daughter-in-law ever; Maria, who reliably laughs at my lame jokes; and Jack, who is a good sport about troubleshooting story endings with me. What would I do without all of you? I hope I never find out.

And to the readers—none of this would mean anything without you. I appreciate the messages, emails, and especially your valuable, thoughtful reviews. I'll keep writing as long as you'll keep reading. Thank you for giving me that privilege.

ABOUT THE AUTHOR

Photo © 2016 Greg McQuestion

The bestselling author of *Hello Love*, Karen McQuestion writes the books she would love to read—not only for adults but also for kids and teens. Her publishing story has been covered by the *Wall Street Journal*, *Entertainment Weekly*, and NPR. She lives with her family in Hartland, Wisconsin. To find out more about Karen and her books, follow her on Twitter @karenmcquestion) or visit www.KarenMcQuestion.com.